CW01095596

WHEN LOVE IS NOT ENOUGH...

A story of adoption, based on real life experience

Hannah Hawthorne

authorHOUSE®

AuthorHouse™ UK Ltd.
500 Avebury Boulevard
Central Milton Keynes, MK9 2BE
www.authorhouse.co.uk
Phone: 08001974150

First published by AuthorHouse   3/26/2010

ISBN: 978-1-4490-9209-2 (sc)

Printed in the United States of America
Bloomington, Indiana

This book is printed on acid-free paper.

*"Wisdom rests quietly in the heart
of him who has understanding."*

(Proverbs 14v33)

Chapter 1
Childhood Memories

Childhood memories can stretch over many years, some perhaps as fleeting, comforting impressions, whilst others form a detailed pattern of clarity, even though decades have passed by. It was usually the sad or unpleasant memories which were the most vivid, and Isabel had plenty of those.

She remembered the freezing, wintry temperatures of her north-facing bedroom with its conventional, sterile wallpaper, the basic utility wardrobe and dressing table of the war years, and no heating of any sort. To be sent to bed, either at the normal time or as a punishment, provided few options for comfort. No radio, television or record player, just books to be read with a torch under the covers because the light had been ceremoniously turned out. The dim landing light filtered through the half-open bedroom door, creating shadows and stimulating fear of ghosts and monsters. Yet when the landing light was finally turned out, it was even worse: total blackness. When sleep evaded her for a time, worries crowded in. When would she have the eye operation to correct her squint, caused by a fall when she was a toddler? Was it true that her right eye would have to be taken out whilst the muscles were repaired? Would she feel the pain, and what about when the doctors took out the stitches? The thought made her feel physically sick. She would never forget having her tonsils and adenoids removed at the age of six during the air raids, the nurse and doctors holding down her arms and legs whilst the ether pad was placed over her face before oblivion took hold. These thoughts were almost unbearable to her, and actually far worse than the operation itself.

She was not an only child, although she had often wished she had been because her brother, Clive, three years older and much stronger than she, was the veritable bane of her life throughout her childhood, adolescence and early womanhood. As a small child she had wondered whether all older brothers were like Clive, but around the eleven-plus age she realized that they definitely were not. Her friends scrapped with their brothers and sisters from time to time, or, as the oldest sibling, they may have been in the blissful position of authority, but the rivalry, which features in most families to a greater or lesser extent, took on an extreme form in her own. She could scarcely remember a day when Clive had not bullied or threatened her. It started as a toddler, when he catapulted her out of her pram. She landed on the hall floor, a screaming bundle. Then, as the years went by, it developed into punching, hitting, half throttling, head banging and tripping up. More than once she went off to school with her eyes blackened. Then came the domineering manipulation, blackmail and violent tempers, much of which her parents could not control, although they did try.

Clive was the family problem. Whenever he returned from school, where he played his part alternately as bully and coward, there was trouble. His undiagnosed personality problem, which manifested itself in lying, thieving, violence, arguing, bickering and domineering behaviour, was difficult to escape in a three-bedroom semi. On most evenings, doors would be slammed and the whole house would shake. Even as an adolescent, when the family was taking its annual holiday at a boarding house in Teignmouth or Eastbourne, his behaviour did not improve. Regular outbursts, kicking his father or mother under the table whilst having a meal in the company of other holidaymakers, and shouting and screaming in the bedroom, were the order of the day. Counsellors and educational psychologists seemed not to exist in the years following the war, so Isabel and Clive's parents struggled to do what they could to help. He was an intelligent boy. They listened to him and reasoned with him, providing encouragement or punishment where they thought appropriate, and they took an interest in his school work and hobbies. They were good, but not perfect parents.

Isabel longed for peace and a happy family life like that of many of her friends, and very occasionally there were glimpses of it, but for the most part, misery reigned. For whatever reason, Clive possessed an uncanny ability for nastiness. Domineering and controlling tactics, if thwarted, turned quickly into violence, verbal abuse or both. The most painful wounds he inflicted were always intended to lower Isabel's self-esteem and to make her feel worthless. By the time she was eleven, she had become a sensitive child, lacking in confidence, and eager to find comfort with her friends outside the home.

She remembered VE Day very clearly, not because of the street parties, the bonfires and the fun, but because her father's duodenal ulcer perforated on that day, and in agony, he was rushed into the local hospital. At the beginning of the war he had failed the army medical, but in spite of not serving in the forces, he had held down a full-time job as secretary to his firm's superannuation scheme and had shouldered much responsibility. The evenings and weekends were spent mostly with the Home Guard and the Air Raid Wardens. Isabel could remember, too, how he had fitted out Clive and her with Mickey Mouse gas masks.

Many a night the family would rush down the garden to the air-raid shelter under the plum tree, staying there until the familiar strains of the siren moaned out to announce that the immediate danger was over. Sleep was lost on a regular basis, undermining an already fragile constitution, and by 1945, Isabel's father was paying the price for over-work, stress and insufficient rest. He recovered slowly from the operation, which from what Isabel could gather at the time, patched up the ulcer rather than removed it, but he never managed to eat normally again. Dairy products, fish and white meat were acceptable to the stomach, but red meat, fatty, spicy or acidic foods were not. Post war short-ages provided few choices, so he ate sparsely and slowly, often relying on Benger's Food which was supposed to coat over the inflamed parts of the stomach lining, and tempo-rarily relieve the pain or discomfort.

During Isabel's teenage years, her father developed a look of exhausted, silent suffering when he returned from the city in the evenings, far from ready to face the onslaught of Clive's violence to his mother or sister, his feckless attitude to study and his tyrannous behaviour. Either by nature not especially aggressive himself, or perhaps incapable of commanding discipline due to poor health, Isabel's father seemed unable to get through to Clive or to flex his parental authority with any degree of skill. Occasionally he would lose his temper and lash out, but he immediately regretted it, and suffered the guilt and pain of his actions for days afterwards. Each evening he would sit for a time in his armchair, pale and drawn, his eyes closed. To Isabel it looked as if he wished he were elsewhere.

She loved and respected her father, despite his failing efforts to understand and motivate his son. She appreciated his general knowledge quizzes, his humour, his comical jokes, some of them much repeated, his sense of the ridiculous and his sensitivity. She shared his love of singing and sacred music, and she admired the way he could provide a kind of instant alto to almost any melody she chose to sing. At the age of fourteen she was thankful that he allowed her to have singing lessons, and together with her mother, he attended her competitions, school concerts and operas. She also felt compassion for his failing health, but in a rather imperfect way because, at the time, she was a self-absorbed teenager.

Ructions continued as the years went by, as Clive, too unstable and flamboyant a personality to be articled to a firm of chartered accountants, created trouble wherever he went. Music was his passion; auditing and accountancy were deadly subjects to avoid, although he had personally taken the decision to become articled. He was out all hours mixing with company his parents disapproved of, the consequences of which were confrontations, violent rows, continual door slamming and staying out for days. Isabel, a pupil at a direct-grant convent school, fervently pleaded with her parents to allow her to become a boarder to avoid Clive's bullying, but they could not afford the extra money.

By the time Isabel was eighteen, her father's health had progressively deteriorated; the duodenal ulcer had somehow become cancerous, spreading to the bowel and liver. During Isabel's first teaching practice at training college, he died. She returned home immediately to be with her mother and to help arrange the funeral. Her mother's weeping, together with her own, and the continual sleeplessness were unforgettably sad. Of the six close friends in her home town, no one else's father had died, and it was not the first time that Isabel realized the unfairness of life.

After returning to college, she tried to pick up the pieces of her course as best she could. Her tutor was supportive and understanding, and her fellow students were much like they always were, which was comforting and normal, but no matter how hard Isabel tried to concentrate on her essays, lesson notes and dissertation, her mind wandered off to thoughts of home, her mother's grief and loneliness, her late father's pallor and emaciated frame, the utter hopelessness that she would never see him again, Clive's threatening and unpredictable presence, and the future. Finally, despite everything, she passed her examinations, and qualified as a teacher, though not as well as she would have liked.

For the most part, her friends, once qualified, had set their sights on leaving home, to share a flat, at first in a distant town, sufficiently far flung from the family home to discourage interference. It was a chance to make one's own way and mark in life, without parental advice or checks. Birmingham was short of 600 teachers at the time, so the joke was that if all else failed, they would all meet up in Birmingham. They would be minus Isabel because there was no likelihood that she could break out into freedom and independence when her mother was so lonely and emotionally overwrought most of the time. So, for two years she returned home to be with her and managed to obtain a local teaching post.

By this time all her old school friends had moved out of the area to pursue studies or jobs elsewhere, returning only at family times such as Christmas and Easter. Social life in that town during the late fifties and early sixties was virtually a non-starter without her old contacts, so Isabel threw herself whole heartedly into her first teaching post, and for light relief, joined the local dramatic society. Nevertheless, she spent many evenings and weekends nursing disappointment and loneliness within. Her mother was very insistent that every household rule should be rigorously observed to the letter, and nothing else would do. Even the new television had to be turned off at nine thirty if that was her mother's wish. Isabel, who contributed to the family finances, would sometimes rebelliously turn it back on again, and then her mother would turn off the main switch, leaving the whole house in total darkness. No chance to read or listen to the radio. Isabel would lie in bed on winter nights in a pitch black, unheated room, wondering how she could improve her life, or escape.

The trouble with Clive did not cease as he became an adult, supposedly leaving behind the uncontrolled and violent behaviour of his teenage years. If anything, the situation worsened, particularly as he was more often than not under the influence of alcohol. One wrong word from his mother would send him berserk: he would pin her to the wall and hit her or half throttle her. If Isabel tried to intervene to defend her mother, he would blacken her eye and throw her to the floor. She was no match for a strongly built fellow over six feet tall. Both she and her mother tried everything they could think of to improve the situation. Talking to him to get to the bottom of his problems produced no solution whatsoever.

Realizing their failure, they agreed to keep fairly quiet when he was around, and certainly not say anything the least bit provocative. That technique failed too, because he would deliberately find ways of flaunting his fury and venting his violence on both of them. The daily dread of what else could happen when Clive was home filled Isabel with a depressing sense of injustice, worsened by the fact that the prospect of any improvement in the situation seemed hopeless. After one of the many occasions when he had bullied mother and sister, Isabel decided to contact the rector of her parish. Outside help seemed to be the only possible solution, and yet she felt obsessed with the guilt of divulging her problems outside the home for the first time. Somehow or other she had been able to keep the worse parts of her brother's behaviour from her own friends. Following the rector's advice and counselling, Clive became less aggressive for about a fortnight, and then the whole vicious cycle started all over again.

When Isabel finally returned from college to begin her first teaching job, she found that Clive had completed his National Service, and had reinstalled himself in the family home too. A feeling of unease filtered through her at the prospect of more inevitable and unavoidable trouble in the future. Having failed his examinations several times, Clive was forced to admit that accountancy would not become a living for him, and yet what could he do? As it was for Isabel, Clive's passion was music, but at the age of twenty-three, without qualifications, contacts or training, his future in that direction did not look promising. He tried a number of jobs, one of which was the direct result of his late father's impeccable professional reputation, but he was fired from all of them. It would have been difficult to have found a less motivated employee, so much of a square peg was he.

At home, frustrated, and constantly expressing antipathy towards his mother and sister, his behaviour rapidly deteriorated. Isabel became aware that his violence was becoming increasingly more dangerous, and that she would have to take definite action before something terrible happened. She was certain that the rector would no longer have any influence over Clive, and so one eye-blackening night, with her mother's permission, she contacted the local solicitor and poured her troubles out to him. When Clive received the solicitor's letter warning him to desist from the domestic violence which he had perpetrated for such a long time, he lit a bonfire the following Saturday afternoon. When Isabel returned from a shopping expedition, she discovered that her prized eighty-page college dissertation, representing a year's work, had disappeared from her bookcase and was smouldering at the bottom of the garden.

CHAPTER 2
FRANCESCA

The nest was wedged between a ceanothus and an entwined solanum high up on a southern wall in the garden, safe from predators, at least for the time being, and there sat a mother blackbird, dutiful and devoted, intense even, certainly single-minded about the task ahead of her. No one could question her raison d'être. There was no conflict of interests there, only a steadfast concentration.

Francesca appreciated both the concentration and the seeming loyalty of blackbirds. Whereas during the winter months, nuts, seeds and bread attracted finches, tits, thrushes, sparrows and robins as well as blackbirds, they all took flight when supplies lessened in spring and summer, leaving the blackbirds to make themselves really at home. Of course, visiting doves made an occasional appearance, attempting to botch a hopelessly messy nest, and then, giving up, cooed off elsewhere in search of another "des res." A lonely pheasant had once lost his way in their coastal area and paused for rest on the thatch, and pied wagtails sometimes fleetingly passed across the lawn, but it was the blackbirds that stayed and endeared themselves to Francesca. She was sensitive, too, to their collective high-pitched, frantic chirping when danger was near, but for the moment all was calm.

Francesca Bedale gazed fixedly at the bird's total absorption, almost in a reverie, and told herself that she was incapable of such devotion at her tender age. As the youngest child of a large farming family, she had been sent away to a convent boarding school until she had finished her A levels. Structure, rules, study, duty and religion had been her daily grind for seven years, and grind it was. Although not without intelligence, Francesca could not be described as academic. Her strengths were in things practical. She loved to sew, to cook and to draw, and although not particularly interested in playing hockey, tennis or any other sports for that matter, she would delight in riding across her father's fields, feeling the breeze of freedom in her hair. Not for her the dry discipline of a university education, or the cramping, soulless mediocrity of office work, or the shame and embarrassment of a shop job. She would do what everyone wants ideally: earn her living doing what she really enjoyed. In her case it was dressmaking. She had counted the days to the end of her final term, and had anticipated her imminent freedom with great excitement.

She planned that she would begin by making clothes for the numerous members of her family. Before long she would become known locally and her circle of clients would widen. With luck she would be able to start her own business later on, more easily if her father could be relied on to provide her with some capital.

Father had proved to be the stumbling block. Whereas all her older brothers and sisters had, as she had, been sent away to school, unlike her, they had all excelled academically, and were able to choose relatively high-flying careers. Their parents basked in the pride and satisfaction of knowing that all the years of fee paying would reap their just rewards and the family honour would be maintained, even enhanced. Francesca felt a failure when comparing her achievements with those of her brothers and sisters. They teased her unmercifully, though not intentionally with cruelty, poking fun at her dressmaking whilst they were busy pursuing law, medicine, agriculture and architecture. Not surprisingly, she developed an immovable sense of inferiority, and worse still, when her A-level results arrived, she invoked the disappointment of both parents, and particularly that of her father.

Mr Bedale, a gentleman farmer and also a magistrate, held very definite opinions, and some would say Victorian ones, about the upbringing of children and how they should behave.

He was a proud and disciplined man and a pillar of the community, so to speak. His demeanour and attitude appeared somewhat archaic in the seventies when many of his contemporaries had adopted a softer, more indulgent method of raising their children. Perhaps it was because he had six children, and to educate them all at independent schools meant working seven days a week, that he became a fair, stern father rather than a loving one. The children knew exactly where they stood with him and what their boundaries were. Mrs Bedale was necessarily more approachable and less authoritarian than her husband, but the complex domestic running of the farm and their social life as a couple, coping with the regular problems and crises which children bring, in addition to the minutiae of daily life, meant that she was always busy.

Throughout her childhood Francesca had longed for more time on her own with her mother, the time of feeling special, which we all crave as children. Something, whatever it was, always prevented it: the ironing, the farm accounts, a family squabble, a tradesman calling, the phone ringing, someone's holiday homework requiring supervision, or a score of other potential reasons.

Francesca felt she suffered from maternal deprivation in the holidays, although she would not have described it as such, until she was packed off to school again at the start of term. Both at home and at school she definitely felt one of a crowd as she interacted with her siblings and her peer group, under the supervision of either her parents or the nuns. She was accepted; she conformed and she was overlooked. That special intimacy of trust and communication which develops both relationships and individual confidence were missing in her life. She respected and feared her father, felt disappointingly distant from her mother, and like many other boarding-school pupils, she had learned independence from an early age.

On that summer's day in 1974, Francesca turned away from the garden to enter her parents' home, the seventeenth-century farmhouse she had known and loved all her life. Removing her boots, she padded across the tiled floor into the kitchen. As she filled the kettle, she appreciated the luxury of being alone in the house, in fact, of taking care of it whilst her parents were away and her siblings were else-where; yet it was an indulgence marred by her own uneasy thoughts. Nevertheless she welcomed the chance to weigh up those thoughts, to sit and stare through the mullioned windows of the spacious, old kitchen which had witnessed so much living, not only of her immediate family, but of her ancestors, because the Bedales had farmed in Norfolk for five generations. She could wander aimlessly in the orchard and think aloud if she wanted to, or she could cry, and then sleep from the emotion and exhaustion of it all, without being asked what the matter was or being forced to talk.

Since she had left school her ambitions had not turned out as she had hoped. First, her father, unconvinced that her plans for starting up a dressmaking business were sound, refused to provide her with the capital she needed. He muttered something negative about not investing money in what was clearly a pre-ordained failure. She had explained her case and pleaded; he had shot holes in her argument and remained adamant. A bitter row followed during which Francesca accused her father of favouritism towards her older brothers and sisters, and especially the boys, at her expense. She claimed that a great deal of money had been spent on their university education, but virtually nothing on her future since leaving school. Her father pointed out that she should have worked harder at school to gain university entrance and a respectable career, instead of pursuing her "damned dressmaking".

Caught up in uncharacteristic fury, she had stormed out of the farmhouse across the yard to the shelter of the orchard summerhouse which had long been her place of refuge when family rows or crises became too suffocating. She could feel more private and cut-off there than in her bedroom, not least because the door could be locked from the inside. Bert, the farm border collie, had followed her, and curled up sympathetically on the mat near the door. She had collapsed in bitter tears on the old camp bed for what seemed like several hours, listening to the breeze fanning leaves gently against the windows, and the chirping of the blackbirds in the boughs above her, until the sun had gone down and the dog had whined to leave, not wanting to miss his evening meal. Francesca, however, had stayed in the summerhouse until she had calmed down and could think clearly, resolute that she would no longer live at the farm, but instead find her own job, her own accommodation and her own independence.

Within three weeks she had managed not only to find herself a job in Norwich working in a music shop, but also a tiny furnished flat in Benedict Street, which fortuitously, she was able to share with Sarah Buxton, an old school friend of hers who like-mindedly was itching to gain her independence, and whose family home was not far away from her own in Burnham Market. Sarah, an attractive nineteen-year-old, had just completed her gap year travelling in Europe and was ready to start a music degree at the University of East Anglia.

The quarrel between Francesca and her parents had cooled down, and during those interim weeks before moving, there were no raised voices or even heart-to-heart talks. Life seemed to carry on normally, perhaps even phlegmatically, though there was no demonstrable compromise on either side. Francesca intended to do design and dressmaking in the evenings and with the money she earned at the music shop, after deducting her contribution to the expenses of the flat, she would be able to save the capital she needed. She would show her father and he would finally respect her.

Life was turning a corner for her; new hopes and aspirations lay ahead. It was a time of courageous optimism and she felt confident about her plans.

Initially, the two girls got on well together despite the minuscule size of the flat and the resulting lack of privacy. Francesca enjoyed her job meeting the public in the music shop and she also enjoyed learning about music categories, publishers, performers and conductors. One evening a week she would study fashion design at evening class and then as planned, most other evenings would be spent dressmaking. Sarah's music lectures at the University of East Anglia sometimes took place in the evening, as did her choral practices, instrumental groups and concerts, which meant that Francesca spent a great deal of time in the evening on her own in the flat.

To make matters worse, the vivacious Sarah quickly found herself a boyfriend, a fellow student, who persuaded her with no trouble at all to share his flat, located much nearer to the university itself. Within two months of moving, Francesca had lost her flat mate and found herself completely responsible for the rent and utilities.

Pride would not allow her to ask her parents for help, especially not her father from whom she would receive short shrift, and her older brothers and sisters had long since left Norfolk to return only for Christmas, family reunions, baptisms, weddings and funerals. Sarah's fun-loving and dizzy personality, which at first had been such a refreshing boon, had turned out to be irresponsible and selfish, and Francesca spent several restless nights worrying about how she was going to cope financially.

"It's not the end of the world; you'll soon find somebody else," Sarah had called out callously as she left the flat for the last time.

After some thought, Francesca decided to put her plan into operation. Since she only received a modest salary from the music shop, she would have to take a part-time job to supplement her income, but what? She could cut back on food a bit and lose a few pounds, and nothing would be spent on entertainment. Her dressmaking would have to be temporarily put on hold, except for making her own clothes, that is, necessities. The most obvious way to solve the problems would have been to find another flat mate, but who? Her negative experience with Sarah, whom she had trusted, caused her to be both nervous and cautious about her unknown replacement.

A chance remark regarding her plight to one of her colleagues at the music shop produced the suggestion that she should look for part-time bar work at the Golden Fleece, one of the city-centre pubs. Evidently the publican was always looking for staff, and quite prepared to train suitably enthusiastic and trustworthy applicants. This was just as well because Francesca, though motivated by her accumulating debt, was totally inexperienced.

After a couple of lunchtime visits to the pub for a half of cider and a roast beef sandwich, she plucked up the courage to speak to a plump, friendly looking woman of about forty-five who was serving at the bar, and emphasized that although she had no previous experience of bar work, she really needed the job. She assured the woman that she would quickly learn how to pull pints and recognize various ales, lagers, vintages and cocktails. Whatever the job required, she would learn, and quickly. There was something about Francesca's earnest and unworldly plea which made the publican's wife smile, and she kindly suggested that if Francesca were really interested in a job she should call in at the pub that evening after work to meet the publican.

By half past six, Francesca had met the gentleman, received a preliminary teaching session about what's what in a bar and discussed hours and pay. It was decided that she would shadow an experienced barman for a couple of evenings, and then she should be able to cope. It all seemed so easy, and Francesca's relief was palpable. Now she would be able to pay off her debts, and while she was waiting for a suitable flat mate to emerge, she would be able to keep the flat going on her own. As a bonus, there would be less time in which to feel lonely. Even though she was a quiet, introverted girl, she thought she would enjoy the cacophony of relaxed pub chat, repartee and peals of laughter from youngsters celebrating the end of the week and the break from work.

At first Francesca's desire to try hard and do her best produced a counter-productive result, since she was unsure of herself and all fingers and thumbs, but after a few days she gained a little confidence and even started to smile, falling into the rhythm of pulling pints and opening bottles.

Totting up the price of a large round was one challenge, as was the skill of pouring drinks and chatting amiably with the customers at the same time. When offered a drink by a customer, she accepted with thanks, but saved the money to augment still further her improving finances. At closing time, after clearing up the bar, she would quickly walk the short distance to her flat, to bed and oblivion. Holding down two jobs was certainly exhausting, yet cathartic at the same time.

As the weeks went by, she had not only managed to pay the bills, but putting aside some money for material, had skilfully designed and made a jacket, skirt and trousers for herself, to broaden her wardrobe for the workplace. She had her hair restyled at a central Norwich hairdresser and felt her self-confidence nudge upwards. She even phoned home to reassure her mother that life was going well, omitting the details which she knew her mother would not want to hear or would worry about. She did not speak to her father.

Music lovers hailed from all sections of the community, so meeting the public, for the most part, was an interesting and stimulating experience. Francesca appreciated how well informed some of the customers were, not least one of her colleagues, and she also realized how much she did not know about classical music, although it had been a favourite subject at school, but she was gradually becoming more informed about various recordings, rifling her way through catalogues and listening to classical music whenever possible, quite often in the shop. A fair number of customers were students and teachers of varying ages who were studying or teaching music to degree standard and beyond, and instrumentalists, singers and academics who required a wide range of both printed and recorded music.

Following late evenings at the Golden Fleece, Saturday mornings had become a time of hazy thinking and suppressed yawns for Francesca who operated almost trance-like on auto-pilot at the music shop until about half past eleven when she had had two black coffees. Only then did she feel truly alert to what was going on around her. Christmas was not so far distant, and several customers, aware of this, purchased or ordered tapes and records of their choice.

"Do you by any chance have the recording of Elgar's *First Symphony* with Sir John Barbirolli conducting the Philharmonia Orchestra?"

Francesca looked up to see who had posed the question, and despite her fatigue, took in the young man who was smiling at her across the counter. He was about twenty-two, she thought, slim and of medium height, with a wavy shock of chestnut-coloured hair and quite magnetic eyes. She also noticed that his hands were sensitive and the fingers long. That recording was not in stock, but Francesca assured him that an order would arrive by the following Saturday. He seemed delighted, placed his order, and then asked about a copy of Haydn's *Maria Theresa Mass* which he needed fairly urgently. She led him to the vocal scores, and after tripping over a box of sheet music which had been carelessly left out by previous customers, they caught each other's eyes and giggled. Then Francesca successfully produced the Haydn.

That initial, brief meeting remained detailed in her memory throughout the coming week, as she looked forward to the following Saturday when he would collect his Elgar recording. She already knew his name from the order form: Michael McKenna. She enjoyed whispering the soft alliteration of the name to herself. Although she hardly knew him, she was certain that he could become more important to her than any of the young customers she had met, either in the music shop or in the pub. The opposite sex had not really interested her before, since she had lacked confidence in her ability to relate to males, with the exception of her brother, Sebastian, or to attract them. Not to try is not to fail, she had thought. Although on this occasion she had made no effort at all, yet there had been an instant moment of rapport. Was she deluding herself, or maybe her imagination was working overtime? Perhaps this Michael McKenna flashed his magnetic eyes wherever he went, and what she had thought was a special moment was one of many to him. She tried hard to banish him from her mind, to be rational and sensible, but he persistently returned to her thoughts, and she could not wait for Saturday to come.

When the day finally arrived, she got up early, took care with her appearance, and reached the music shop more punctually than usual, given that it was Saturday morning. Soon a steady stream of customers invaded the shop, intent on collecting or placing their Christmas orders before departing to pursue their next shopping mission. A small group of browsers remained, but on the whole, business was brisk at that time of year and the turnover fast. By lunch time he had not arrived, so she eagerly anticipated the afternoon. Whenever she was not involved with a customer, she kept one eye on the door, but by five o'clock, when he had not made an appearance, she was genuinely angry with herself for feeling so disappointed.

After spending an uneventful weekend feeling flat and lonely, even when she was working at the Golden Fleece, she returned to the shop on Monday, her spirits low and confidence sapped. The one fillip to the weekend had been a letter from her mother reminding her of the family Christmas she was organizing, and Francesca was unquestionably expected to return home. Evidently much would be packed into a short time, with Christmas and post-Christmas visits to and from the numerous aunts, uncles and cousins on both sides of the family. Present buying was a nightmare with so many relations to think of and with such a modest sum to spend, so Francesca made a quick decision. She would buy token presents only for her parents, brothers and sisters. The extended family would not be included, but perhaps her more affluent siblings would be able to make up for her feeble finances.

These practicalities and the short time in which she had to cope with them, at least forced romantic thoughts about Michael McKenna to the back of her mind. The publican at the Golden Fleece had been very accommodating about her short Christmas break, which she had organized more or less to coincide with that of the music shop. On her very last day, when a veritable mêlée of customers was purchasing last-minute gifts, and she was multitasking in all directions, he suddenly appeared in front of her, as cool as a gin and tonic, with magnetic eyes still working overtime.

"That recording is a surprise for my best girl, so I hope it's come in!"

Francesca averted her eyes, said nothing and quickly produced the package. The transaction completed, he wished her a happy Christmas, and was gone. Her low spirits reached rock bottom.

Although she had partly dreaded Christmas, the holiday turned out to be far better than she had expected. All her brothers and sisters converged on the farm in suitably exuberant spirits, and were pleased to see their parents and each other again. For the most part, they helped out with chores and meal preparation whilst exercising their considerable wit and repartee. They sang carols around the piano with great enthusiasm, sometimes singing in parts or with descant, they attended Midnight Mass, and ate and drank their fill. It was a time when Francesca felt glad that she was one of a large family, no matter what problems had occurred in the past. She at least had some confidence in her identity; she was one of the clan, and she felt secure and supported in that knowledge. After her experiences during the last few months, she had realized for the first time in her life just how important her family was to her. Although unpleasant arguments and rows broke out from time to time, when the chips were down and trouble involved those from outside the family, the clan closed ranks and clung together with steadfast loyalty against the world.

Francesca was required to return to Norwich after just a few days, whereas her brothers and sisters were able to stay longer in the family home to reunite briefly with their cousins, aunts and uncles. She had always felt close to her eldest brother, Sebastian, twelve years her senior, and she would have liked to have spent more time with him. His disposition was kind, calm and rational, enhanced by a mischievous sense of humour. The age gap between himself and Francesca was sufficiently wide to prevent any sibling rivalry, and together they shared a sense of the ridiculous to the extent that Seb, as she called him, often cracked the most impossible jokes, delivering double entendre in a sotto voce bass voice, which sent her into fits of suppressed giggles and which, certainly in her adolescent years, she had great difficulty in controlling. He had taught her a special language, too, which meant they could communicate without other people understanding. It worked like a dream, and was particularly useful in her childhood when she had fallen out with one of her sisters. You simply took any word, and placed the sound *irag* between each syllable. So, "How are you?" became "Howiragow ariga youiragoo?" Despite its simple formation, it was surprisingly incomprehensible to others. Although Seb was now newly married to Heather, a lawyer like himself, and they were living in York, he still felt protective towards his youngest sister, and enjoyed a special bonding with her.

Shortly before the New Year snow fell throughout Norfolk, and east winds blew, as it seemed, directly from the Urals right across the low-lying county. It was bitterly cold, and Francesca trudged to work each day zombie-like with her head down, collar up and woolly hat pulled well over her ears. The pre-Christmas spending spree in the shop had been replaced by relative stagnation, and the hours passed very slowly indeed. She was, therefore, surprised and glad when Sheila, a colleague, quite unexpectedly invited her to a New Year's Eve party in the Earlham Road, close to the university.

"Do come, and bring a bottle. More snow is forecast to-night, so you may have to stay over. Is that okay?" she asked cheerfully. Francesca sadly had to decline the invitation because she was on duty at the Golden Fleece. "Well, join us later. It'll be an all-night affair. You know my address."

Francesca imagined she would be on her knees with fatigue by the time the pub had closed, and therefore hankering after her bed, but then the thought of a new year and a fresh start inspired her to disregard sensible ideas like having a good night's sleep, and concentrate on the potential excitement of the rest of the night. So, clutching a bottle of red plonk, she took a taxi to the party address. No-one could have mistaken it for another. Pop music was blaring out, all the lights were on and young people were coming and going. She did not recognize any of them, but peals of laughter and raised voices inside rang out above the persistent beat of the music. Sheila caught sight of her, made her welcome, offered her a drink and introduced her to one or two pimply students standing nearby.

Despite all the vibrant activity in the room, they were a bit tongue-tied, not long released from their mothers' apron strings, Francesca imagined, and so, losing interest, she turned to watch the dancing.

There he was! The frenetic tempo which had assaulted her ears on arrival changed to a smoochy adagio as he looked up, caught her eye and immediately came over to her.

"Hello, hello again! A happy New Year, or nearly! May I have the pleasure of this dance, oh lady of the beautiful name?"

He bowed somewhat theatrically, and dazzled her again with his twinkling eyes. She smiled, but made no reply, as his arm went round her, guiding her onto what had become a small but crowded dance floor. She felt a sudden frisson of excitement which she had never felt before in her entire life.

"Who told you my name, Mr McKenna?" she asked teasingly.

"Ah! Now that would be telling, Francesca."

Then silence reigned between them as they concentrated on enjoying the music, the closeness of each other's bodies, and dancing as one. It was intoxicating, and she wished that this feeling would go on for ever

Midnight struck and everyone was ready to toast the New Year with great spirit, hilarity and the nearest drink they could find. A great deal of hugging and kissing preceded "Auld Lang Syne" and Francesca wondered which of the girls present was Michael's girlfriend.

Then gradually, it was all over. The music stopped and late-night reality returned. A few conscientious characters staggered towards the kitchen carrying tumblers and wine glasses, whilst one young man with a greenish pallor aimed for the bathroom and only just made it. Francesca went to retrieve her coat from upstairs and discovered couples in all the bedrooms. Others were bedding downstairs or leaving for their own student accommodation nearby.

It had been snowing heavily, and the full moon lit up the thick, white expanse which was the Earlham Road. She stood for a moment in the doorway and wondered what to do. Michael was mysteriously nowhere to be seen, and she imagined that he had discreetly disappeared with his girlfriend, whoever she was, without bothering with even the courtesy of saying goodbye. She had no option but to walk back to her flat in Benedict Street, and sadly she set off in the snow.

Fortunately, other people were tramping home, so the road was not empty or frightening. Her shoes were not robust enough to withstand snow, and her feet were already freezing to the point of numbness. She wondered how she was going to survive the long walk back to the flat, considering herself a total idiot for accepting an invitation to a party where she knew hardly anyone, and the ones she did know were scarcely responsible or hospitable. Perhaps she should have stayed curled up in a bathroom or airing cupboard rather than face this lonely walk home. She was in no mood to appreciate the wintry silhouette of the snow-laden trees in the moonlight.

Suddenly she heard a male voice call out to her from some way away.

"Francesca, wait! Francesca." Turning, she saw Michael ploughing through the snow towards her, dressed in a heavy overcoat, scarf and boots, clearly prepared for arctic conditions.

"Why did you race off so quickly? Did you say you live on Benedict Street? You can't possibly walk all that way on your own."

"Well, I couldn't find Sheila, and I thought you'd gone off with your best girl, so I decided to brave the elements."

"My best girl?" he queried in mock puzzlement.

"Yes, you know, the one you bought the Elgar recording for as a Christmas present." answered Francesca.

"Oh, that's my mother." He grinned broadly as her face expressed obvious disbelief.

"I always call her my best girl. She's a bit of an Elgar fanatic, you know."

"Your mother!" Francesca giggled in relief, caught his eye, and then they both burst out laughing.

He insisted on taking her home, and explained that since his student accommodation was full to bursting with visitors, he could not invite her to spend the night there. They plodded on in companionable silence, trying to keep warm, and within an hour they had reached the flat. By this time, it was nearly three o'clock, and the snow was still falling. Francesca had no intention of allowing Michael to go one step further, so she invited him to spend the night in her flat. If her parents knew, they would probably have had an apoplectic fit, but they did not know and she did not care. They were both frozen to the bone and the flat was empty.

The night-storage heaters were no longer pumping out heat, but nonetheless the flat felt quite warm compared with the subzero temperatures outside. Her shoes were all but ruined, and her feet ached with pain as the warmth seeped in and the feeling in them was restored. She scurried round making cocoa and filling hot-water bottles. Michael was relieved not to have to return to overcrowded lodgings, or to have to sleep on the floor. Instead he slept in Francesca's bedroom in the other twin bed,which had been left vacant by Sarah's departure. Unsurprisingly it was not long before she could hear the steady, rhythmic breathing of his sleeping a few feet away from her, and before oblivion overwhelmed her exhaustion, she marvelled at how events had turned out, and sleepily, she looked forward to a really happy new year in 1975.

She woke late at about eleven o'clock, and glanced over at Michael who had not stirred, and looked as though he might stay in a dormant position until further notice. Outside it was no longer snowing, but all was frozen up, since the night temperatures had dipped several degrees below freezing point, and very little traffic was passing down Benedict Street. Turning around into the bedroom again, she felt very mixed emotions. It was new and strange to her to share her bedroom with a man. Her strict and conventional upbringing had stamped its mark on her, and she realized, too, how little she knew about him. And yet as she gazed down at the boyish face on the pillow, so peacefully sleeping and unaware of her thoughts, she also considered that she was now twenty years old and well able to make decisions for herself. After all, some girls or women of her age were wives and mothers, and needed to make important decisions every day of their lives.

She pulled on her housecoat and headed for the kitchen, and by the time she had prepared tea and toast on a tray, he must have heard her movements and awakened. He smiled sleepily at her as she placed the tray on a small white stool close to his bedside.

"Would monsieur prefer zee tea or zee coffee?" she asked, affecting an overblown French accent.

"Since we are in England, I shall take zee tea," he replied drowsily.

"Just as well, monsieur, *parce que* that is all we 'ave." They found themselves laughing again, which for Francesca dissipated the slight unease she had felt about his staying in the flat.

Neither of them was expected anywhere in particular for the next hour or two, and so they spent the time talking, learning a great deal about each other in a short time. Whereas Francesca was the youngest of six children born in Norfolk, Michael was an only child and born in Finchley.

He was twenty-one, an organist, and in the final year of his music degree, but in addition to gaining an academic qualification, his main wish was to continue his studies as a performer, perhaps abroad, but most likely in an English cathedral. At the moment he was able to gain practice at the cathedral in Norwich, and also at the beautiful fifteenth-century church in the market place, St Peter Mancroft, claiming to be the largest parish church in the country. Michael's parents were divorced.. His mother lived in the family home in Finchley. His father worked in real estate and lived in Paris, and so Michael had not had close and regular contact with his father for some years.

Francesca felt drawn to him. Perhaps it was her maternal instinct making her feel protective about an only child of divorced parents, for no matter how confident or academic he was, he was virtually alone in the world. Unlike Francesca, he was not bolstered psychologically by a large clan, but had to have a very independent spirit, whether he liked it or not. Despite his boyish charm, magnetic eyes and recurrent sense of humour, he neither showed his feelings nor talked about them.

Francesca imagined and hoped that if their relationship developed, he would open up more to her. As it was, he gave her a few facts about his family, work and friends, but no feelings or opinions about them. His friends, unsurprisingly, were mostly to be found in music circles, at the university, in Norwich or in London. Since she had acquired knowledge about newly released recordings and famous ones of great works during her months of learning at the music shop, they shared a common bond in music, and also in the wild North Norfolk landscape which Francesca knew so well.

She talked to him about the wild life, about the twitchers who came in their droves to North Norfolk to watch rare sea birds, about the seals on the sandbanks off Moston Quay near Blakeney, and the terrible flooding of East Anglia during her parents' time in 1953. She was surprised at herself for talking to him like this about her Norfolk heritage. It was not something she remembered having done before, but the truth was that he was an attentive listener and seemed genuinely interested in what she was saying. Nevertheless, she spared him a narration of the lives of the more famous sons and daughters of her home county, namely Lord Nelson, Elizabeth Fry and Edith Cavell.

As the conversation finally drew to a close, he took the opportunity of thanking her repeatedly for her hospitality, mentioning that he needed to get back to his university lodgings, to recover his property and check out his habitat before any more time elapsed after that famous party. He knew that she worked a few evenings a week at the Golden Fleece, and suggested that he could easily contact her there. No phone had been connected in her flat, which had made communication difficult, but Francesca was determined to remain solvent until she found another flat mate. As the earnings outweighed the expenses, she would have a phone installed, but in the meantime she would have to do without. She had given her parents her two work numbers for emergencies and important messages.

She rose and took the mugs into the kitchen, and when she returned he had already pulled on his coat and scarf. She noticed that his shoes had not dried properly from their snow trek across Norwich. As she turned to open the door, he swivelled her around in his arms and kissed her fully on the lips. She had anticipated this moment and let herself relax blissfully into the drama of it. It was her first real kiss with someone as good looking and mysteriously exciting as Michael McKenna. She could not believe this was happening to her; he surely could have any girl.

"Thanks again," he whispered. "I'll see you soon."

Then he was gone, and through her window she watched him trudge up the street in the snow past the church, and disappear into the distance.

Her heart was pounding and her mood exultant. She sat down, trembling slightly, as she mentally retraced the events of the previous twelve hours.

He had spent the night or part of it in her flat, and he had not admitted to having another girl friend. In fact he had all but denied it, and he had actually kissed her. The adrenalin was flowing as she slumped back on the settee in a state of dreamy euphoria. She could not wait to see him again, and as she was unable to contact him easily, she had no choice but to wait until he contacted her.

Finally, exhausted with emotion and lack of sleep, she dozed off with nothing and nobody but Michael McKenna on her mind and in her dreams.

A few days passed uneasily for Francesca and then, true to his word, Michael dropped in for a drink at the Golden Fleece at about ten o'clock one evening, after having accompanied a rehearsal for one of the city's choral societies. It was evidently worthwhile practice for him and a way of boosting his student income. He waited until Francesca's shift was over, and walked her back to the flat, holding her hand in his and occasionally stopping to kiss her on the way.

Although she felt as if in heaven itself, her silent hopes of romantically spending time with him in the flat evaporated when he explained that he was getting up very early the next day in order to travel to Carlisle for an interview and music examination at the cathedral. He would return on Saturday, and hoped to see her then. Their final kiss in the darkness of the courtyard was insistent, passionate, and to Francesca, addictive, leaving her weak physically and yet elated in spirit.

Her emotions continued to be in turmoil over the next few days. Her appetite had all but disappeared. She was almost desperate to see Michael again, although she did not want to admit it to herself, and at work she forced herself to be focussed on the jobs in hand for fear of losing them.

She and Sheila at first had very little to say to each other following Sheila's disappearance after the party. Francesca did not ask for an explanation and Sheila did not give one. There was no mention of Michael McKenna. In the music shop they each went about their work independently in the normal way, but a coolness existed between them.

Francesca's shy, introverted and secretive nature meant that she was not in the habit of broadcasting her business and her emotions to others, but on this occasion her feelings were so powerful that she longed to share them with someone, to receive another opinion, outlook or advice, and unburden herself. She could not tell any of her brothers and sisters, and certainly not her parents. She had her pride. After all, she was trying to prove her independence to them, and that included emotional independence. She might have been able to tell her brother Seb, but he was 200 miles away in York and incredibly busy. She had fallen out with Sarah for letting her down over the flat, and Sheila had shown herself to be irresponsible too. Most of all, she could not risk telling either of them for fear of her thoughts being communicated back to Michael at the university or over a drink. So, she bottled up her emotions and got on with living, since there was no other acceptable option.

This state of not being able to confide in anyone caused Francesca to turn in on her own thoughts. Her reverie was so intense, as she dreamed and thought constantly about Michael, that she became incapable of interacting fully with her colleagues and friends. She existed on the surface of things, but her real life was in her own thoughts and hopes. She had never felt like this before. She was still eating very little, and the fact that he might not be really interested in her, filled her with panic. Saturday finally came, and she felt sick with excitement and apprehension. Michael's arrival at the music shop late in the afternoon, though, caused her spirits to soar, particularly when he mentioned that he would like to see her at the Golden Fleece that evening, adding that he had something to tell her.

Saturday evening at the Golden Fleece was usually a lively affair, with theatre and concert goers adding to the regulars and predinner customers. All the bar staff, including Francesca, were busy serving throughout the evening with scarcely any let-up until closing time. She was grateful to be so occupied when Michael made his entrance and last drinks were called. He had attended a concert in the city after returning from Carlisle and once again waited for her shift to end.

Despite her fatigue after having worked for so many hours, both in the shop and in the pub, Francesca felt herself alive and elated in Michael's presence. She kept telling herself that she had never felt like this before. As they walked back to her flat, arms and hands entwined, he told her that he thought his interview and examination at Carlisle Cathedral had gone well, and that maybe becoming an assistant organist there would be his first job after graduation. Within minutes, they had reached Benedict Street, and as she inserted her key into the lock, she knew that he would stay the night despite the disappearance of the snow.

The flat was certainly bijou, yet full of character, furnished by the owner to an attractive level of good taste and comfort, with side-lighting providing a welcoming and mellow ambiance. Francesca was just about to choose an atmospheric record to play when Michael miraculously produced a bottle of wine and a gift.

"A present for you," he said. "It's Brahms's *Sextet in B flat major*, and the theme music of a riveting French film I saw in Finchley during the last holidays. It was called *Les Amants (The Lovers)* and I just know you'll love the music."

Francesca hugged him with thanks, delighted with the thought of his giving her a present, and fetched two wine glasses from the kitchen, as he prepared the record for playing.

"The theme is in the second movement, the andante moderato section, not in the first," he commented with enthusiasm.

They snuggled up together on the settee, sipping the wine and kissing tenderly whilst listening intently to the intermingling movement of the violins, violas and cellos, as they rose and fell in alternately delicate and insistent emotional cadences. Francesca felt that up to that point, her life at best had been a tolerable existence, preliminary to the real life she was to have with Michael in the future.

Then the second movement, dominated by the cellos, changed to the passionate theme music of *Les Amants*. Michael was deeply affected by the music. Tears rolled down his cheeks, and they both felt a powerful emotion, uncontrollable and compelling in its force. He moved her from the settee gently onto the rug, and Francesca was completely helpless in his arms. All her pent up longings of the previous weeks poured out as he undressed her, and then with great passion, he overwhelmed her and completed the act of love.

A week later Francesca had mixed thoughts about losing her virginity, and it was because she did not have a totally clear view on the subject that she felt irritated with herself.

Michael had returned to his studies by necessity, and she to both her jobs, leaving her with little time on her hands except for thinking. She wondered how she could have so quickly become totally magnetized by him, and felt guilty for allowing him to unleash in her such a powerful physical need of him that she knew she could not control. She ached for him all the time, and thought of him constantly, her emotions proving too strong for her mind at that point.

When would she see him again? She hardly knew. He was busy studying for final examinations at the University of East Anglia, and anyway, there was no phone in her flat.

Personal phone calls were not encouraged in either the music shop or the pub, and to make matters worse, she found that the communal phone in Michael's student accommodation often rang incessantly. It seemed that either everyone was out or indifferent about answering it. Occasionally, when using a public phone box, she did manage to contact him only to have the briefest conversation. His time, he said, was crammed to the last second with lectures, tutorials, essays, revision, instrumental practice, rehearsals, and practical examinations. The list seemed endless to Francesca. He would be unable to see her for at least a fortnight.

He was, of course, terribly sorry about it. He would miss her as much as she would miss him, but his life was so full at the time that he had no choice but to honour his commitments and prepare for final examinations, ready to pursue his career. He would contact her when this present spate of musical activity had calmed down, and then they would have a loving reunion.

Francesca's decision to exist for the next fortnight until they were reunited did not improve her heightened emotional state, particularly as she felt there was no one in whom she could confide. Sheila might have been her confidante, or even Sarah, but they had both proved themselves to be unreliable and untrustworthy. Sheila, particularly, had gained the reputation of being a gossip, and nobody's private news or finer feelings were safe with her, so Francesca lived in her own inner world, even though she was busy most of the time, work being her salvation. She lost her appetite and suffered from insomnia, which was very unusual for her as she normally fell asleep shortly after her head touched the pillow. Her thoughts were only of Michael, and her accumulating emotional exhaustion often reduced her to tears. Each day she hoped and expected she would hear from him, just the briefest of phone calls. Each day she was disappointed.

Two weeks passed, and then a hurried note arrived from him through the post, telling her that he would shortly attend more interviews involving travel away from Norfolk, and therefore he would be unable to keep their date, but would let her know as soon as possible on his return. In the meantime he was looking forward to that day. She read and re-read the note to take in every word and nuance, and at night she placed it under her pillow which was often wet from her tears. If a definite date for their reunion had been mentioned, she would have been able to go about her daily duties with some optimism and fortitude, but the uncertainty and disappointment of the situation increased her emotional exhaustion to the extent that her colleagues and friends commented on her loss of weight and unusually pale complexion.

Francesca bravely disregarded their observations with a quip about managing to lose her puppy fat at last, and marvelled at herself for guarding her privacy so effectively, or so she thought. At both the music shop and the pub, customers with whom she had become friendly over the past months invited her to join them at a concert, meal or play from time to time, but she always had the perfect excuse of being too busy, or needing to catch up on her sleep. Her thoughts and priorities were only with Michael, and she did not want to unburden her soul to any of her newly found friends.

Unbelievably, after waiting so long and although it would have halved her expense, she turned down an offer to share her flat from Emma, a pleasant and newly qualified primary school teacher who like many young people of her age wished to leave the family home for freedom and independence. Francesca told her that that her sister, Deborah, was to stay with her for an indefinite period, and unfortunately the flat was too tiny to accommodate three of them – a white lie. The truth was that she wanted the flat free for Michael's visits as unpredictable as they were.

Finally, after what seemed like eternity to Francesca, but was actually three weeks, Michael again turned up in time for last orders at the Golden Fleece on Saturday evening and escorted her back to the flat. Her joy to be reunited with him, her first and only love, was so overwhelming that she disregarded any questions that she might have asked him, content only to fall into his arms and express the passionate yearning aroused by his absence from her life. The earlier uncertainty she had felt about him following their first love-making, coupled with a tinge of guilt for having doubted him, were now replaced with the strongest, unspoken desire that what she now wanted from life was Michael.

He stayed with her the rest of the weekend, making meals and making love, without going out until early on

Monday morning when he left to attend his first lecture of the week.

He had actually wanted to return to his student accommodation on Sunday evening, to prepare for the coming week, particularly as he had been away periodically. Francesca, however, had pleaded, and he, succumbing to her charming entreaties, had relented, even though the single bed was cramped and uncomfortable after a while. For future contact arrangements, they decided that she would phone on certain evenings when he was fairly confident of being in, and when study, work and commitments allowed, they would see each other. He emphasized that his future prospects were at stake and he did not want to let his parents down. Although Francesca was tearful about saying goodbye again so soon, she nonetheless felt calmer and less nervous about their developing relationship, and consequently approached her work with a cheerful heart.

A few days later she received a letter from her sister, Deborah, asking to be put up for a weekend before heading south from Norwich to London to spend the Easter holidays with friends in France. It was ironic that the lie she had told Emma about her sister's coming visit turned out to be reality, even for a short time. Unfortunately, it also meant that she would be unable to see Michael at the flat that weekend. When she telephoned the news to him, he seemed somewhat disappointed, but then came the shock.

The following week he was to fly to Paris to spend the Easter holidays with his father, combining the visit with sightseeing, and he hoped, a large dose of la cuisine française. Without sparing her feelings, he added that he was looking forward to it because his life had recently become so pressured and hectic that he needed to wind down and relax. He looked forward to seeing her at the start of the summer term, or maybe sooner.

Her cheerful spirits spiralled downwards, and without much success she rationalized with herself that it was not so very long to wait. She was incredibly busy with both her jobs, and her sister was coming to stay, if only for a short time. She also needed to focus more on her dressmaking ambitions which she had neglected for some weeks, and seriously plan what she wanted to do in the future. Deep down she felt confused and even angry. It seemed that he had suddenly and coolly delivered a news bombshell that was designed to depress and unnerve her just as they were becoming closer.

After a few days these thoughts and feelings lessened in intensity, and she was again partly able to rationalize the situation. Michael, after all, was a very busy student, close to finishing his degree course and maintaining additional music commitments, and since his father lived in Paris, it was quite natural that they should want to spend time with each other there.

Deborah's visit came and went uneventfully and Francesca mentioned not a syllable about her love affair with Michael. Of her three sisters, Deborah was the closest to her in age. Just eighteen months separated them, but they were not close in any other way.

During their childhood there had been considerable rivalry between them which had continued into their adult lives. At the root of it, Francesca was jealous of her parents' admiration for their ambitious and talented daughter's study of architecture, and in turn, Deborah considered Francesca to be the spoilt baby of the family who had been indulged unnecessarily and should have focussed more single mindedly on her education and career prospects. Francesca usually muttered that Deborah sounded just like an echo of their father and did not know what she was talking about. On this occasion, Deborah did not criticize her. She was clearly glad to be staying in Francesca's flat over the weekend and must have noted that her sister was very busy indeed.

A Norfolk winter emerged into a windy Norfolk spring, with daffodils predictably following the crocuses, and early camellias and grape hyacinths blooming at the Bedales' farm where Francesca spent Easter. A mass of yellow celandines carpeted the spinney at the bottom of their garden, and the Lenten roses she had planted with her mother two years before nestled among the ferns under the sumac tree near the summerhouse. Her parents were pleased to see her, especially as their other offspring, apart from Robert, had made plans to spend Easter elsewhere.

Robert was in his final year at agricultural college and had returned home during the Easter holidays to help his father at a busy time of year. After his graduation Robert would work full-time. The plan was that he would take over the farm when Mr Bedale retired within a few years. Father and son got on very well together, their temperaments and opinions were similar and they spoke the common language of farming, though the industry was no longer a matter of muck and mystery, as in days gone by, but had become very much an industry of science and efficiency.

A happy-enough supper was spent together on the first evening, during which news was exchanged. Francesca made certain of carefully editing what was going on in her life, remembering to tell her parents and Robert only the wholesome snippets of information of which they would approve. As usual she was forced to talk superficially, avoiding any kind of controversy. Predictably, the latest news of the achievements of her brothers, sisters and even cousins were totally praiseworthy.

Sebastian was forging a most successful legal career for himself in York and was considering being called to the bar. Emily, after years of studying medicine, had become a qualified doctor and was now specializing in anaesthesiology in London. Deborah had miraculously won a special award for her teamwork in an architectural project. Caroline, too, would shortly take her law degree, and was expected to pass with flying colours since she had always been brilliant. Robert's love of and ability for farming pleased both his parents. Even the cousins were distinguishing themselves, though the one piece of unfortunate news was that Cousin Jack had broken his leg in a skiing accident, his freedom and adventures being temporarily curbed. No doubt he would spend the time studying profitably, and reap the just reward of his academic prowess and motivation. God, thought Francesca, if only I had some achievement of real worth that would please my father.

After helping her mother with the dishes, she stepped out into the garden as dusk was falling, and headed once more for the summer house, her place of sanctuary. Only Bert, the dog, followed her. She opened the door and sat down on the familiar, old rocking chair whilst Bert curled up on a rug beside her. He had always especially loved Francesca because, unlike the others, she had treated him like a pet and not like a farm dog, giving him titbits, stroking him, kissing the top of his muzzle and even telling him her secrets.

And so it was in the fading light of the summerhouse that she told him all about Michael and how she longed to see him again; how she had missed her period and was desperately worried that she might be pregnant, although her menstrual cycle had never been regular; how she could not tell anyone and especially not her parents; and how she would not see Michael for at least another two weeks on his return from Paris. Unlocking her secrets to Bert released her tightly controlled emotions, and tears poured down her face for several minutes. Despite being a member of a large family, she felt very much alone. Realizing that something was wrong, Bert whined in sympathy, and sprang up into her lap. She hugged him tight, as her tears flowed onto his coat.

"Dear Bert," she whispered, "what a comfort you are. I've missed you, you know."

Her parents were socially busier than ever now that their children had grown up and moved away. That evening they were to attend a Conservative Party function, and as they were both preparing to go out, Francesca was able to nip back to the house via the kitchen without attracting attention to herself, and arrived in time to wish them a cheery goodbye as they departed. She was asleep when they returned.

Although her Easter holiday was very short, Francesca did not trust herself to maintain this false cheerfulness in front of her family for long, particularly as anxiety nagged at her all the time. So, on the day before her return to Norwich she asked her mother's permission to borrow her car to spend a day out on the North Norfolk coast. She desperately needed time to be free of responsibility for a day, to have time to think and to be soothed by the wild beauty of that coastline, but she also needed some company. So, gathering together a thermos of coffee, a packet of sandwiches, some dog biscuits and stale bread, she jumped into the car with Bert and drove out of the farmyard, already sensing relief that she could spend the day how she wished,and just be herself.

After a few minutes' drive, she reached her favourite village in that area. It was special because of its picturesque cluster of thatched cottages with gardens full of floral colour and interest that appeared as if no one had planned them, but had just effortlessly and enchantingly appeared. She parked the car and headed for the small lake on the north side of the village with beloved Bert at her heels, delighted to be free of the farm and noticeably enjoying his day out.

The sight of the lake, shrouded by blossoming trees interspersed with evergreens, gladdened her heart, as she looked across the water to a small island where mallards, moor hens and Canada geese were seemingly nesting in peaceful harmony together. Francesca walked all round the lake and sat down on a sturdy bench in the sunshine, noticing that it had been donated by a local resident who had loved the spot but was now deceased. Who could not love it?

Despite her pressing worries and the guilt about deceiving her parents, she was able to push these thoughts temporarily from her mind with the arrival of a mother mallard in search of breakfast or lunch, followed by eight tiny ducklings, all paddling like the clappers behind her.

Smiling, she reached down for the stale bread in her bag and broke it into crumbs before throwing them to the expectant family until all was gone. Any intruding male mallards intent on gate-crashing that lunch were sent off smartly by mother mallard's beak, snapping at their tails. It was such a delightful and amusing scene that Francesca wished she could stay forever, or at least visit more often. She also thought that nature, although often cruel, can have a cathartic influence on us all, and that places such as these were important for comforting the soul. Bert remained on impeccable behaviour at a safe distance from the ducks, his gaze never leaving them until it was time to go.

Once back in the car she headed for Holkham beach, one of her favourite places on earth a few miles away. Her great need was to think through the anxious turmoil of her mind and to work out a plan of sorts. She had found in the past that she could do this best by walking. Somehow the peace of covering a fair distance on foot calmed down the emotions, and at the same time set in motion a rational thinking process.

After parking in one of the usual public car parks, she and Bert hurried along the widespread dunes to that wonderful, massive stretch of pure sand which is Holkham beach. Surprisingly, although the weather was sunny and bracing, few holidaymakers were to be found there; perhaps as yet, it was too early. Just the occasional dog walker on the dunes, some horse riders in the distance and a father and son enjoying kite flying were all that could be seen. She saw Norfolk at its best, on a beautiful day, with billowing clouds, wide skies and the waves rolling onto long stretches of perfect sand. But for her worries, she would have been happy.

Strolling along the beach with Bert, she wondered what she should do, and occasionally she voiced her thoughts to him before they were whisked off onto the fresh, salty breeze. Perhaps she was worrying without cause, since her periods had often been late or irregular in the past, and when two or three years previously her mother had suggested consulting their doctor about it, Francesca had adamantly refused, blushing red with embarrassment and claiming that she was perfectly all right.

Perhaps then, this period was just a little bit later than usual as it had been before and the curse would arrive in a week or so. For once in her life it would be greeted with joy and relief. If it still did not arrive, she would see a doctor, but definitely not the family one who hobnobbed with her parents at the local Conservative Club. She would have to register with a Norwich doctor with whom her parents had no contact at all. What of Michael? Should she tell him of her fears on his return from Paris, or wait in case those fears proved groundless? She decided on the second idea, and anyway she was uncertain of the precise date of his return. He had not been specific about that. Again she told herself that most likely she was worrying for nothing, but that in the future she would need some contraceptive advice.

The walk along the beach, together with her decision-making, had invigorated her with renewed energy. After playing duck and drake with pebbles as the white-crested waves rolled in, she returned to the shelter of the dunes for lunch, much to Bert's delight. Propped up against tufts of marram grasses, she relaxed with coffee and sandwiches until Bert shook his wet coat all over her. Shrieking with mock indignation, she threw a dog biscuit just far enough to prevent a second round of unwanted spray. Lunch finished, she lay back sleepily in the sunshine, and dozed off for a few minutes.

She awoke to find her peace and solitude disturbed. The sunshine and the beauty of the seascape had inevitably attracted holidaymakers to the coast with the added interest of visiting Holkham Hall nearby. She jumped to her feet, after noticing that Bert had parked himself dutifully by her side while she was dozing. Seeing her move, he sprang into life expectantly, seemingly wondering what further adventures lay in store that afternoon. The car park was full. Francesca was glad to reverse out of it and be free from picnickers and excited children. They all had as much right to be there as she did, she knew, but in her present mood, she felt unsociable and in need of peace on her last day of freedom before returning to Norwich.

As she drove along the coastal road to Blakeney, she realized that her chances of being alone on that day were minimal, since too many people had the same idea as she did. Rather than return to the farm too soon, she headed for Moston Quay. She knew there were regular boat rides around the sand banks in that area for the purpose of viewing seals and their habitat. Fortuitously parking was easy, the tide was in and the boat was due to depart within a few minutes. After buying tickets, she and Bert clambered aboard the small craft with a number of other sea adventurers just as the engine started up, and they were off to circumnavigate the sandbanks in the continuing sunshine.

At first Francesca closed her eyes, pretending to be alone while holding tight to Bert's lead, as she enjoyed the gentle rise and fall of the boat and the mild breeze in her hair. When she heard delighted gasps from a group of children near her, she opened her eyes to see that the boat was nearing the first of the sandbanks, and dozens of seals of varying dimensions had come into view. What a sight it was! A large number were sprawled languorously in the sunshine. Two massive male specimens were fighting and snarling at each other, while others of more modest girth were intent on slipping off the sandbank into the sea to perhaps catch their next meal.

Others, females according to the boatman, more curious than their friends and relatives, were following the boat for some distance, which fascinated the group of children. Their reaction to the pursuant seals was the same as Francesca's, namely, to sing to them. She, like them, wanted to communicate with those wild creatures whose courage and freedom she admired, and some of them at least responded to song.

The scene on the remaining sandbanks was similar. Numerous ungainly, land-bound seals suddenly became transformed into skilled, agile movers as soon as they entered the sea. Capable of staying underwater for fifteen minutes or more, they appeared confident of their role in this life although it was a limited one. Francesca fleetingly wished that she was like them in that respect.

As the trip neared its ending and Bert showed signs of wanting to be back on terra firma, she realized that the day out had been as helpful as she hoped it would. She had devised a simple plan of sorts, and later, before packing to return to Norwich, she would be able to describe her happy day enthusiastically to her parents before they drove her to the station. They suspected nothing.

Her life in Norwich slotted back into place automatically as far as the music shop and the pub were concerned, and within days she had registered with a medical practice on the Earlham Road.

She had heard nothing from Michael, but rationalized that university holidays were quite long, and anyway he was spending time with his father in Paris whom he seldom saw. She longed to see him, to feel his arms protectively around her and to hear the reassurance of his love for her, which he had expressed so passionately in their lovemaking. She could not contemplate a future without him in her life. Somehow it felt right. It must be, since she was so besotted with him, and they seemed to have so much in common: music, dancing, books and a love of nature and wild life. They were both young and could build a wonderful life together.

Francesca's colleague, Sheila, who had handed in her notice before Easter, no longer worked at the music shop. She was taking time off, she said, before applying for a new job. Presumably she was taking an extended holiday, letting it be known that she did not really need to work at all since Daddy was a very successful business man, and as an only child, she wanted for nothing. Francesca was not sorry to see her depart, but was eager to meet her replacement with whom she hoped she would strike up a better relationship.

A fortnight after Easter, Gemma started her first day at the music shop, and Francesca did her best to familiarize her with stock, catalogues, order forms and general working practice. Gemma was as different from Sheila as she could be and in the most pleasant of ways. Like Francesca, she had left school after A levels, and had not opted to go to university. She loved music and admirably, she possessed not only a sense of humour, but also a capacity for hard work. Each evening she would take a bus home to Sprowston, situated in the north of the city where she lived with her parents and two brothers. She was easy, uncomplicated and unspoilt, and by the end of the first week, Francesca felt that she had made a friend. At least it was the start of a friendship.

Francesca treated Gemma to a meal at an Indian restaurant in the nearby city centre to celebrate the end of Gemma's first week at work. Over a chicken madras and a lamb dhopiaza, they chatted animatedly about their lives, families, taste in music and clothes, though Francesca was very careful not to mention a word about Michael. She felt uneasy about it, and still had no idea whether he had returned from Paris, although she thought that the university term was about to begin, if it hadn't begun already.

After their meal, Gemma went off to catch her bus and Francesca to start her shift at the Golden Fleece. She felt lethargic and tired, and had to force herself to work to the end of the shift. The publican's wife commented on how exhausted Francesca looked and she did so with some regret, since that weekend the pub was very short-staffed and Francesca's help was particularly needed. Nevertheless, she withdrew from the pub scene the minute she had finished her last chore and plodded home wearily, hoping that after a decent night's sleep, she would feel fine in the morning.

The alarm did not go off at seven o'clock since in her fatigue the night before she had forgotten to set it. When she awoke quite naturally after a deep sleep, she noticed, to her horror, that the time was nine thirty. She should have been in the music shop half an hour earlier. She wondered what her boss, Keith, would think and say about her unreliability and dashed to the bathroom. The long night's sleep had not made her feel better. In fact, she felt decidedly worse.

As she looked at her unusually pale face in the bathroom mirror, an unexpected queasiness overwhelmed her and she vomited in the toilet bowl. After a few minutes of retching and mouth washes, she left the bathroom and slumped onto the bed. By the time she felt less nauseous it was almost ten o'clock. Breakfast was out of the question, so she dressed hurriedly and on her way to work found a telephone booth from where she could phone her boss and apologize for her lateness, cursing the curry of the previous evening as she went.

"Fortunately Gemma is here on this busy Saturday morning," Keith commented sarcastically, "and you've certainly taken your time phoning in. Can we expect to see you any time soon?"

Francesca mumbled her apologies and explanation, feeling duly humiliated that Keith's strident tones would have been heard by Gemma and any listening customers, but she assured him that she would arrive at the shop very quickly. Once there, she was greeted with the information that she would lose two hours' pay from her weekly wages for lateness, and that Gemma, who had suffered no ill effects from the curry of the previous evening, was beavering away efficiently, completing orders and advising customers as if she'd been in the job for years, much to Keith's admiration. With typical British stiff-upper lip, Francesca said nothing, and resumed her duties.

It was from that Saturday onwards that Francesca managed to stay on the wrong side of Keith, and she noted anxiously that all his approval and praise was now directed towards Gemma who was a junior assistant and less experienced and knowledgeable about the music business than Francesca. A week later, when she asked Keith for a half day off for personal reasons without telling him the precise nature of her request, his comments were brusque and disparaging.

"The trouble with you is that you have taken on too much work, trying to hold down two jobs instead of doing one properly. I've noted for some time now that your punctuality leaves much to be desired, and when you do turn up late, you appear exhausted and unmotivated, hardly a credit or good advertisement to an important city store. I advise you to get your act together PDQ."

Keith never minced his words. He noted her half-day absence and did not pursue the matter further. For all her apparent good nature, Gemma could not resist a triumphant, little smile, knowing that her own status in the shop was strengthening by the minute.

The truth was that Francesca had been feeling unwell and exhausted for over a week, particularly since the curry episode, and knew that the decision to see her new doctor, with whom she had recently registered to have a medical, was the wisest course to take. She knew that her mother had suffered from anaemia a few years earlier, and had seemed permanently tired before her treatment. That was exactly how Francesca felt. Perhaps she, too, was anaemic.

After a full medical examination, blood and urine tests, Francesca faced the fatherly-looking doctor in his surgery, expecting him to prescribe her a course of iron pills. He seemed to be forming what he wanted to say quite carefully before doing so. He looked at her steadily over his bifocals, and after a lengthy pause, he said,

"Well, young lady, we shall have to wait for the blood test results to be returned from the hospital laboratory, but I am willing to stick my neck out and say they will confirm that you are a very healthy twenty-year-old. However, your urine analysis reveals that you are pregnant."

Francesca sat there in a state of shock, barely capable of taking in his comments, advice and directions, all delivered in a monotone. When he had finished speaking, she softly thanked him and without seeing the receptionist as he suggested, she rose and walked out of the medical centre towards Benedict Street in a trance-like state, aware only that the tingling in her breasts was confirming the doctor's diagnosis.

CHAPTER 3
ISABEL (1961–62)

Two years after her father's death, Isabel felt a desperate need to break out from the restricted existence of living with her mother in the town where she had been born, and she left home to take up a teaching post in London. She missed her father so much, his advice, support, humour and insight.

She was not envious by nature, but she was definitely envious that her peer group had fathers and she didn't. She did not particularly covet the cars they drove or the holidays they took. It was not having a dad that gnawed away at her and filled her with emptiness. The thought of his dying in pain at the age of fifty-three, after a domestically disturbed and unfulfilled life, often flooded her eyes with tears. Those who knew her thought enough time had passed for her return to normality, as if bereavement had a date on it. She had to get away, to feel less pain.

She had always been a religious child, even though her parents were not practising Christians. She took the daily instruction at her convent school quite seriously, and yet at church she immersed herself in her own Anglican tradition. Believing or not believing in the Immaculate Conception, the doctrine of the Assumption, or papal infallibility and transubstantiation, were matters of importance to her. She wanted to be clear cut and not foggy minded about it all. She was a bit of a zealous Protestant in the company of Catholics, and more than a bit Catholic in Protestant company.

Her peer group, at least those at the convent, were similarly minded. The churches were well attended in the fifties and ecumenism had not as yet made much of an impact. As much as she liked to learn and discuss religious doctrine, the emotional pull for Isabel lay in the rich tradition of Anglican church music composed since the Reformation. It included the works of Tallis, Byrd, Gibbons, Weelkes, Tomkins, and later Boyce, S. S. Wesley, Parry, Elgar, Vaughan Williams, Stanford, Bairstow and many others. Much later her soul would be sent into raptures by the very Catholic music of Palestrina, Victoria and Lassus, but as yet, she had not encountered these composers.

At the age of twenty-three, despite her religious background, Isabel completely lost her faith, and railed against God in her anger. Why did so many blameless people, like her father, die of disease, never to reach old age? Why did good people often languish in pain and agony, and thousands of innocents perish in floods, earthquakes and pestilence scarcely before they were aware of life itself, or later in poverty and starvation? She talked to a few knowledgeable clerics on the subject, but nothing they said could convince her that God was up there and involved with humanity. Her reading did not help either. She could only agree with Voltaire who became an agnostic in the eighteenth century, following the great earthquake of 1755 in Lisbon in which thousands of people died, many of them infants and babies, untouched by sin and therefore undeserving of divine retribution. As an unbeliever she felt a hypocrite singing in church, so she did not go at all.

Even in the early sixties life was rough in parts of South London, and when Isabel was assigned to a secondary school close to the Elephant and Castle by London County Council, she received a few shocks for which her suburban and convent upbringing had not prepared her. A badly maintained, dark, dingy building, seemingly dating back to the days of Charles Dickens, harboured problems of all kinds: endemic thieving, continuous disruption, vandalism, real poverty, flagrantly coarse and vulgar language, milk-bottle fights between Greek and Turkish Cypriots in the playground, racial tension generally, a low standard of education, a high turnover of staff both permanent and supply, and an indecisive headmaster. After two years of unsupported struggle against what seemed to her to be overwhelming odds, she felt drained physically and mentally with an exhaustion that a few nights' sleep would not correct.

Yet her mind and conscience were torn between the motley collection of South London teenagers who craved uninterrupted care and sound teaching, and her own health and survival.

The long summer holiday provided her with the opportunity to go youth hostelling on the continent with Mary, an old school friend, to feel the freedom and excitement of travelling to the unknown, and to recharge her batteries. Their main objective was to travel through France as quickly as possible so as to spend the maximum time they could afford in Tuscany. Isabel had already been drawn to Italian from her interest in opera, and had studied the language for two years at City Literary Institute evening classes with a Neapolitan *professoressa*.

Despite the blistering August heat and oversized backpacks, they were both dazzled by the beauty of the Tuscan landscape, the friendliness of the people and the seeming drama of every Italian conversation.

Isabel loved the trattorie with inexpensive and delicious food, and the lambrettas with girls sitting side-saddle on them, clinging onto overconfident boyfriends. Both Isabel and Mary were exhausted by the glories of Florence: the Uffizzi gallery, the Pitti Palace, the Piazza della Signoria, the churches of San Marco, San Lorenzo and Santa Croce, and the majestic and dominating Duomo with its campanile. It was a very different culture to what Isabel was used to, certainly to the near squalor of her professional life as a teacher in South London. All this Florentine beauty was located in a compact city with virtually no difficulty of access or transport. From the elevated Piazzale Michelangelo they could see the entire city below them, easily identifying the river Arno and the famous Ponte Vecchio of Puccini's aria, "O mio bambino caro" from the opera, *Gianni Schicchi*.

When the unforgettable holiday finally drew to a close, Mary appeared to be perfectly satisfied to return to her comfortable and uninspiring life with her parents in their three-bedroom semi until her boyfriend decided to propose marriage, or perhaps wait to visit Spain the following year. Isabel, however, who was hooked on Italy, could not get enough of it and was reluctant to return to London where a plethora of problems awaited her, with no let-up for good behaviour and all encompassed in dreadful weather.

An added Italian bonus was the new Florentine boy-friend she had acquired whilst on holiday and who was so sorry to see her departure. Italian men were so much more attentive and romantic, full of laughter and wit, she noted. They really appreciated women and knew how to treat them. She was delighted when Giovanni insisted on exchanging addresses, promising to visit London sometime soon. This turned out not to be an idle promise made in haste. He did, in fact, visit London twice, whilst Isabel spent the following Easter in Florence, staying in a small hotel near to his home, able to meet all the members of his family.

She found their rapid speech and Florentine accent difficult to understand at first, but imagined that her comprehension would improve with time. She also realized that they were genuine, well-meaning working people, though barely educated. Giovanni, who was ten years older than Isabel, had set up in business with a close friend living in Fiesole, and they had done well for themselves. They imported televisions from America and sold them, together with Italian-made models, from a large sale room situated near Piazza Santa Croce. Next to the sale room was a workshop for repairs, and their clients hailed from all over Florence as well as from the villages around. Most of the business was carried out between September and Easter, with Christmas creating the most demand, and summer the least. Giovanni worked hard and was eager to build up the business. He was also keen on Isabel, on getting married and starting a family.

Over the months of exchanging letters and visits, she had become fond of him, and had completely fallen in love with Italy at a time when life in the Elephant and Castle sapped her energy and joy in living. Daily confrontations in school on weekdays were followed by bitter rows and violence if she went home at the weekends, and Clive was in residence.

The flat in Tooting that Isabel shared with three other girls was small, shabby, claustrophobic and cheerless. The prospect of continuing to live there, whilst achieving negligible progress despite massive effort with classes at school, was bleak, and filled her with despondency.

A few days before the end of Isabel's Easter holiday in Florence, Giovanni proposed marriage and Isabel accepted. Together they planned that she would resign from her teaching post on her immediate return to London, and arrange a registry-office wedding, to take place shortly after the end of term in August. Meanwhile, he would find them a flat situated in a newly built block on the periphery of the city overlooking the Tuscan hills. It seemed that out of hell or purgatory, she had discovered paradise.

Isabel's mother arranged a modest wedding reception at a country club near her home in the Kent suburbs for their few relatives, friends and small Italian contingent which had journeyed to England by car. Surprisingly, Clive who had already married some months before did not ruin the day. In fact, it was one of a very few days in Isabel's life that he had not blighted somehow, or downright ruined. Throughout the marriage ceremony and reception she seemed to exist in a nervous haze of nagging anxiety and guilt, whilst Giovanni looked permanently confused. He could speak no English at all, and neither could the friends who had accompanied him. If Isabel was not immediately available to translate, the two groups did not interact conversationally, though dancing helped, and the special day passed off happily enough.

Many guilty thoughts crowded in on Isabel's mind. She blamed herself for leaving her mother to the mercy of Clive, for leaving those South London teenagers after only two years to take up a so-called easier life for herself, instead of committing herself to five or even ten years of consistent teaching, thus contributing to the improvement of educational standards in that part of London. Instead, she had joined the high turnover of staff statistics. She now felt uncertain about her feelings for Giovanni. Had she accepted a marriage proposal from someone she did not love so as to run away from her problems? Perhaps, as was the case for many brides of arranged marriages, love would grow with time even if it were not there initially. She would just have to make the best of it and persevere. In the meantime, she examined her conscience and felt very ashamed for not being really honest with Giovanni.

Preparing to leave the country, she acted out the happy goodbyes to her mother, relatives and friends, when in her heart she felt sick with anxiety and nerves, homesick even before leaving England. Weeks and months later, she only retained a sad, hazy memory of the journey back to Italy, covering hundreds of miles of French soil during which time Giovanni and Stefano took turns driving, and she made forced conversation with Gabriella in the rear of the car. As each mile passed, Isabel realized with sickening confirmation that she had made a terrible mistake, a disastrous mistake.

She recalled no significant details of the journey, where they stayed or what they ate. She slept quite a bit in the afternoons. She vaguely remembered that after they reached Italy the hairpin bends in the Apennines made her feel sick. What she did remember with clarity, though, was her own disinclination to have sex, and Giovanni's unquenchable need for it. She was a virgin, and during their brief courtship he had respected her virginity. Now that they were married, once they were in the hotel bedroom, he seemed to want it all the time: on the bed clothed, against the wall, on the floor and several times during the night, often without her consent. If she objected, he became rough with her rather than loving, and she had the uncanny feeling that he would have struck her had they not been in a cheap hotel with paper-thin walls. As it was, she submitted, and dreaded their arrival in Italy, her body aching and sore from his frenzied penetration. She longed to be back to all the familiarity of her life in London, warts and all, instead of peering into this unknown which, at first, had seemed so enticing, but in fact, was turning out to be yet another hell.

She missed her friends, particularly the old ones from her own school days, her singing lessons, the choral singing, the snatched evenings at Covent Garden queuing for tickets in the gods, her pupils at the Elephant and Castle and her efforts to motivate them, and the laughter and repartee of the staff room. She missed her mother despite the fact that she could sometimes be ultra fussy and dictatorial. Her mother had always given her love, but not confidence, a trait which seemed to be characteristic of her mother's generation. She still missed her father although he had been dead for a few years

. If only she could lean on his protective sanity right now. She did not miss Clive.

As expected, the flat was newly built and situated on the periphery of Florence, along with other similar apartment buildings, creating a new area served by a few local shops and a bus route. The flats were constructed around a courtyard, and Giovanni had chosen a one-bedroom flat on the first floor, with sitting room, dining room, kitchen, bathroom and two balconies. The rooms were spacious with marble floors, and painted in calm neutral colours. The high kitchen windows looked out onto the courtyard, and on three sides Isabel could see activity all the way up to the sixth floor.

Signoras passed the time of day with each other, shook dusters, prepared food or indulged in one of those dynamic Italian conversations which might be expected to end in a fight, as excitable tones compete with each other to reach a conversational climax. Old grandfathers nodded off on the balconies and infants screamed. The views from the two balconies off the bedroom and sitting room looked out onto typical and beautiful Tuscan countryside. In the distance, sun-parched hills with terraced cultivation, vineyards and a few small white-washed, red-roofed houses showed signs of human habitation and industry. Isabel would have liked to paint the peaceful, rustic scene, but doubted her talent, and she would have to leave out the foreground, which included a car park, a children's play area and newly built shops.

The flat was far better-equipped, cleaner and more attractive than anything Isabel had seen in South London. In fact, she had been ashamed of the Tooting flat she had shared with her friends when Giovanni had visited her earlier in the year. Perhaps she would adjust to her totally new life in Italy if her mother and close friends could visit once in a while, but there was no second bedroom, and come to that, no second bed. It would be expensive for them to stay at a hotel, and since she was no longer working, she could not hope to pay for their stay. Most of her savings had been spent on the wedding dress, veil, shoes, flowers, going away outfits and presents.

When she mentioned to Giovanni how much she would appreciate a visit from her mother or friends in the future, he either showed no interest or claimed that he had not understood her Italian, which not only infuriated her, but made her feel that it was hardly worth speaking at all. After a few unsuccessful attempts, she decided that she would only speak when she was spoken to, and in the meantime she would continue studying the language. She could not help thinking that Giovanni claimed *non capisco* when it was in his interests to do so.

Every morning at eight o'clock he went off to work, leaving Isabel to her own devices until lunchtime, and after a siesta, he would not return again until seven or eight in the evening. She spent the mornings and late afternoons with little human contact as she cleaned, coped with the laundry in the basement of the apartment building, wrote letters home, learned Italian on her own or struggled with newly acquired recipes, ready to present them at lunchtime. She was not experienced even in cooking English food, least of all Italian dishes, and most of the time Giovanni was not impressed with her efforts. It was not so much what he said, but the disapproving look on his face told all. Very soon he took her to lunch at his mother's house, situated closer both to the city and to the river Arno, where at regular intervals he could rely on being served some of the delicious meals of his youth: saltimbocca, escalopes alla milanese, minestrone, tagliatelle, bistecca alla fiorentina, spaghetti alla carbonara - the list was endless.

Isabel felt ashamed and demeaned that she could not please Giovanni in the culinary sense, although it was hardly surprising since her own mother had not given her any opportunity to cook, wanting to control the kitchen herself. Anyway, the meals she prepared were simple English fare, and would not have helped Isabel to conquer the wealth of recipes which she imagined every Italian housewife could effortlessly produce as and when.

Giovanni's mother, who was in her late sixties and looked older, lived with her daughter, son-in-law and granddaughter. Among her varied duties she prepared lunch for them every day. It was their most important meal, invariably substantial with three courses. They all ate large quantities with great relish and it was no wonder they needed a nap afterwards, particularly in the stifling summer heat. The family members were hospitable and friendly, but somehow Isabel caught the impression that she and they knew that she would never be like them, no matter how hard she tried. She was a foreigner.

The conversation at table was rapid and idiomatic, but as with total immersion, it was a quick way of learning, since no one spoke a word of English and Isabel had to communicate. Staying on her own in the flat for so many hours of the day was a lonely business. She tried out her newly acquired vocabulary on the family, and became aware that the Florentine accent and dialect omitted the letter *c* from words which began with that consonant, and replaced it with the letter *h*. Therefore, a simple word such as *la casa*, meaning *house*, or *la carne*, meaning *meat*, would be pronounced *la hasa* and *la harne*. That took a bit of getting used to, but as the weeks passed, her understanding of the family's table conversations improved. She usually caught the gist of what they were saying, but missed the quick repartee and some idiomatic expressions.

In some ways she was glad to be in the family's company at those lunchtimes because it shortened the siesta time she had to spend with Giovanni. It was not only his insistence on having more sex at that time of day which she dreaded, but also his anger and subsequent sulkiness if she refused. On one such occasion he hit her across the face, and so thereafter she submitted without complaint, staying in the flat for days until her face showed no signs of his abuse. Conversationally they struggled too. She listened with interest to his comments about his family, friends and the business, but suddenly, in stark contrast to his pre-marital interest in her, he had become totally indifferent to her family, friends, profession or, indeed, to almost anything she said.

He communicated to her that she was now living in Italy, and her previous life was of no consequence to him. Even worse, he was not interested in books, singing, music, art or languages, so there was no meeting of minds or shared interests. His work absorbed him for many hours of the day, and at the weekend he enjoyed going hunting in the Tuscan countryside with his brother-in-law. Isabel silently felt disgusted by this hobby. She had seen too many featherless songbirds displayed in butchers' shop windows, and apart from wondering if there were any birds left in Italy to shoot, their bodies were so thin and lacking in meat that the whole barbaric operation seemed pointless.

Isabel noticed that Giovanni was more and more absent from the flat, but she continued with her daily schedule of completing her domestic duties, studying Italian, reading books and writing letters home. She felt terribly alone, and guilty that she had consented to marry someone with whom she had virtually nothing in common. The affection that she had once felt for him had faded away and turned to disgust. Perhaps all the sex he wanted was absolutely normal for newly married couples who were in love with each other, but she had discovered that she did not love him and certainly was not *in* love with him.

As the summer turned into autumn her depression increased. She rarely went out, and only to buy meat and groceries at the local shops.

She would have liked to pursue a course in Italian at the University of Florence, but her own funds would not allow it, and since Giovanni was disinclined to spend his money on her education, she was forced to remain in the flat. No friends called, and those in England, imagining that she was happy and settled in her new life, did not contact her much. On the other hand, Isabel felt ashamed of her failure, and reluctant to be the bearer of bad news, rarely wrote to them. Even letters to her mother did not express her unhappiness.

Her appetite had all but disappeared, and the thought of food, or even the preparation of it, filled her with nausea. Most of the time that Giovanni was out of the flat she allowed herself to cry, hoping that in releasing all her pent-up emotions, she would feel better able to cope with her life.

Sometimes, however, he would arrive unexpectedly and find her in floods of tears which did not improve his temper.

He could not for the life of him understand what she had to cry about. After all, she was lucky enough to have him, a lovely flat with views, and his family who lived ten minutes away by car. Surely that was enough for any girl and she should snap out of her melancholy straight away. Isabel listened to him, and feeling very guilty indeed, promised him that she would try hard to overcome her problems with homesickness and loneliness, but she did not mention the problem of his persistent need for sex and her revulsion, for fear that he would strike her again.

True to her word, she made a concerted effort to be more cheerful in the few weeks that followed.

She tried to pre-empt any potential criticism from him by keeping the flat spotlessly clean, and organizing the laundry with care. Following Italian recipes, she presented meals to the best of her ability, though she could eat little herself. Both Giovanni and his family noticed that she was losing weight, and seemed genuinely worried about it, but Isabel just could not force herself to eat more since she could feel the nausea rising in her throat.

Then, unexpectedly, she fainted, and all the family thought she was pregnant, but Isabel knew better. Her periods had continued to arrive every twenty-two days, with painful cramps and a heavy loss of blood. Despite valiant efforts to face life more positively and to avoid Giovanni's anger, she felt weaker each day. On several occasions she could feel herself losing consciousness, so she no longer went out in case she fainted in a busy street. She confined her tears to the bathroom, so that Giovanni was less likely to notice or erupt with fury.

Then, as luck would have it, she caught flu and was confined to bed for a few days with a high temperature and a raging headache. She found that she could no longer harness her concentration for learning Italian or reading books. As she was drinking only water, and sleeping intermittently throughout the day, unfit to cook or do anything constructive, she was not surprised that Giovanni went to his mother's house for lunch during his working day, even deciding not to return to the flat for his siesta.

One evening he returned at about eight o'clock and told Isabel that he and the family had spent some time discussing her problems. They were all convinced that she was suffering from a spell cast on her by one of Giovanni's previous girlfriends who was jealous of their marriage.

In short, she was casting the evil eye on Isabel and making her ill. Perhaps, he reported, she wanted Isabel dead, and therefore something had to be done, and quickly.

Despite protests from Isabel, the whole family, vociferous in their opinions and comments, were convinced that she would have to seek advice from a *donna di cura* who would know exactly how to lift the spell or curse, and also prevent another from being cast on her. All then would be well; the marriage would be successful and fruitful. As soon as Isabel had recovered from the flu, Giovanni made an appointment for her to visit the miracle woman, insisting that he should not only accompany her, but also be present at the examination.

The premises were located in a dark, dingy street in a poor part of Florence, which Isabel had never seen before and was way off the tourist track. Remains and smells of rotting fruit and vegetables on the cobbles suggested that a small market was held there regularly. Isabel retched with nausea as Giovanni directed her up a side alley to the surgery. As he opened the door of the waiting room and confirmed their arrival for an appointment, Isabel noticed that the small room was crowded, and scarcely a spare seat remained.

The first impression was one of poverty. Three elderly, peasant grandmothers dressed in black, each with her hair drawn back into a bun at the nape of the neck, were chatting together in a corner.

They looked weary from a life-time of hard work and resigned to their lot, as if they had shared each others troubles many times in the past. Occasionally one would crack a joke and the others would nod knowingly, revealing toothless smiles, clucking with laughter. Isabel thought of *Macbeth*. A young man with only one leg stood on crutches by the door, presumably for support, and was soon called into the surgery. A pale-faced, emaciated, middle-aged woman stared straight ahead, and next to her sat a crippled old man with a stick and a large boot on his right foot. In the opposite corner an anxious mother was pacifying a toddler with Down's syndrome next to a tearful, young mother cradling a jaundiced baby whom Isabel imagined to be scarcely more than two weeks old. In all, they were a sad collection of human suffering, in need of compassion, and she wondered if they would receive help in that place with its grimy, paint-chipped walls and depressing, oppressive atmosphere.

After some little wait, her name was called out and she and Giovanni were ushered into a tiny, sombre surgery, as shabby as the waiting room, but littered with books whose titles she could not decipher, together with bags and boxes of dried herbs, two old chests of drawers, a table and two simple kitchen chairs. A small gypsy-like woman of about fifty with jet-black hair, a swarthy skin and dark, penetrating eyes was seated behind the table. She indicated that Isabel should take the other seat whilst Giovanni remained standing close to the door. The woman did not introduce herself. Instead she immediately asked Isabel what the matter was and why she had come to seek her advice.

Of course, Isabel had not gone voluntarily, and she was just about to harness her thoughts into decent Italian sentences when Giovanni launched forth into a long-winded description of all their marital problems: the home-sickness, the loss of appetite for food and sex, the loss of weight, the fainting, the influenza and the continuous melancholy and tears. Despite help and renewed efforts to improve the situation, there had been no improvement, so that he and his family could only conclude that one of his former girl-friends, disenchanted with his marriage, had cast a spell on his wife.

As he was speaking, Isabel noticed that the donna di cura was wearing a gold chain around her neck with a pendant in the form of an eye. When Giovanni had finally finished speaking, the woman nodded pensively, as if she understood not only what the trouble was, but also how it had come about. After a long pause and with some gravitas, she stated that spells of this kind were relatively common and used by rejected lovers who failed to heal from their broken relationships and move on. It was necessary, therefore, to protect oneself from the spell that had been cast, so that no further misfortune would be inflicted.

The woman stood up, went over to the chest of drawers, and took out a few bunches of dried herbs and what looked like a glass eye, similar to the one she was wearing around her neck. She explained that the dried herbs had two uses. First, they should be combined with water and thrown over the exterior threshold of the flat's main door so as to prevent evil spirits from entering. Second, the dried herbs should also be rubbed into the thighs at night to prevent evil spirits from having a disastrous effect on the physical side of marriage. Finally, the glass eye should be kept on Isabel's person at all times to protect herself from the evil spell.

Completely satisfied with the given instructions, Giovanni thanked her, paid her fee, and then he and Isabel departed, clutching the bags of herbs and the glass eye. Not a word was spoken in the car. She was dropped off at the flat with the booty, and he promised to return for lunch in a couple of hours.

He arrived at one o'clock, whistling, and tucked into his lunch with a cheerful optimism that had been missing from his character for several weeks. As far as he was concerned, the problem would be solved if they followed the donna di cura's advice. Therefore, it was perhaps unwise of Isabel to comment over the pasta that she would have nothing whatever to do with the mumbo-jumbo black magic she had encountered that morning, and that ten kilos of herbs on the doorstep would not make the slightest difference to their marital problems or her condition.

Giovanni's facial expression suddenly contorted with fury as if his self-control battery had snapped. With unpredictable speed he hurled his plate of pasta against a kitchen wall, and seizing Isabel's hair, dragged her into the bedroom where he beat her around the face, head and arms more times than she could count. The shock and pain of the assault completely silenced her and she lay stunned on the marble floor, her head throbbing and her heart thumping fast in her chest. She felt too weak for any retaliation, and anyway she knew it would make the whole situation even worse. Giovanni left her lying there, and spitting out what she thought was a torrent of swear words in dialect, as yet unfamiliar to her, he slammed the main door and was gone. After several minutes, she gathered enough strength to pull her aching frame onto the bed where, after sobbing for some time, exhaustion overcame her and she fell asleep.

She awoke with a gasp at five o'clock, having dreamed that Giovanni was standing over her, but in fact, the flat was empty. Her immediate decision was to leave the marital bedroom, except for access to clothing, and transfer herself and a few belongings to the small sitting room with the balcony so as to be as far away from Giovanni as possible. One of the room's advantages was the sofa, which was long enough for her to stretch out on, and the other advantage was that right next door was the bathroom where she could lock herself in, if need be.

She looked at herself in the bathroom mirror. Her face was swollen and bruised, one eye was almost entirely closed, her lips were bleeding and her head ached. Mercifully though, she could still move her limbs and fingers, albeit painfully, so perhaps no serious damage had been done - yet. Aware that she was alone and vulnerable in a foreign country, her need to survive came strongly into play, and she was forced to pull herself together whenever floods of tears enveloped her. So, she set herself some tasks to complete before Giovanni returned.

First she bathed her face and whole body carefully, and put on fresh clothes. Then she cleaned up the mess in the kitchen, and after peeling the dried pasta off the kitchen wall, she washed the dishes and put away the crockery and cutlery. When everything was spotless, she made tea for herself and took some aspirin. Then finally, she stretched out on the sofa, and as she gazed listlessly at the Tuscan countryside, she made a firm decision. In spite of being very fearful of Giovanni, she now felt a sense of unspoken defiance towards him. She also remembered her brother's violence and tyranny years before, and knew that she could not live with another violent man, a battered sister replaced by a battered wife.

It was ten o'clock before Giovanni returned, and then not a word was spoken. He did not apologize, and she had nothing to say to him. At least silently, he seemed to accept that she would want to sleep in another room, and for that she was relieved. She knew now not to inflame the situation, but to wait. It seemed to her that she could not sleep at all the entire night, her mind and body aching with confusion and pain. As she watched dawn break over the Tuscan hills, she prayed that the new day would bring her clear thinking and physical strength.

Yes, she actually prayed. Isabel who had joked that God had lost her phone number, and who, after a seriously religious education, had lost her faith and had ranted and railed against him for his lack of interest, finally prayed for forgiveness and help. "Out of the depths have I cried unto thee. O Lord hear my prayer," she murmured in her tears, again and again, until she fell asleep.

When she was awakened at nine o'clock by the sunshine flooding into the small sitting room, she instinctively knew that Giovanni had already left the flat for work. Another look at herself in the mirror confirmed her belief that she would have to remain in the flat until her face had healed, a sensible idea, since she felt exhausted all the while, and needed time to recuperate her strength. To achieve that she would have to eat, so she prepared herself some breakfast: a piece of stale bread, a few grapes and a cup of tea. There was little left in either the cupboard or the fridge, but at least it was a start. If she ventured down to one of the shops located on the ground floor of the apartment buildings, she thought she would die of the shame of displaying her facial bruises and black eye to the customers and proprietor of that much-frequented delicatessen. No, she would just have to stay put.

No members of Giovanni's family came to visit her, but he sometimes started to bring back groceries at lunchtime: milk, bread, cooked meat, cheese and fruit, - and then he would depart until quite late in the evening. Occasionally, he would burst into the flat unexpectedly, and threaten her with violence if ever he caught her with a man friend taking advantage of his absence. When, in her physical weakness she cried for fear of being battered again, he would leave her alone, slamming the front door as he left. She rested a great deal, ate a little at the appropriate times, and as the days passed, her cuts, bruises and black eye gradually healed up, although she still felt light-headed, even dizzy when she stood up.

One evening at about nine o'clock, Giovanni returned to the flat with a priest, Dom Pancetti who worked for him as a part-time electrician and repairer of televisions. It was common in Italy for priests of poor parishes to supplement their income by turning their hands to something practical, a bit like St Paul and his tent making. On that occasion they had dined together after work, and it was clear that Dom Pancetti was well informed about Giovanni's domestic situation. In Isabel's opinion, Giovanni had deliberately waited to introduce her to the priest after her injuries had healed, the physical ones, that is.

When she offered him some coffee, he quietly declined, and intimated to Giovanni to leave the room. As he did so, the priest launched into a veritable eulogy about his employer, insisting that he was a good and honourable man who would not harm a fly. Having observed Isabel's rapt attention to what he was saying, he gained confidence and raising his voice, he advised her to appreciate her husband's kindness and gentleness, and do the right thing by him. If the marriage failed, he finally emphasized, Giovanni would be a ruined man, utterly finished, because there was no divorce in Italy, and he could not, therefore, hope to marry anyone else. He repeated this in case she had not understood the first time, and then asked her if she had anything to say. Isabel had read about the Spanish Inquisition, and thought that his biased monologue must bear some similarity to it, but she simply answered that she had understood. With that he rose to his feet, and stony-faced, bade her good night.

At his departure Isabel felt pressured and distraught, and wondered if Giovanni had confessed to having beaten her black and blue more than once, but it was hardly likely after that verbal delivery. Her guilt about marrying the wrong person obsessed her, but just as strongly she knew deeply within her soul that she could never love this man. She, therefore, had to escape as soon as possible. It would not be easy because Giovanni turned up at the flat unpredictably, hoping to catch her out at something.

The next day he looked for an improvement in her attitude and behaviour, and was glad to be told that she was feeling better, that in fact, she would like to take the bus into the city centre to enquire about Italian language courses at the University of Florence. He seemed to approve of the suggestion, and would have offered to take her there by car but for an important business engagement in Arezzo. Her luck was in.

On arriving at the university reception area that morning, she read a pamphlet which informed her that the language courses were in progress and would not recommence until the new year. The pamphlet would at least prove that she had actually been to the university, as promised, thus reassuring Giovanni that she intended to enrol in the advanced course in January and that perhaps her mother would give her a contribution to the cost of it as a Christmas present. She hated herself for being duplicitous. It was foreign to her nature and upbringing, but she could not risk being battered again. She had to act quickly.

Her next port of call was a travel agency, CIT, where she received information about the times of the trains to Milan, and the sleeper trains across France to Calais. Fortunately she had brought her money with her, and decided there and then to buy a rail ticket for the following Friday morning so that Giovanni would have less time to suspect what her intentions really were. The thought of what his reaction would be if he found out sent her pulse racing and filled her with panic, but now that she had made the decision, she had to see it through.

Distractedly she wandered off in the direction of the Piazza del Duomo to visit the great cathedral for the second time. As she knelt to confess her sins to God and to ask forgiveness and help to carry out her decision, she heard a choir from the Netherlands practising Arcadelt's *Ave Maria*. The simple, mellifluous harmonies of the sixteenth-century motet moved her to tears. What a mess she had made of her life so soon, and more importantly, she had ruined somebody else's life too. She could still hear the priest's words of the previous evening. Giovanni would be a ruined man. He could never marry again, not in Italy.

She withdrew from the Duomo when she had composed herself. The tourists, visitors and Florentines, taken up with their own concerns, did not notice her. She headed for Piazza San Marco from where she would catch her bus.

Giovanni had not returned from Arezzo when she reached the flat. In fact, within a few minutes of her arrival, he phoned to tell her that he would arrive much later than expected, and therefore she would not need to prepare anything for him that evening. With several spare hours to herself, she sat down and thought out her plan. First of all she would make sure that her passport and railway ticket were sewn into the lining of her winter coat, in case Giovanni looked into her handbag on one of his checking-up exercises. She had already placed her English pounds sterling inside the lining of her handbag so that he would see only Italian lire in her purse. Rather more difficult was the packing of her clothes, and she quickly took down just one of her cases from the top of the capacious wardrobe. It would be cumbersome carrying more than one case, and since her health was fragile, she knew she could not manage two. Sacrifices, therefore, had to be made. She decided to leave her light summer clothes behind in the wardrobe so that Giovanni would not suspect. Her underwear, night clothes, toiletries and winter outfits would fit into the one case, and she would wear one of the warmer outfits. It was late November, and in England it would almost certainly be very cold. Wintry weather had not so far reached Italy, although there had been some rain. When she had half packed the case she placed it back in its original position in the wardrobe. Then she took a bath, washed her hair, put on her housecoat and prepared some supper for herself. She was so jittery at the thought of what she was doing that her hands would not stop shaking, and she had to force herself to eat something.

Before retiring to bed on the small divan, she placed the university pamphlet in the kitchen where Giovanni would see it, and exhausted from her day of drama in the city, she fell fast asleep. On the Thursday morning, after many hours of rest, she felt calmer than the day before.

Over coffee Giovanni mentioned that he, his partner and employees were particularly busy at that time of year. Leading up to Christmas many people either wanted to buy televisions, be they Zenith from America or the home brand, Italvideo, or have defective ones repaired. Then there was the constant all-year-round selling of fridge-freezers, keeping up with the supply and demand of his customers. Isabel wondered if that really was the situation or whether he was using it to mask something else. Whatever it was, on the surface she expressed understanding for his overwork, adding that business must be very good, and secretly she felt extremely grateful that her plans could succeed without too much fear or hassle. Only one more day! Before leaving the flat, Giovanni added that his business life would have to slow down at the weekend, since he and his brother-in-law intended to go hunting. With that he was gone.

She still did not finish packing the case because he would be back that evening and might check her section of the wardrobe, but she did order a taxi from a company she hoped he did not know. With any luck Giovanni would leave the flat on Friday morning at around 8.30 a.m. She would then finish packing the case and wait for her taxi at 10.15 a.m. She would hide the case under the bed until the last moment, should he return unexpectedly. In the meantime, she wrote him a note that she was returning to London for good, and that she could not tell him to his face for fear of being battered again. She was truly sorry that she could not live with him, although she had tried. She was returning the engagement ring, wedding ring and gold bracelet that he had given her because she did not merit wearing them as a wife, and selling them could be of some financial compensation to him. She wished him happiness in the future, and asked him to convey her apologies to his family.

Once written, she hid the note in a book until it was time to leave.

The hours passed unbelievably slowly. Alone in the flat, with no one to speak to, she was forever checking her watch and the kitchen clock to see how many minutes had passed. She could not concentrate on reading, and it seemed futile to write home since she hoped to be in England soon. She decided not to ring her mother from the flat in case, out of worry, she phoned back when Giovanni had returned. He would immediately suspect something. She was sick with apprehension and nerves at the thought that something might go wrong and her plan would be scuppered with dire consequences. Suddenly the phone rang. It was Giovanni telling her again that he would be late due to pressure of work and not to cook for him. The phone went dead. Was he testing her? Did he intend to drop in unexpectedly again, or was he making a genuine phone call? Why did the line suddenly go dead? He did not phone back to explain why.

To fill in time, she cleaned the bathroom and the kitchen very thoroughly so that he could gain a good impression of how she had spent her time that day, and she made sure that her preparations to leave were well hidden. By the time Giovanni returned to the flat just before ten o'clock, Isabel was nearly asleep on the divan with the Italian television ads blaring out. He volunteered that he had been dining with his business partner, Alberto, after spending an exhausting day both at the sale rooms and in the repair shop. Business would be frenetic until Christmas, followed by a gradual slow down. He seemed to need to give her an explanation, although she did not question him in any way. At least he did not appear to be in an aggressive mood, merely somewhat thoughtful and taciturn, so Isabel who was genuinely exhausted from the emotion and worry of her duplicity, closed her eyes, and he left the room.

Although she managed to sleep for several hours, she awoke at six, but did not get up until after seven. As she tiptoed to the kitchen, she noticed that the door of the main bedroom was open.

Giovanni was still fast asleep. What if he slept late that day, what on earth would she do? She would have to cancel the taxi, and if he heard her on the phone, he might demand to know who she was talking to. She had to behave normally. The best thing to do was to wake him up by making domestic noises in the kitchen. Ten minutes later he was awake, and he asked her why she was up so early.

She replied that she had slept many hours and could sleep no longer. Her nerves were jangling inside her, but she tried her best to conceal her anxiety and above all, not to provoke his temper. He seemed to want to know her plans for the day, but was reticent about his own. When she asked him whether he would be home for lunch, he prevaricated, saying finally, that he was unsure. By 8.45 he had left the flat, and from the landing window just outside the front door she watched him get into his van and drive off in the direction of the city centre. She immediately took down the case, finished packing it and checked her passport, ticket and money in her handbag. She decided to place the case back in its stored position in the wardrobe.

Her heart seemed to miss a beat when she heard his key in the lock. She quickly threw her handbag in a drawer, closed the wardrobe doors and started to make the matrimonial bed with great care and precision. He told her that he had called in at his mother's house, and that she had invited them both to lunch there at one o'clock. He added that he was pleased that Isabel's health seemed to be improving, and that she was committed to continuing her wifely duties once more. With sudden dexterity, and before she could turn around, he tipped her over onto the bed that she was making and pinned her down with one powerful arm whilst with sex-driven speed he tore aside her knickers and penetrated her violently. She knew better than to resist. In fact, she tried not to show her feelings of disgust at all and said nothing. After climaxing, he lay panting on top of her for a few minutes, and then obviously realized that he had a day's work ahead of him, so he adjusted his clothing and told her that he would collect her at lunchtime. Her smile of assent masked the contempt she felt for him.

When he finally left it was almost ten o'clock. Tears streamed down Isabel's face as she washed herself, changed, left the note and rings on his bedside cabinet, took down the case and placed it with her handbag and coat in the hall. Then for safety's sake, she phoned the taxi company again to remind them of their 10.15 appointment to take her to the station. All was in order, and she waited. She dried her eyes, applied a little make-up and then the doorbell rang - down the stairs, into the taxi and away to freedom, avoiding the staring eyes of the delicatessen customers.

CHAPTER 4
ISABEL (1962–1968)

After a painful time in Italy, Isabel's return to the London suburb where she had been born was clouded by guilt, conflict and, above all, a sense of failure. Whilst her mother went to work, she stayed at home, spending much of the day in tears. It was difficult getting out of bed in the morning to perform the few domestic tasks which her mother asked her to do, and the thought that she had ruined Giovanni's life never left her mind. She was unable to sleep by night and refused to see anybody by day. The apprehension of meeting friends and acquaintances in the street, answering their questions and then breaking down uncontrollably in her distress, kept her at home. She was guilty, guilty, guilty, and she was powerless to improve the situation. To return to Italy would be hell for her, to stay in England meant that Giovanni's life was ruined. She was unquestionably suffering from a nervous breakdown.

Her mother understood that Isabel was unfit to go out, and after a week, was worried enough about her to call the family doctor. He listened attentively to a summary of what had happened in Italy, and observed Isabel's tearful appearance, loss of weight and depressed, anxious condition. He then took her blood pressure and found it to be rather low, which probably explained her light- headedness and fainting attacks. He advised complete rest and regular meals, and he prescribed some sleeping pills which she could use temporarily until she had re-established her sleeping pattern. In two weeks she should have a follow-up appointment at his surgery, so by then she would have to make the effort to go out. For the time being though, she wanted to stay in the house and leave the phone unanswered until her mother returned from work.

Fortunately there was no contact from Italy, and Isabel doubted that Giovanni would leave his business in the run- up to Christmas to pursue her to England and try to take her back to Florence. At the very thought of it, she felt sick in the pit of her stomach. Her hands trembled and her heart beat wildly. The sleeping tablets helped a great deal since she was able to blot out her anxiety and guilt for a few hours, and by day she sought refuge in books. She ploughed through many of the nineteenth-century classics in her parents' bookcase, which had been left untouched and unread for years: *Barchester Towers*, *Silas Marner*, *The Mill on the Floss*, *Mary Barton*, *Ruth*, *The Professor* and Elizabeth Gaskell's biography of Charlotte Brontë. Books were such a comfort to her. She could immerse herself in their world, relating to the lives of others, and simultaneously forget her own worries for as long as her reading concentration lasted. Some of the plots were deeply absorbing and the narrative so expertly written, demonstrating such a depth of understanding of the human condition that Isabel would either continue to turn the pages until her head ached, or be moved to tears with the pathos as the story unfolded.

The family troubles weighed heavily on Isabel's mother. As a widow she was forced to return to work for a pittance after thirty years of being in the home. Then there was her daughter's failed marriage. Clive's marriage had failed, too, after only a year and the birth of twins, a boy and a girl. His young wife, worn down from the birth, from being physically abused and neglected and forced to look after the twins with no support and very little money, left him to live with a much older and prosperous man who would be able to look after them all in comfort, and protect her from Clive's tyranny. Clive was rarely at home in the evenings. He played in orchestras and sang in choirs. Somehow he imagined that it was perfectly acceptable to leave a young wife all day and most evenings shortly after the birth of twins. When he was fired from his work, she made the decision to leave him since she had to protect her children.

Following the failure of his marriage, Clive's presence in the family home, even for weekends, was a time to be dreaded by both Isabel and her mother. Within minutes of his arrival, rows blew up owing to his refusal to observe simple house rules; his liking for alcohol, and his allergic reaction to his mother, often resulted in highly abusive language and violent behaviour. Whenever Isabel intervened to prevent her mother from being hurt she, too, was thrown to the floor and punched. She tried to persuade her mother to say nothing in the least provocative to Clive to avoid his wretched outbursts and maintain some form of an uneasy peace until his departure on Sunday evenings, but this strategy rarely worked because his inner anger always had to engineer trouble of some sort. It was as if he were forever looking for a target on which to aim his fury. Apart from that, his only contribution to the household was a motley assortment of weekly washing, which his mother never failed to launder.

When, after two weeks, Isabel kept her appointment with the doctor, she already knew that she was not pregnant. Her period had arrived a few days before, and so she was able to tell him that pregnancy would not be an added complication. She was simultaneously relieved and disappointed.

She knew she was in no condition to look after a baby at that time, and she also knew that the birth of a child would have to involve Giovanni. It would be his right. Her disappointment centred on her marital failure and her desire to have a baby some time, though not with Giovanni. She could scarcely believe that she was not pregnant after all that sex.

The doctor kindly advised her to invite one or two friends home, so that she could start to face up to life by explaining to them what had happened. Now that she had made her first attempt to go out, she should gradually do so more often until she had established a normal social life.

She totally rejected the idea of creating a social life for herself. She was far from ready to do that, but she did phone two friends that she had known since their infant reception class. When they visited her, they were both sympathetic and non-judgmental. She could pick up her friendship with them from where they had left off before her marriage and she was grateful for that. Such friendships were valuable beyond words.

Christmas was a very low-key affair, spent mostly with her mother, although an elderly uncle shared Boxing Day lunch with them. Clive was away somewhere, but he had not bothered to say where. His absence was a relief, and a sort of depressed peace hung over the household.

Isabel yearned to sing carols, or at least to hear them sung, but she dared not go to the church her friends attended because she still did not trust her emotional control when faced with a group outside the home. She wanted to believe in God again, more especially because knowing that he had a purpose for her in life would be heartening, and also because church music could be so uplifting. Yet, doubts always seemed to crowd in on her, and she felt constantly aware of her guilt and inadequacy.

Fortunately, she still had some money in her bank account, saved from her teaching before her marriage, and she was able to buy her mother a decent Christmas present to cheer her up. She also had sufficient money to pay her way for room and board, but not for long. Two weeks after New Year she would have spent everything. Over the Christmas holidays she knew that she would have to conquer her anxiety about facing her friends, acquaintances, her mother's friends and future employers. Her first thought was to speak to a solicitor about changing her married name back to her maiden name by deed poll. It proved to be incredibly easy and not strictly necessary in the case of reverting to a maiden name, but it made her feel better. Then she set about the task of informing all parties who needed official notification. By a stroke of good luck she discovered that, due to a maternity leave, a secondary school in the next town needed a temporary teacher in English and French for two terms. A phone call, an application form and an interview secured the post and a source of income for the immediate future, for which she was truly relieved. She could catch a bus at the top of her road early in the morning with little chance of meeting anyone, and teach in the next town where she was not known at all.

Before the start of term she familiarized herself with her timetable, the courses of her various classes and what stage of the syllabus they had reached. Then she prepared lessons with care, bearing in mind that she might at first be called on for a flexible approach to be able to assess the ability of each class. The school was a mixed secondary modern, pre-dating the comprehensives of the l970s. Unlike her former pupils at the Elephant and Castle, these children wore uniforms and, for the most part, took a pride in their appearance. There were less discipline problems, and fewer uncooperative, disruptive pupils. Local private-housing estates alongside council housing indicated employment and a higher standard of living, though not excessively so. A tradition still existed of having separate staff rooms for male and female members of staff, which Isabel thought very strange, and on the first day she felt awkward in the female staff room, though not for long.

Teachers popping in and out for tea or coffee, en route to somewhere else, were friendly enough, and nobody asked her any awkward questions. They were far too busy.

Isabel had made a seating plan for each class, so that by the end of the week she would recognize all her pupils by name, and be able to treat them as individuals. She planned what she hoped to achieve with each class for a whole term, and organized her lessons in detail for a week. She also set homework from the start, so that her pupils would become accustomed to doing it. After two days of introducing herself to all her classes, getting to know them and attempting to move them forward with kindness and determination, she felt better than she had done for months.

Over the following two terms until the summer holidays, she threw herself into her teaching, and continued to live with her mother. Motivating teenagers was an absorbing challenge which she enjoyed, and she appreciated their cheerfulness and quick-witted repartee. She was conscientious about her planning and marking, which her pupils appreciated, as much as adolescents can.

Despite her professional satisfaction, she still felt unable to attend church and mix with her friends. It was as if a chapter had finished, and yet she still could not bear to talk about it. Her only social outlet was an amateur dramatic society in the next town. The company was rather ambitiously putting on a performance of Arthur Miller's *The Crucible*, a play she could get her teeth into, if ever there was one. Isabel really appreciated the power of the plot and thought herself well cast as the down-trodden Mary Warren. The temporary lack of music in her life was barely tolerable, and she hoped vehemently that singing opportunities would happen in the near future.

With the onset of the summer term, knowing that her present job was only temporary, she applied for a permanent position as teacher of French in a secondary school in Bethnal Green. Her intention was to travel in by train for a term or so and then look for a bedsitter or tiny flat, whatever she could afford in London that was closer to her place of work.

As expected, the first term in Bethnal Green was tough, challenging and sometimes demoralizing. Fortunately, the school had a strong headmistress who united and supported her staff in the troubled school in that socially deprived area, but too many teachers, unable to inspire, control and discipline the pupils, did not stay the course and left after a short time. This led to large, permanent gaps on the timetable, which had to be filled by a steady stream of supply teachers. Predictably, they were of varying teaching ability, and the less able or less charismatic ones were so overwhelmed by the disruptive hostility of certain adolescent classes that they did not return the following day. The London County Council, therefore, had to send a replacement, and often the same scenario was repeated. In fact, in the upper school, classes would predict how long Miss Smith or Mr Brown would stay and then orchestrate a way of bringing their prediction to reality. Supply teachers hailed not only from various parts of Britain, but also from the Commonwealth and beyond.

Unprepared, yet highly qualified, some would make their entrances like lambs to the slaughter. They were almost literally voices crying in the wilderness, as pupils cheered or jeered, desks banged and chaos ensued. At the end of the day, the teachers were wrung out and the children had learned nothing.

Despite this unsatisfactory situation, a hard core of mature, permanent teachers seemed to have an unspoken vocational commitment to improve the educational standards and career prospects of the children at this school. It was a hard uphill task, however, and progress was slow, yet Isabel, realizing the worthiness of the cause, felt herself dedicated to working with this group, and to embracing their ambitions.

The hour-and-a-half journey from home to school, involving the tube, a bus ride and walking, and requiring her to get up early and return late, was exhausting. By half-term she had managed with the help of colleagues to rent a tiny furnished flat in George Street just off Baker Street for £5 a week, for which she was truly delighted. It comprised a bed-sitting room, a tiny kitchen and a tinier bathroom and was situated in an ideal location. Finally, she was independent and the feeling was exhilarating. She moved out of the family home, promising to spend Christmas with her mother within a few weeks, and to phone regularly in the meantime.

Isabel was satisfied with her newly discovered freedom to paint the walls of her new abode in the colours of her choice, to buy a carpet on the never-never (hire purchase), and within a very limited budget, to organize her flat as she wanted it. On the one hand, she was delighted that its location was so central, since her nearest underground was Bond Street, which enabled her to take the Central Line every weekday directly to Bethnal Green. On the other hand, the rent took up to twenty-five per cent of her income, and there were so many other expenses that at the end of the month she could save nothing.

She began to think about a weekend job. Discussing this with colleagues who had now become friends, she learned from Leah who taught music and who augmented her income by singing soprano at the West London Reform Synagogue that there were vacancies for altos. Non-Jewish singers were acceptable provided they were keen to sing phonetic Hebrew, were sympathetic to Judaism and would present themselves for practices, services and weddings. So Isabel, accompanied by Leah, auditioned one Sunday morning and fortunately passed. The choirmaster showed her the music for both the Friday-evening and Saturday-morning services, together with the sequence of Jewish liturgy. It was both fascinating and challenging to sing unfamiliar music and to learn about Jewish culture in detail, as well as to be earning the money she needed.

Isabel spent the next five years teaching in Bethnal Green, living in her bijou flat in George Street, and singing every weekend at the West London Synagogue. Her Majesty's Inspectorate enabled her and the whole Bethnal Green staff to optimize their teaching skills and to broaden the pupils' horizons. In Isabel's case this meant introducing Italian as well as French to the timetable, and developing syllabuses for both languages to the level of the CSE and GCE. To become properly academically qualified she studied advanced French and Italian two evenings a week at the City Literary Institute, and gradually worked towards taking a French degree at the Institute of Linguists.

Life was very full, which was exactly what she wanted it to be. Friends sprang from school, from the synagogue, from the City Literary Institute and also from the neighbourhood around her flat. A social life gradually developed.

It was inevitable that she thought back to her experiences in Italy and the abysmal failure of her marriage. She wondered if Giovanni had come to terms with her departure, and how he would be able to face marital failure in a country like Italy. She had also discovered from a lawyer friend that she would have to wait five years before initiating divorce proceedings in England. Most of all she realized yet again how much she loved children and how her own biological clock was ticking by.

CHAPTER 5
ISABEL AND JERRY
(1967–1975)

O n Saturday afternoons, unless she was visiting her
mother in the suburbs, Isabel would meet her local
friends in a restaurant on Marylebone High Street. Some
would lunch there, whilst others might drop in later for
coffee and pastries, all congregating around a large, circular
table in the centre of the restaurant. Harry, a tax adviser, was
particularly interested in speaking to her, when she arrived
after the synagogue service on that Saturday afternoon in
July 1967.

"Isabel, I've been meaning to phone you, but mislaid
you number. This evening I'm throwing a party to celebrate
nothing in particular. Just getting together as many friends
as poss. Can you come? Please say you can!"

When Isabel replied that she had no other engagements
that evening, Harry was most enthusiastic.

"Well, do come. You'll be most welcome. No need to
bring a bottle, just yourself. I'd like you to meet some of my
old contacts. Two Americans who used to be at LSE, and
various chaps I know in the City, as well as this dishevelled
lot here! Do come! We're short of women!"

"How can I refuse an invitation like that?" quipped Isabel.

It was at that party that she met Jerry. He was introduced as an American who, after visiting Athens, had stopped over in London to maintain contact with his old friends at the London School of Economics before returning to the United States. Evidently he had studied for his doctorate at the London School of Economics some years earlier.

The party atmosphere bordered on the frenetic with many people juggling glasses or bottles, talking animatedly in far too small a space, elbowing each other good-naturedly towards the nibbles and dips, or less charitably away from crashing bores absorbed in their own importance. There were quite a few of those and Isabel was glad that she had arrived late to avoid many of them. It was the custom to adjourn these parties to the local Indian restaurant which she knew well, and so at 10 p.m. she found herself sharing poppadoms with Jerry, a tall, dark American of Greek extraction. He was not exactly good looking, and his hair was noticeably thinning, but he certainly had a presence, intelligence and a sense of humour. Although numerous partygoers had returned home, enough curry fans had stayed to fill up the entire restaurant, and waiters were running hither and thither, taking orders and delivering exotic dishes with amazing speed and dexterity.

During the meal Isabel learned that Jerry was to spend another week in England before returning to the United States to lecture at summer school. He invited her to accompany him to his old haunts and stomping grounds in London, which he had frequented over six years earlier. At the age of thirty-six he wanted to recapture the carefree excitement of student days, which he still hankered after, in contrast to his sedate life as an academic at the University of Pennsylvania (Penn) with its demanding timetable and publish-or-perish burden. He had dutifully visited his mother who had quite recently retired to live in Athens, and was more than ready to enter into the holiday spirit for a week before preparing for summer courses. Isabel was still busy at her Bethnal Green school, finishing off the summer term, but she kept him company in the evenings, introducing him to the Proms and Covent Garden. They dined out at Italian restaurants in Soho and Baker Street and at Simpsons in the Strand, and Jerry bought tickets for them to see *The Boyfriend* at the Haymarket. It was a wonderful action-packed and culture-filled week, and combined with the end of term, was totally exhausting for Isabel. When Jerry finally checked out of his hotel and took a taxi to Heathrow, he and Isabel felt sad to part from each other, and promised to write as faithfully as possible until Christmas.

From then on she looked forward to his letters on her return from school, during the holidays, and even more to meeting him off the plane a few days before Christmas.

First of all he stayed with her in the flat, squashed into a single bed, and then when they arrived at her mother's house on Christmas Eve, it was a case of separate bedrooms. At least it was a chance to make up for sleep deprivation. The lack of central heating made a memorable impact on an American staying in an English semi during a particularly cold winter, since the living room and the kitchen were the only heated rooms in the house. When they finally said their goodbyes to Isabel's mother after Boxing Day, Jerry claimed that he had turned into an icicle, and was relieved to return to Isabel's tiny, electrically heated flat. Their feelings for each other had become serious, and they both knew they wanted a future together, a loving, meaningful relationship which would lead somewhere; to marriage perhaps, and a family, but those thoughts were as yet premature and unspoken. Jerry poured out the detailed and sometimes amusing sagas of his previous girlfriends to her, and Isabel in turn, related her brief and bitter marital failure to him.

More than five years had passed since that disaster and she had finally managed to initiate divorce proceedings. Progress had been slow and unsurprisingly, Giovanni did not cooperate, mainly by refusing to acknowledge receipt of the divorce documents. The costs were spread out over a two-year period and Isabel was ever more grateful to be singing at the synagogue for the additional income, enabling her to remain financially independent and not have to ask her mother for a loan. Her recent promotion to head of modern languages at her school had brought her increased income as well as extra responsibility. By a stroke of luck, her solicitor actually took time out from his annual holiday in Tuscany to serve the documents himself whilst on a visit to Florence. Isabel was very touched and appreciative of this kindness because it meant that the whole tortuous divorce process, such as it was in the sixties, could go ahead.

Early in 1968, after Jerry had returned to the United States, he made enquiries at the Immigration Service about the kind of visa best suited for Isabel's permanent entry into the United States. It was a lengthy business, seemingly full of obstacles, requiring much form filling and a few visits to the American Embassy in Grosvenor Square. With cooperation and persistence on both sides of the Atlantic, the visa was finally processed by the time Jerry arrived back in London at the beginning of July.

Isabel spent the last three weeks of that month preparing to leave her mother, her Bethnal Green school, her friends and her flat. She was, in a sense, sorry to leave her life behind her. She felt so much part of her east-end school family in which several years of children had gained confidence from a caring, committed staff. She would miss her colleagues and friends, her tiny flat, her singing lessons and her friends at the synagogue, where she had been happily singing the services for over four years. She would certainly miss her beloved London. Maybe she would be back, as yet she did not know, but she felt convinced that she had to go on to a new life with Jerry in the United States. She would be able to write to her mother and also visit her in the summer holidays. So, Jerry and Isabel sailed to New York at the beginning of August, and travelled on to Philadelphia to begin a new chapter of their lives.

Philly, the city of brotherly love, as it is known, presented Isabel with a definite learning curve, when she found herself living with Jerry on the twentieth floor of a high-rise apartment building in the city centre. The difference in culture was immediately discernible. She had to listen attentively to what people said so that she understood what they were talking about. It took about three months before she really grasped their humour. In her own efforts as raconteur she would naturally use British phrases unfamiliar to Americans, to find that they would stare uncomprehendingly as her jokes fell flat.

She had to admire their vitality, their capacity for hard work and their conviction that anything is achievable with motivation and application. On the minus side, the city had a high crime rate, and in contrast to London in the sixties, it was unsafe for a woman to walk alone on the streets at night. In spite of American wealth, there were large areas of poverty where unemployment, violence and drugs were endemic, although in the city centre prosperity was evident. There were businesses, luxury department stores, a plethora of restaurants, bars, cinemas, sports centres, theatres and two opera companies.

Jerry returned to his job as a senior lecturer at Penn, whilst Isabel sent her curriculum vitae to as many schools as possible. It was late August and most institutions had already hired their staff for the coming year. Nevertheless she persisted, and was delighted to attend and pass an interview to teach French and English at a convent school in the suburbs, starting at the beginning of term. This meant leaving the apartment very early in the morning to take two street cars, one passing through a dangerous area, followed by a longish walk at the other end.

The school was situated in glorious countryside, and the nuns were both charming and helpful. They laughed at her English-isms, appreciated her accent, and with prompt efficiency presented her with syllabuses and a timetable. The pupils were between the ages of six and seventeen years, from Pennsylvanian Catholic families and were a delight to teach. It was expected that all would benefit from a university education. As the days passed Isabel realized that many of her American pupils were no brighter than those she had taught in Bethnal Green, and yet none of those East Londoners would go to university. They would become telephonists, machinists, shop girls or worse. She realized, too, that one's good fortune is determined by where and to whom one is born.

"Hey, madam, would you like a lift?" called a smiling, uniformed seventeen-year-old out of the window of her smart Corvair one morning in the first week of term. Isabel had just alighted from the second street car in pouring rain, and was grateful for the offer to avoid the lengthy walk. She laughed and thanked her pupil, adding that it seemed unusual for a student to offer a lift to a teacher and not the other way round.

"Gee, no. It happens all the time," the pupil replied, and it did.

The lower and upper departments at the convent school were separate, but on the same site, and Isabel was responsible for teaching French to groups of senior girls as well as English to younger pupils aged nine, ten and eleven years. She quickly settled down, getting to know her pupils and thoroughly enjoying the challenges of her new work. Both staff and pupils alike were friendly and welcoming, and she relished the lively to and fro of conversations at recess and lunch. It was shortly after her arrival that she grasped just how well organized and business-like the nuns really were. Evidently all members of staff were signed up to a one year contract, and if their pupils failed to make the anticipated progress, the contracts were not renewed, regardless of whether the teachers concerned were sole providers for a family of six, or comfortably endowed with a private income. This was independent education. It was a business, and the nuns were well aware that inadequate teaching could quickly close the school down.

As fall progressed, and the autumnal leaves displayed the most vivid colours that she had ever seen, Isabel felt optimistic about her new life in America. Although Jerry could look taciturn, even morose sometimes, and as a couple, they could not be described as soul mates, they mostly got on well together. They enjoyed weekend trips to New York for shopping, for seeing the sights and for visiting Jerry's brother and sister-in-law in Manhattan. How exciting it was to browse in famous department stores such as Macy's, Bloomingdale's and Bonwit Teller, to enjoy shows at Radio City, art treasures at the Metropolitan Museum of Art or sip a Manhattan on top of the Rockefeller Center. Isabel really loved New York. She enjoyed every minute spent in its dynamic vitality, and looked forward to attending a performance at the Metropolitan Opera House.

A few weeks before Christmas Jerry proposed to Isabel. She accepted, and as they were both over thirty and living together, they thought it sensible not to delay the wedding. Since Jerry claimed that he was allergic to churches of any sort, particularly Greek Orthodox ones, and Isabel thought that she could not be remarried in an Anglican church, and neither of them warmed to the idea of a registry office, he invited the Episcopalian chaplain of Penn to marry them right in their apartment with no fuss at all. Only Jerry's mother, brother, cousin, and a few friends attended, but nobody arrived from England. Isabel felt that she could not subject her mother or anyone else to another wedding after the previous disaster, and her mother understood.

Jerry, like many Americans, was absorbed in his job, and lived to work, rather than the other way round. He enjoyed talking to Isabel about the courses he was organizing, his lecturing techniques and the papers he hoped to publish. One of his professional requirements was to keep abreast of current affairs and finance, so the New York Times and the Wall Street Journal featured on his daily reading menu. Their first row was about Vietnam, and whether American forces should be there. Isabel thought not, and Jerry's eyes blazed with threatening fury, so she decided not to articulate her opinion on that subject again, noticing that his brooding temperament took a few hours to return to normality after a flare up.

To her great delight, she discovered two opera companies in the city: the Lyric and the Grand. They were sponsored by private industry and international singers were invited to sing in performances of grand opera. The choruses were drawn from local talent in the city and paid as semi-professional singers. Isabel auditioned for both companies and was accepted. It was an opening she would not have had in England, and she was overjoyed with the opportunity. Rehearsals were two evenings a week, and since the performance of each opera lasted a few days only, the practice and on-stage time were not too onerous. Her knowledge of French and Italian was a great boon to learning the libretto quickly, and over a three-year period she learned the synopsis, libretto and music of several operas, including *Aida*, *Nabucco*, *Norma*, *Macbeth*, *Die Fledermaus*, *Die Meistersinger*, *Carmen* and *Il Trovatore*. The learning and the camaraderie were not to be forgotten, and Isabel was certain that in later life she would look back on her operatic experiences with tremendous gratitude. Jerry was not overjoyed with her spending two evenings a week rehearsing, despite the fact that he was busy writing and preparing lectures during that time, but he did enjoy the performances.

Friends were made so easily at school, at the opera companies and at Penn that Philadelphia had become the city of opportunity and friendship for Isabel. She was both gratified and amazed that for the first time in her life she was able to save money. Every month in London her salaries from teaching and singing were only sufficient to pay for her expenses including the divorce. Try as she might, she could never save anything, although her disciplined upbringing influenced her enough to remain debt free and always in the black – just! Yet in Philadelphia, after opening an account at a bank in Rittenhouse Square, she took the greatest delight seeing her savings grow each month. It gave her a sense of security and it was deeply satisfying to be able to accumulate capital, albeit a modest amount, and not have to watch every penny of her spending.

From Isabel's reunion with Jerry in London the previous July right through to their marriage in December 1968, they had enjoyed vigorous, unprotected sex, which they both hoped would lead to conception as soon as possible. Each month, just before her period was due, she hoped that her bloated waistline and tingling breasts predicted pregnancy, but each month she was disappointed. When the period arrived, it was as if the intense pressure within her body had been released only to add pressure to her mind and emotions. She recalled bitterly her time in Italy, and how she had not conceived in those few months. Now seven years later, it seemed as if she had been given another chance, and yet her ardent wish to have a baby was being thwarted.

Sometimes she would stay in the bathroom at period time and cry, washing her face carefully afterwards and applying a little make-up, in the hope that Jerry wouldn't notice, but he did.

"Gee, what's the matter? Have you lost a dollar and found a dime?" he joked.

"Do you think I'll ever get pregnant?" Isabel blurted out, and then burst into tears. Her emotions were so raw and on edge that Jerry put his arms right round her, and looking her straight in the eyes, he said,

"Listen, you're not the most patient person in the world, but you may have to develop patience. Just forget about trying to get pregnant. Enjoy life, and before you know it, you'll get pregnant."

Isabel was grateful for his comforting advice, but she was very much aware that her biological clock was ticking away fast.

The next week she decided to withdraw some money from her bank in Rittenhouse Square and find a gynaecologist. She had made insufficient contributions to be covered by insurance, and there was no national-health scheme in the United States. Even in England, Isabel doubted whether infertility was covered by the National Health Service in the nineteen-sixties. After collecting a short list of three consultants with Jerry's help, she chose one specializing in infertility at Pennsylvania Hospital, where the surgery was conveniently open several evenings each week. She was grateful not to have to take time off from school and explain the reason to the nuns, and she was equally thankful to be given an almost immediate appointment. A first-rate gynaecologist would soon identify the problem, if indeed there was one, and lose no time in treating it. Her mood became optimistic, even upbeat. This was the United States, which lead the world in surgical and medical expertise and where problems were solved and dreams came true.

Predictably, and much to Jerry's chagrin, the first examination involved a semen analysis. Since this produced positive results, he was eliminated from the potential problems of conception. Then they were given a temperature chart, a thermometer and advice on optimal sexual positions, followed by a brief examination of Isabel's abdomen. When her temperature rose slightly in the middle of the menstrual cycle, it indicated the ovulation period and the best time to have sex, with the vagina tilted upwards and the lower abdomen raised on a pillow.

This technique was used over a period of several months with two disadvantageous results. Their sex life became predictable, clinical and even stressful, and Isabel did not conceive. There were more tears in the bathroom each disappointing month, heavy, painful periods and a feeling of frustration and failure. She tried to take comfort from the happiness of her married life with Jerry, from her job, and from her music, but try as she might to relax and forget all about pregnancy, the desire to conceive never left her mind.

The next piece of advice from the gynaecologist was for her to be admitted to hospital for a D and C, a dilation and curettage, in which the cervix, or neck of the womb, is dilated under anaesthetic so that a scrape, or endometrial biopsy, could be taken. Isabel and Jerry arrived at Pennsylvania Hospital early one Friday evening, and once they had completed the reception formalities, they were directed to a ward on the first floor. Once there, Jerry kissed Isabel goodbye, and wishing her luck, promised to collect her the next morning.

Isabel looked around the small room, noting that a curtain divided it in two, and on either side were two single beds and two lockers. A table, a television, two chairs and an en suite were the only extras. As yet the other bed was unoccupied, and a nurse drew the curtain right back as she breezed in.

"Take a shower, honey, then put on this gown and jump into bed." So saying, she smiled and swished off to her next port of call. With a bit of luck, thought Isabel, the other bed will remain vacant, and I ll have the room to myself. She went into the en suite, and sobbed self-pityingly for a few minutes under the shower, certain that nobody could hear her.

Why was it so difficult for her to conceive? Her own mother had given birth to twins, even though one did not survive, followed by a third child, herself. As with many families, it was often a limited budget which restricted the size of the family, not infertility. Oh, she wanted a child so badly!

As she turned the shower off, and began to dry herself, she heard pop music blaring out on the other side of the en suite door. She quickly put on her white hospital robe, brushed her hair and cleaned her teeth. The music was still blaring out as she collected her toilet bag and clothes, and opened the door. An attractive auburn-haired girl of about twenty was stretched out on the other bed, chewing gum and watching a television pop-music programme.

"Hi hon, I'm Sandy." She waved a hand.

"Pleased to meet you. I'm Isabel."

"Is that a British accent you got there? Geez, it's kinda cute. Are you in here for the same thing as me?"

"Well, I've come in for a D and C actually," Isabel answered.

A doctor entered at that point and drew the curtain back into position, so that the room was once again divided in two, thus creating a little privacy. He examined Isabel, and told her that within half an hour she would be admitted to the operating theatre, and would not spend long there.

"It's only a D and C," he commented. "These semi-infertility cases don't take long. You'll be back here in no time, and home tomorrow morning," he added encouragingly before leaving the room. The pop-music programme continued unabated, but the curtain remained in position. Within minutes a nurse administered a premed injection and within half an hour, Isabel was trolleyed off to the operating theatre.

When she came round from the anaesthetic, she was back in the room she shared with Sandy who was still stretched out on her bed, fully clothed, consuming an enormous cheeseburger and fries. The television was still blaring.

"Howya doing, hon? So, you're finally back? Would you like me to order a burger for you? Ida waited only I didn't know how long you'd be. Geez, you look pale, hon. Are you okay?"

"Yes, I'm okay. Are you allowed to eat before your operation?" Isabel asked weakly. "I thought it was nil by mouth."

"Me? I've been and come back, hon. Abortions don't take long yer know."

Isabel felt her mouth go dry, reached out for a small kidney bowl on the bedside cabinet and was retching into it when a nurse came in, turned down the television volume control and pulled the curtain back into position to divide the room once more.

Jerry collected her the next morning, and after spending the weekend resting, Isabel was ready to return to school on Monday morning as if nothing had happened, and nobody knew. Normal life resumed, entertaining friends, visits to New York and preparations for an August holiday in England. Isabel was stimulated by her teaching programmes and her pupils. She fitted in well with that particular American private-school system, and was delighted at the end of the final semester when her contract was renewed. Half a dozen teachers were let go at the same time. It was also a joy and a challenge to learn more operas and to broaden her repertoire.

When Jerry first entered the academic life, after having worked for General Motors for several years, he had no problem in publishing papers relating to economics, but more recently, publishers had refused his work for various reasons, and he was frustrated, angry and uncomprehending. The publish-or-perish reality obsessed him at a time when his colleagues were not only publishing papers to their satisfaction, but books as well. He was often uncommunicative on his return from work, silently brooding over his meal and refusing conversation. He needed to study at home as well as at the university, but the open-plan layout of the apartment did not encourage privacy.

The kitchen was open to the living room, which faced directly onto the bedroom, there being only three doors in the apartment: the front door, the bathroom door and the balcony door. Consequently neither Jerry nor Isabel could ever find any private space. After finishing the evening meal, decisions would be made as to whether they would study, read, watch television or go out. Jerry rarely wanted to go out in the evening, preferring to persevere with his academic papers, whereas Isabel was required to attend opera rehearsals twice a week leading up to a performance.

Instead of cheerfully optimizing the time when Isabel was out to concentrate in peace and quiet on his work, Jerry took a negative and disapproving attitude. Before they were married, he approved of her involvement with Philadelphia's opera companies; now that they were married, he did not. Isabel tried to reason with him, unwilling to give up this wonderful musical opportunity, but without success.

Summer brought the end of the opera season and a visit to England, and Isabel fervently hoped that a relaxing holiday with an opportunity to reunite with her mother and friends, as a joy in itself, would also produce the desired conception. After all, so many babies were conceived on holiday, she told herself, and the results of the D and C were certainly encouraging. She did ovulate and she did not have endometriosis.

"The consultant said there was no reason for me not to conceive," commented Isabel.

"Let's hope this vacation will give us a break," replied Jerry, unemotionally.

Reuniting with her school friends in England, Isabel discovered that a number were producing their third or fourth child, having been married a few years. She envied the unofficial maternity club they had joined and the bond of the children they had in common. She longed to share this mystery, but she no longer felt at one with them. Despite their school history together, she felt something of an outsider, partly because she no longer lived in England, and partly because she was childless. Even her mother had hinted that she wanted grandchildren, particularly now that her daughter-in-law had escaped with the twins to live with a new partner far away in Northumberland, leaving Clive to his own devices. There would be no reconciliation, and it would be highly likely that Isabel's mother would not see the twins in the future, since their mother wanted no family connection with Clive.

When they flew back to JFK Airport at the end of August, both Jerry and Isabel retained memories of a pleasant few weeks, first of all in the London area, enjoying the West End shows, concerts and restaurants, before hiring a car to tour the Lake District and Scotland. Predictably the weather had been mixed, but Isabel always felt more energetic in English summers than in American summers. She sometimes found the American June-to-August heat overwhelming and could well appreciate the need for air-conditioning.

Jerry's brother, Andy, met them at the airport and drove them to his apartment in Manhattan, where they would stay the night before driving down the New Jersey Turnpike to Philadelphia the next day.

"Well, it's great to see you, though you don't look very suntanned!" Andy joked, and smiled broadly.

"Did you manage to take off your raincoats at all in good old Blighty? Anyway, for a special celebration, I'm treating us all to dinner at my favourite Greek restaurant, and you can tell Sue and me all about your holiday."

"What are we celebrating?" asked Isabel.

"You'll have to wait until later." Then he added to Jerry, "It's the one near Radio City with the dancing and the broken plates!"

The atmosphere in the restaurant was dynamic, with waiters moving at agile speed amid vibrant, conversations between animated couples, and the strains of Melina Mercouri in the background. When they had each chosen from the menu, and ordered a bottle of retsina, Sue ,who was looking particularly radiant that evening, suddenly exclaimed, "I really can't wait any longer to tell you. I'm so excited. We're going to have a baby in March, and we're going to ask Jerry to be godfather!"

"Congratulations to you both. I'd be delighted," beamed Jerry.

"Yes, congratulations! What wonderful news!" added Isabel.

Isabel did not begrudge Sue's happiness at becoming pregnant, but the arrival of her period a week after she and Jerry had returned to Philadelphia smashed all their hope of conception during the long summer holiday. Isabel broke down with anger and frustration when Jerry was not in the apartment, and her body shook with bitter sobs. Why, why was she not conceiving? The consultant had reassured her that she was gynaecologically healthy, and Jerry's sperm count was normal. What was preventing pregnancy, she could not fathom. She cried herself into exhaustion, and finally fell asleep until Jerry returned from Penn to find her a picture of dejection with swollen eyes and blotchy skin. He guessed the cause of her distress before she told him and he, too, looked very disappointed.

During the fall, the opera season recommenced. It involved learning the *Aida* choruses for the Lyric Opera Company, and *Die Meistersinger* for the Grand. Isabel was delighted to reunite with her singing friends after the long summer vacation and to face the challenge of committing the new operas to memory. However, when two of her soprano friends became pregnant and decided not to return for the season, she envied their fecundity and missed their friendship. Even a colleague at school seemed to have produced a pregnancy out of nowhere, would be leaving at Christmas and was already "carrying all before her." The wives of some of Jerry's colleagues at Penn were also pregnant. To Isabel it seemed that pregnancy was everywhere, but it evaded her, and she was obsessed day and night with her frustrating failure.

The temperature-chart technique to detect and optimize the ovulation period continued over the next few months, and spontaneous lovemaking became a thing of the past. The need to achieve conception was so important to them both that they became tense and stressed, which they knew was counterproductive, but which they could not control. Finally, Isabel decided to return to the gynaecologist at Pennsylvania Hospital to inform him of her lack of progress and to seek his advice, emphasising that her biological clock was ticking away fast and she wanted results. He advised a laparoscopy which involved inserting a laparoscope, or telescope, into the abdomen under anaesthetic to view the uterus, ovaries and fallopian tubes in order to diagnose any specific problems. In Isabel's case there were no problems. In fact, after the operation, the consultant described her as "disgustingly healthy", advising her to give it time, and then adding what she did not want to hear, namely, that some couples did not produce children even if no detectable reason could be found.

That depressing piece of information incited Isabel to seek a second opinion. There must be a medical reason for her inability to conceive, and perhaps it was a problem that, with treatment, could be rectified. She and Jerry were advised to consult an eminent, infertility specialist practising in the city centre. To ascertain the exact nature of the problem, she was asked scores of questions relating to her general health, her gynaecological history, her sex life and her psychological condition. An endometrial sampling followed a vaginal examination. A narrow tube was inserted into the womb, without anaesthetic, to examine cells from the womb lining. Endometrial cancer was eliminated, and again no specific problems were discovered. After three appointments, a beaming, middle-aged gynaecologist informed Isabel that he had every confidence that she would conceive, and would more than likely go on to have three or four children.

"Try to be patient and just give it time," he added finally. Time, time, time.

After dinner that evening, when Isabel was washing the dishes, Jerry said, "I've got some news for you. I've decided to apply for a job in England. How do you feel about it?"

For a second Isabel was stunned because this was an out-of-the--blue comment. He had never even hinted at such a decision before, not even when she was a bit homesick during the first year. Now in her third year in the United States, she had thoroughly adjusted to the American way of life, and was making the most of the teaching and musical opportunities which Philadelphia offered. Nonetheless, she did miss her mother and her old friends.

"Gosh, that's sudden. You mean you've applied already?"

"Yep! I thought you'd enjoy being back in England."

"Whereabouts in England?"

"Manchester. Senior lecturer in economics. Aren't you pleased?"

"Er ... yes of course."

She knew not a soul in Manchester, and thought it to be about 150 miles or more from London, her mother and all her friends, but she did not want to give Jerry the impression that she was reluctant to move back to England. It was clear, though, that his decision to leave Penn was by no means due to her. His temper, always on the verge of becoming trigger-happy, had recently become difficult to live with, mostly because he could sulk for days after a flare-up over something Isabel considered to be trivial. What was bugging him?

At first she concluded that her inability to conceive for no apparent reason must be the cause for his anger and melancholy. When asked, he refused point blank to admit that anything bothered him, except that the academic world had its fair share of super-ambitious, back-stabbing bastards, and he wanted to pursue his future elsewhere. The publish-or-perish problem would not go away and Jerry, still having no success with producing articles and papers, was under constant pressure and strain. Since his mother had already retired to live in Greece, the only close relatives to leave behind in the United States were his brother, Andy, his sister-in-law, Sue and their new baby daughter. They all agreed that England was nearer to Greece than New York, and therefore advantageous to their mother.

Isabel had no idea what to expect of Manchester, only that they would have to live in furnished and serviced accommodation in the south of the city whilst they searched for a house. When they finally moved in, Jerry took off to the university every day whilst Isabel had to fall back on her inner resources in a characterless flat with orange, plastic armchairs, dripping taps and noisy neighbours.

Packing up and leaving Philadelphia had been harder for Isabel than she thought it would be. After three years she had met and enjoyed the company of a few of Jerry's friends, but had formed many happy friendships of her own with those on her staff at school and at both opera companies. Life had been full and invigorating in the United States, giving her opportunities that she had not enjoyed in the United Kingdom, and she knew that on her return, those opportunities would disappear. She felt guilty about her mother, though, as a seventy-year-old widow living alone, and she was glad she would be able to live closer to her, even if her London suburb was about 200 miles from Manchester. It was certainly nearer than Philadelphia.

Well, it's here we are and let's start all over again, thought Isabel, as Jerry returned, glowering, to the plastic flat each week-day evening. It was the same moody Jerry in a worse environment. With nothing much to do all day other than contemplate her problems, she suggested to Jerry that she might tackle a bit of supply teaching, but since their move from America Jerry had become noticeably controlling and forbade the idea.

"You have to devote yourself to two important priorities," he said firmly. "One is to find us a home, and the other is to find a gynaecologist, a top man in infertility."

Those final words imprinted their meaning into her soul. She had not managed to conceive after over three years of trying and she felt a failure.

Every now and then Jerry would remind her that she was the party at fault, whereas he claimed his sperm count was completely normal. Isabel set about finding a private fertility specialist in Manchester to obtain an early appointment, and because infertility treatment in the seventies was not widespread on the National Health Service.

In the interim period she visited estate agents and read the property pages of the local newspapers. As she pointed out to Jerry, they could only select houses theoretically. To view properties as widespread as they were in Derbyshire and Cheshire, they would need a car, and after lengthy bus rides and arduous walks in the rain to the disappointing reality of what had looked attractive in photographs, Jerry agreed. In a short time he acquired a second-hand Ford Cortina, and with the help of their wheels at weekends and on afternoons when he was not lecturing, they were able to discover the charms of as many properties as possible before making their decision. They soon realized that they were far from being in control of the house-purchase business.

Although some cottages and houses were picturesque and full of period features, they were either too cramped or required expensive alterations; others with spacious rooms and adequate storage space were box-like and characterless. Isabel could not imagine settling in them with any degree of contentment. Three months after their arrival in England, they had been gazumped and lost two properties, with the accompanying solicitor's fees and no result. Jerry's temper had not improved, and they were still living in the plastic flat with leaky taps and noisy neighbours.

With little luck on the housing front, they had no option but to keep up-to-date with the market on a daily basis and this was left mainly to Isabel. She also received a recommendation from her temporary GP about an infertility specialist practising in St John's Street, Manchester. Since Jerry was working, she was grateful to attend the first appointment on her own. It was so much easier to supply the consultant with her medical and gynaecological history than have Jerry

listening and glowering in the background, ready to correct
a potential blunder. After taking copious notes, the doctor
examined her internally and then, by placing an instrument
through the cervix into the womb, he removed a small piece
of the lining. Once again it was as painful as it had been in
the United States. Despite the fact that she ovulated every
month, chlomid was prescribed to aid ovulation, which
Isabel could not understand. Up to that point no one had
diagnosed why she had not conceived.

Within the next three years Jerry and Isabel bought a
country cottage in Cheshire with half an acre of land, and
spent just over a year in Belgium, where Jerry worked temporarily at a college in Brussels, advising European students
on their doctoral theses in various aspects of economics.
For her part, Isabel had pursued infertility treatment in
Manchester, London and Brussels, at considerable expense
to herself. Finally, she learned that her inability to procreate
was due to polycystic-ovary syndrome. In Jerry's opinion,
both in England and Belgium, she stood a better chance of
conceiving if she stayed at home and rested. At first Isabel
cooperated, but she became lonely and isolated, particularly
when Jerry was abroad, as she did not know many people
either in Cheshire or Brussels. Her sole obsessive thought,
day in and day out, was to get pregnant. She did not conceive, but she did become depressed. Much time was spent
in tears during the day when he was out, and in the evening
when he returned, she had virtually nothing to say to him
since her life was so empty of stimulus. She noticed that he
was having a hard time adjusting to the British way of life
in the north, which bore little resemblance to the London
he had known in the sixties.

For the twelve months they spent in Brussels, Isabel took advantage of enrolling for courses in advanced French at the university, as well as singing with the Flemish Radio Choir which was a joy, and took her mind off her obsession for a short time. Once back in England, it was a different story.

When Jerry travelled into Manchester by car, Isabel was virtually marooned in the countryside where, initially, she had neither friends nor relatives. She really needed to pour out her sorrow and distress about her childlessness to a sympathetic listening ear, but to whom? Jerry who at first had shown her some support and understanding had now withdrawn into his own problems: his workload, his struggle with publication and his consulting, or lack of it. His largely unspoken expectation that a doctorate would serve as a passport to success and riches was a disappointment so far. Life definitely owed him something. After all, he had studied for all those years, passed the examinations, and therefore deserved to win the prizes. The guys back in the United States were making pots of money consulting and publishing regularly, and their wives were fruitful and multiplying.

When Isabel's mother ventured up north to spend Christmas with them, it was not difficult for her to sense the tension between them and notice Jerry's brooding temperament, the speed at which he could be moved to anger and the slowness to return to normality. She could see the unnerving effect it had on Isabel, and it worried her.

"It would drive me crazy spending all day here without knowing anyone," she remarked, loudly enough for Jerry to hear.

"Spend some of that money you earned in America and buy a second-hand car. Then you can find a job and stop thinking about getting pregnant every minute of the day." It was like a breath of fresh air.

"What's happened to your teaching? You were so good at it - and your singing?"

Jerry scowled meaningfully, but since it was Christmas, he decided to treat his mother-in-law's remarks with studied silence rather than lose his temper. Yet, when she had returned home after Boxing Day, he could scarcely contain his rage.

"What the hell does she think she's doing, interfering with our lives?" he yelled. "Why doesn't she mind her own bloody business?"

"She was only giving her opinion. It's a free country and she can see for herself that I'm unhappy," replied Isabel.

"Well, she's just stirring it, and you've absolutely no need to be unhappy. If you were seriously sick, or penniless, or the victim of some terrible crime, I could understand it, but you're not. You're relaxing at home, hoping to get pregnant. That's no reason to be unhappy."

"But I don't want to stay at home. It's lonely and unfulfilling and –" Not waiting to hear her reasoning, he left the kitchen, spewing out invective, and went straight to the study, slamming the door behind him.

The next morning he was up before six with his bags unexpectedly packed. Isabel, tearful about their disharmony, had not noticed him making preparations the evening before. An hour later, she awoke to find a note on the kitchen table saying that a consulting job had come up and he would be away in Brussels for five days. Needless to say, he had taken the car and left it at the airport.

Isabel was marooned, but not entirely without comfort and companionship, since a few months earlier, they had acquired Carmen, a beautiful, black and gold German Shepherd puppy, with large soulful eyes, a prodigious appetite and a delight for exercise. On that morning Isabel whistled for her, locked the cottage door, and nimbly scaled the five-barred gate into the pastureland stretching ahead of her. It was a crisp January morning, the sun was shining, and she could see clearly across the fields to the Macclesfield hills in the distance.

As she strolled towards the copse at the far end of the field, she knew that these unexpected five days of freedom would give her an opportunity to make some decisions and reorganize her life, free of Jerry's control.

She was acutely aware that her marriage was important to her, that infertility was a real confidence-sapping problem, and that one disastrous marital failure was more than enough. Yet, in spite of being married, she had to determine her own life, at least to some extent. Emerging from the shady copse into the sunshine again, she clipped the leash onto Carmen's collar, and headed towards a farm some 300 metres away.

By the end of the week, life had taken on a more encouraging turn for her. She had made friends with her farming neighbour, Jessie, a fair minded, robust young woman in her middle thirties with a terrific sense of humour, and had invited her to coffee. Fortunately they struck up an instant rapport. Jessie was a teacher by training and had married into a farming family. It was not long before she offered Isabel a lift into Macclesfield. Once there, Isabel was able to organize her finances at the bank. Wasting very little time, she bought a second-hand Volkswagen beetle at a garage in town, and surprisingly quickly, the paper work, including the insurance, was complete and the vehicle was actually delivered to her door one evening after the garage had closed. Wheels! Glory hallelujah, she had wheels!

Anticipating her mobility, she had telephoned the local education office to enquire if any supply teaching was available, emphasising in what areas her strengths lay, and a day later, she was phoned with a request to report to the head of St Jude's School in Macclesfield the following Monday morning. The arrival of an unwelcome visitor, her period, was the only bad news in a cheering week. It happened just before Jerry returned from Brussels, mystified by the warm welcome home he received from Isabel and Carmen.

Six years had passed since their wedding day, and now Isabel was convinced that the only way left for them to have a baby was through adoption.

Chapter 6
Decisions

Francesca's near disbelief that she was almost three-months pregnant made her realize that she must have conceived early on in her relationship with Michael. She had to contact him. No luck with the phone in that student lodging house. Most of the final-year students were either in the middle of examinations or due to take them shortly. Those who had neglected their studies during the year were frantically trying to make up for wasted time in the library, so when she phoned, the house was often empty. Failing to contact Michael by phone, she resorted to writing a letter, telling him that she needed to see him as soon as possible. Finally, after she had gone through a week of worried waiting, he replied that he had two more weeks of examinations, and had to cram every minute with study. Consequently he could not see her until the examinations were over. He suggested they met after her stint at the Golden Fleece on a Saturday night and mentioned a date and time.

Francesca felt that she had no option but to agree, since telling him her news could seriously disrupt his examinations. Each morning, as regularly as light dawned, she would feel nauseous and vomit into the toilet bowl, and without taking any nourishment, she would direct her steps slowly down Benedict |Street towards the city centre and the music shop, her mind in turmoil and her energy dwindling. Keith would scowl at her regularly, expecting her to be late or barely on time, whereas Gemma, the golden girl who had to travel in by bus, appeared early every morning, well groomed and enthusiastic.

The music shop was no longer a pleasant workplace for Francesca. She was sickened by the smell of coffee there and was barely able to camouflage her nausea. In the two weeks of waiting for Michael to appear it seemed that Keith was searching for new ways to find fault with her: she was three minutes late coming back from lunch, she had mislaid an important catalogue, and she was uncommunicative. The latter was certainly true. Her worries were locked up inside her, and any non-genius could guess that she was silently preoccupied with something - but what? She worried that she was putting on weight, and her pregnancy would soon be noticeable. Then there was her exhaustion, which a night's sleep did not rectify, and her shifts at the Golden Fleece became something to dread. How long could she go on? Yet she needed the money.

When Michael finally met her as arranged at the Golden Fleece, he was all smiles and in a jubilant mood. She was overjoyed to see him, after waiting so long, and it was taken for granted that he would stay over at her flat. His relief at having completed his examinations was palpable, and he was demonstrably loving to Francesca on the way back. Once in the flat, they fell into each other's arms, kissing tenderly, whilst Michael gradually stripped her until their mutual desire became insistent, strongly passionate and finally burst into a flood of ecstatic orgasm. Shortly after, overwhelmed by loving exhaustion, she fell fast asleep, aware only that Michael's naked body was lying beside her until the morning.

At eight o'clock she awoke to find the sun streaming in the window, and Michael still sleeping and looking attractively vulnerable, his dark hair tousled and his body only partly covered by the sheet. She brought him tea from the kitchen and kissed him gently on the lips, so as to awaken him in the most loving way possible. His eyes opened slowly, and he grinned contentedly at her.

She loved the way his eyes smiled more than his mouth, especially when he was sleepy. Eventually he sat up and silently sipped his tea.

"Well, Francesca mia, what was your reason for phoning me and writing to me during the exams? You should know better," he teased playfully, at last. "Couldn't you live without me?"

"I may as well tell you directly now because I love you and that's all that matters, isn't it?"

"Tell me what?"

"The truth is, I'm over three-months pregnant. We are going to have a baby."

It was as if Michael were suddenly struck dumb by the news. The colour drained from his face, and he just stared ahead of himself, his mood changing in seconds from lovingly playful to morosely silent. After some moments of thought, weighing up the impact of her news, he spoke coldly and dispassionately to her.

"What about birth control? Didn't you think of using any?"

She was alarmed by this sudden chill in his demeanour, and stuttered a defensive whisper in reply.

"What about you? Didn't you think of using contraception, a condom?"

"Well, men don't have babies, you may have noticed," he remarked sarcastically. "It was up to you to protect yourself. Now look what a mess you're in!"

"We're in," she reminded him vehemently. "Michael, please!"

She burst into tears and headed for the bathroom where she retched in the toilet. Feeling completely miserable, she decided to have a bath and wash her hair. It was Sunday, after all, and she told herself that when she felt better and less emotional, she and Michael would be able to discuss the situation rationally and make plans. The news had obviously been a shock to him, news which she had known about for over a fortnight. Twenty minutes later, she emerged from the bathroom wearing a pretty housecoat she had made for herself and a towel round her head. The radio was strangely blaring out favourite hymn tunes, but Michael was gone.

She cried as she had never cried before in her whole life. Sobs engulfed her, body and soul, as she lay on the bed where all the passion and joy of the previous evening with Michael had now turned to desolation and emptiness. What was she going to do? Surely Michael wouldn't abandon her? He had made such passionate love to her that she was certain he must feel something for her, and yet … She would wait a short time to see what he had decided once he had recovered from the shock, but she also realized that being unmarried and pregnant required a number of decisions to be made as soon as possible. If only she could confide in someone, it would relieve the worry and the loneliness, but she dared not trust anybody. The thought of her parents discovering the truth filled her with distress, and the sobs overwhelmed her again and again.

As a magistrate in the 1970s, Mr Bedale's attitude to unmarried mothers was far from compassionate. He had faced an increasing number of them in court, and with a few sad exceptions, considered them to be both immoral and irresponsible. In his view, sexual intercourse should be confined to marriage only, where any child resulting from that union would have two caring parents and be provided with a proper Christian upbringing. A stable society was built on marriage, not on one-parent families who could not cope. If these girls were unable to control their sexual appetites and say no, they should equip themselves with some means of birth control. There was no lack of choice.

Francesca knew only too well that telling her parents of her plight was a lost cause. If, by chance, they learned that she was pregnant, they would disown her without question. Imagine their shame and disgrace at the local Conservative Association, or when the news was hinted at, sotto voce, in the Rotary Club.

"It's all very well old Bedale pontificating in court about morals, but his own daughter's got a bun in the oven," she could hear them sniggering. She could also see that she might alienate the entire family.

The idea of confiding in her sister, Emily, now a qualified doctor, was tempting, but then in her turn she might confide in Caroline who in a family row might feel it necessary to inform their parents. She decided painfully that she would tell no one for the time being, wait a little longer for Michael's revised thoughts on the subject, and in the meantime, she would contact the Golden Fleece to tell the publican that she was unable to continue her duties there, knowing that without the extra money, she would either have to give up the flat or find someone to share the expenses.

A few days passed, and since she had heard not a word from Michael, she decided to take the bus down the Earlham Road to his student accommodation. Why was he avoiding her? Could he not even speak to her? She had no luck at the lodging house and thought he would probably be in the music faculty. Once there, she enquired his whereabouts from a student emerging from a practice room.

"Michael McKenna? Oh yes, he's a final-year student and he's finished all his exams. In fact, I think he's left - found freedom, the lucky devil - but you'd better check at the office. I'm not absolutely sure."

At the office his departure was confirmed. She was told that, following his graduation from the University of East Anglia, he would continue his practical music studies at the Paris Conservatoire. At this news Francesca felt stunned and dizzy, and had to sit down for several minutes to regain her composure, before returning to the flat to shed more bitter tears.

Before the end of the working week she had received an envelope bearing a French postmark. In it was a cheque for £200 which Michael had borrowed from his father. It was accompanied by a short note with no address heading. In it he told her that he was not ready for marriage, that he had come to France specifically to pursue his music studies, and again was horrified that she had allowed herself to become pregnant. Would she use the enclosed money to pay for an abortion? He wished her all the best. It was clear that he did not favour any further correspondence or contact of any sort.

Francesca could scarcely believe what was happening to her. Distraught with sadness and with the agony of hindsight, she realized that she had not only fallen in love with him when he did not love her, but that she had also fallen for his patter. The note was so terse and final, and the realization that their futures would separate for good filled her with unbearable pain.

Abortion. She spent the entire evening and most of a sleepless night thinking about it, remembering clearly what the nuns had taught her on the subject at her Catholic convent school several years before. We are all made in the image of God, and therefore each one of us is precious in his sight. In fact, the first right of a human being is his or her right to life. To remove that right is to commit murder. "Thou shalt not kill" was one of the Ten Commandments delivered to Moses on Mount Sinai. Surely, she reasoned, ending a pregnancy is not the same as committing murder? As soon as the ovum is fertilized, a life is begun. With development, that life will become a person, a human being, and so to kill it, to deliberately prevent it from growing, is to commit murder. Yet, here was Michael, sending her money to do precisely that. He obviously was not convinced about the sanctity of life.

It would be so tempting and convenient to take a short abortion holiday, so to speak, and to recover and get on with life, wiser for having had the experience. Her plans for independence could continue. Nobody needed to know, and a dress-making business could remain her goal. She would have to make enquiries, but perhaps private medical care would speed the process up somewhat. She would have to think up a "compassionate" reason for Keith to grant her the required time.

She had read that many women return to work shortly after an abortion, and, yes, she was young and strong. Another advantage was that she had the money to do it. Many of the pregnant girls facing her father in court for some petty crime like shoplifting, did not. Yet, she felt dreadfully alone, and although Michael had abandoned her, she still loved him, and she could scarcely face up to what was happening to her without him.

Such thoughts persisted all night with no resolution, but Saturday morning brought its responsibilities - the music shop. Her morning sickness continued, and sleepless, she felt lethargic and unwell, fit only to lie down until she recovered to make herself a hot drink. Instead, she went to work and arrived late again.

Keith was bordering on the incandescent, and he insisted on shouting at her in the large stockroom located behind the customer area.

"What on earth is the matter with you, Francesca? You're twenty minutes late, and it's Saturday. I've warned you several times before, and you appear to be impervious to reason. You're a law unto yourself, and I've had just about enough. You are no longer showing the promise of a few months ago, so I'm telling you to go. Yes, go! Collect your things and what is owed to you, and go. Now!

Don't bother to wait until this evening. Your attitude to work infuriates me, and it is better that you go now and have done with it!"

Francesca remained totally silent, giving no defence of herself. Her eyes welled up with tears, as Keith called out, "Gemma, hold the fort in the shop while I phone my niece to help us out. She's finished her exams now, I think."

Pregnant, fired from her job and exhausted, she returned to the flat to sleep, eat and think. In the short term she was relieved to be freed from both her jobs for two reasons. She was so deeply tired all the time, and then she suspected that Keith might have guessed the truth. If she had stayed at the shop any longer, he would have become certain of her pregnancy, and she could not rely on his discretion or Gemma's. The shameful truth could reach her parents by the Norfolk bush telegraph, and she could not allow that to happen. Who would help her now that Michael, her parents, family and friends were definitely not possibilities? In a flash, she realized that one member of her family could be trusted and would help her: Sebastian.

Her brother, Seb, the solicitor, twelve years her senior, with whom she had always felt a special bond and with whom she had shared secrets in the past, was really her only hope. Realizing how much she needed his advice, support and practical help, and the lamentable plight she was in, she broke down in tears again, but not for long. She had to act fast, and could not allow herself the indulgence of falling apart emotionally. Towards the end of the working day, she headed for the nearest phone box in Benedict Street to call Seb at his office.

Fortunately he was not engaged with a client, but was on the verge of leaving the office when Francesca phoned, and since the staff and other solicitors had already departed, he was alone.

Sebastian knew that as much as Francesca loved and respected him, she was not given to making long-distance telephone calls to him without good reason, and certainly not to the office. He was so shocked by the brief account of her condition, the loss of her job and her general emotional state that he promised to take three days' holiday immediately and drive down to Norwich to be with her. It would mean having to tell Heather, his wife, but because Heather was fond of Francesca and thought that she had received a rough deal in the Bedale family, she could easily be sworn to secrecy.

Two days later Seb arrived in Norwich, parking his large Volvo estate car conveniently outside Francesca's flat. She was so relieved to see him and to feel his generous support and concern that she burst into tears again. Noting her obvious distress and anxiety, he spoke to her calmly, yet with loving authority.

"Francesca, listen to me: first things first. Whatever you decide about the baby later, the top priority at the moment is for you to leave Norwich as soon as possible."

She knew he was right, and over a meal they discussed their immediate plan of action. She would settle the utility bills and a month's rent with Seb's financial help, and any overlap of payment could be forwarded to the landlord later. The two bonus points of not needing to arrange the removal of furniture or inform employers meant that they could make a speedy departure for York the next day.

Seb slept on the spare bed overnight, and his only phone call from the Benedict Street box was to Heather. Their parents and siblings must, at all costs, suspect nothing, and not having a phone in the flat definitely helped. With no sudden incoming calls or the need to make excuses or even tell lies, the delicate situation was more under their control, and as lonely in her despair as she had been before Seb's arrival, Francesca was now very relieved that she did not have a host of friends who could knock on her door at any moment.

Their departure the following day was only delayed by Francesca's morning sickness, the need to clean the flat and strip the beds. They finally loaded her cases, bags and boxes into the Volvo estate car with surprising speed, and were gone shortly after the city rush hour was over. Francesca would post the keys back to the landlord as soon as she arrived in York.

The approximate 200-mile journey to the north passed in amicable silence between them. When she was not looking at the map to aid Seb with navigation, she had much on her mind to think about, whilst her brother was giving all his attention to unfamiliar roads and returning safely. It was not the time to discuss anything. Francesca realized that the final decision about her pregnancy rested with her only. Nevertheless, she was very dependent on the generosity of her brother and sister-in-law for an uncertain amount of time, and this made her uneasy.

Sebastian and Heather, as successful young lawyers, had done well for themselves by buying an attractive, substantial Victorian house in Heworth, a suburb of York, with easy access to the city centre where they both worked in different legal practices. The numerous rooms, their high ceilings and characterful features provided an atmosphere of spacious comfort to which Francesca immediately warmed on her arrival. Her bedroom, recently decorated in light colours, and appealing with its quirky shape and original fireplace, looked onto the back garden, which she thought seemed unexpectedly peaceful for a suburb of York.

The garden was medium-sized and cleverly landscaped at the far end with trees, both evergreen and deciduous, together with mature shrubs and wild flowers to produce the effect of a wood or copse and to attract wild life. Both Seb and Heather were green-fingered. It was not merely the law which they had in common - and they had completely fallen in love with the garden. In fact, it had clinched their decision to buy the house, since gardens of that maturity and beauty took years to achieve. Their appreciation was total.

The young couple helped Francesca with all her luggage, and what was superfluous to her present needs was stored in their dry cellar. Many of her important odds and ends, including her radio, record player, sewing machine, china and kettle, all found suitable niches in that delightful bedroom, and when everything was in its place, she suddenly became overwhelmed with fatigue and relief, stretched out on the bed and fell fast asleep.

She was awakened at 6 p.m. by Seb bringing her a cup of tea and telling her that Heather was cooking a meal which would be ready in half an hour or so. He suggested that afterwards they should have a mini-Bedale meeting. A Bedale family meeting in the past usually involved all the Bedale family, was presided over by their father and something to be tolerated or dreaded, rather than enjoyed.

When she joined Heather in the kitchen for the first time, she was delighted to meet a smooth-haired, black and tan dachshund puppy, named Chipolata - Chip for short.

"Oh, how adorable he is!" she cried as she scooped him up in her arms, licks abounding and tail wagging prestissimo.

"Yes, he's quite a character, and we couldn't resist him when we saw the litter three months ago," replied Heather. "He made a bee line for us straight away, almost jumped out of the whelping box and said 'Buy me!' We just knew he was meant for us.."

I wonder how they cope with Chip when they are out all day, thought Francesca, but she politely did not ask. She was keen to get on well with Heather as she had done in the past.

Once the meal was over, and they were relaxing in the living room, Francesca, answering their questions, filled in her story with greater detail. When she reached the part where Michael's father had sent her a cheque to cover the cost of a private abortion, Sebastian asked, "How do you feel about an abortion?"

"I'm not sure."

"Well, you know it would make life a great deal easier for you in many ways. It's a relatively simple operation. You're young. You would recover from it quickly, and be able to resume your life with no encumbrance - sadder and wiser, maybe. Mum and Dad would never know, nor the rest of the family, nor your friends. Obviously, it would be unwise to return to Norwich in the near future, so you could stay here until you are more settled, and can find yourself a flat in York. Turn over a new leaf, start a new life."

Seb was considering what was best for Francesca, not what was best for the baby, and this unresolved decision had been whirring around in Francesca's head for weeks.

"But I don't think I want...."

"Francesca, you don't intend to keep the baby surely?" interrupted Heather. "How would you cope?"

"You can't keep the baby," Sebastian added vehemently. "It's impossible. You must realize that. Mum and Dad would be appalled. How could they accept from you what they cannot accept from others? Unmarried mothers are their bêtes noires - you know that - and to them, partly responsible for the potential breakdown of civilized society. And what would you do for money? They would cut you off with the proverbial shilling, and furthermore they would refuse to see you again. It would split up the whole family. Heather and I would be next on the list to be sent to Coventry for helping you. There's a great deal at stake here, and you need to think it through. Imagine the situation. You've already lost Michael who you thought was the love of your life. Do you want the poor child to grow up with no father, no family and virtually penniless? Think, Francesca, think!"

Tired from the journey and the physical and emotional demands of her pregnancy, Francesca could only sob. She suggested that she would prefer to discuss her decision with them when she had rested and calmed down, and she thanked them for their help and concern before retiring to bed.

The next day Heather went to work, but one day of Seb's holiday still remained which gave Francesca and her brother a chance to discuss the problem on a one to one basis. As much as she liked Heather, she was glad of this important time alone with him, and after a sound night's sleep, she felt better able to face her problems. It was not long before their discussion started once more. When Francesca told her brother that she realized keeping the baby was no longer an option, he heaved a sigh of relief.

"Thank God," he murmured.

Secretly she knew that she would have loved the baby with all her heart and soul because he would have been Michael's, and she still loved him and hoped that he would have a change of heart, not that she had his address, and he would no longer have hers now. Yet reality had struck with the arrival of that cold cheque, and the likelihood of him changing his mind was minimal. Sebastian pressed on.

"Fran," he said softly, "if you are going ahead with an abortion, we really ought to make arrangements as soon as possible because these things take time, you know. You will need to be examined by two doctors and..."

"I'm not having an abortion," Francesca replied emphatically.

"What?"

"I'm definitely not having an abortion, so we won't need to make any arrangements. Why should I put an end to this baby's life because I have been careless and stupid? Carelessness and stupidity are forgivable, but murder is much more serious. This baby will be a person, Seb, just like you and me, and I cannot, will not, deprive him of his life. I could not live with myself."

It was as if Seb was suddenly listening to a mature adult instead of his little sister. There was no convincing answer to her credo on the sanctity of life, and he was sensitive enough not to try to give one, realizing that, along with millions of others, her suffering had caused her to grow up.

When it was clear that Francesca had finally made an unwavering decision, many practical issues had to be discussed. First of all her stay with Seb and Heather in Heworth would be much longer, waiting to give birth, rather than recovering from an abortion. Before anymore time passed, she would have to phone her parents and lie to them about there being more favourable dress-making prospects in York than in Norwich, and how happy she was to be staying with Seb and Heather until she found a flat. She would add that York was such a fascinating place and the people so friendly that she might stay and settle there. During the actual phone call, the conversation went well enough. Her mother seemed glad that Francesca was with Seb, and relieved that she had finally made contact. Francesca was well aware that had she not called her parents, her mother would have phoned the music shop in Norwich to find out if everything was all right. That problem had been pre-empted just in time.

It would be easy enough for Francesca to be registered with Seb and Heather's family doctor, and have her pregnancy monitored, but how would they explain her increasing girth and unmarried state to their friends, neighbours and colleagues? The ever-practical and generous Heather produced her late mother's wedding ring, which fitted Francesca's finger perfectly, and together they concocted a story of a tragic traffic accident in which Francesca's husband had died a few months before, not even knowing that she was pregnant. They would say that she was still so upset with grief that she could not bear to speak about it. She agreed that it was probably wiser to remain in her room when guests came to visit occasionally.

The house was large enough for them all to guard their privacy when necessary. Inevitably Francesca was anxious about paying for her room and board to avoid becoming something of a parasite for several months. Again Heather came to her rescue.

"We'll just love having you here," she said, "and have no qualms about making yourself useful.

First of all I won't have to organize a dog sitter for Chipolata during the day. You seem to have really taken to each other, so I can rest assured that he will be well taken care of and adore your company."

"Then there's the odd meal you can cook," suggested Seb with a twinkle in his eye. "You know how useless I am in the culinary department and it will give Heather a break sometimes."

"Before I forget, you may have noticed that although this house has many rooms, only a few of them have curtains. As Seb and I decorate them, we hoped you might make the curtains for us. We know it's your forte. Please say yes."

"Of course, I will. What a wonderful idea! I shall be delighted," replied Francesca.

She relaxed with the relief of being able to give as well as take, and felt her spirits rise a notch.

How fortunate she was to have the security of staying with Seb and Heather. Perhaps things could work out satisfactorily after all. Yet nagging at her all the time was grief over the loss of Michael, and guilt. To give a child up for adoption was surely to abandon it. How would that child feel as an adult, when he realized that his genetic father had turned his back on him, and finally the mother had too?

It was betrayal.

Alone in her bedroom, Francesca tried to put herself in the situation of a rejected child and felt totally wretched. What else could she do? After all, there were surely hundreds of childless couples out there who would not only shower her baby with love, but would provide him with so many opportunities that she could never give him. And yet he was hers, not theirs, and always would be.

Then again, her parents and large family were all important to her, and she could not do without them. The choice lay between her baby and her family, and for many nights she cried herself to sleep with these conflicting thoughts.

One evening a few weeks later, when Seb returned from the office, he remarked that he had confidentially acquired information about adoption societies from one of his colleagues. On that very evening Francesca felt the first fluttering of the baby in her womb.

CHAPTER 7
JERRY, ISABEL, FRANCESCA
AND LAURA (1975)

A chilly autumnal wind was blowing over the Cheshire plain as Isabel trudged home across field after field with Carmen, her faithful German Shepherd dog. To leave the confines of the cottage just temporarily was always a joyful release to her, no matter what the weather was like, excluding blizzards or torrential rain. After climbing the first five-barred gate, a symbol of boundary and control, she always savoured the relief of being free in the countryside to think and feel what she wanted. Sometimes she would walk through the copse, alert to bird calls and unidentifiable noises, smiling at the antics of the squirrels, or perhaps noticing a fox's brush disappearing into a ditch. At other times, she would take the route by the lake, and enjoy the moor hens and mallards gliding in and out amongst the reeds, before walking more purposefully towards the fields and woods which lay beyond. There she felt free. She rarely saw anyone, perhaps a farmer in the distance, but that was all. She was free to speak her inner thoughts, to plan, to substantiate half-formed ideas, or to sing, to cry even, for there had been many tears of disappointment. On the days when she felt her wavering faith strengthening, this freedom seemed God given, a gift of his nature inspiring courage and hope in her.

To keep tight hold of her sanity, Isabel had continued to teach, much to Jerry's disgust, and as luck would have it, despite all the investigations and infertility treatment, she did not become pregnant. Well-meaning friends told her that if she adopted a baby she would almost certainly conceive. Et voilà! Her family would be complete.

She researched the names and addresses of adoption societies in the north of England, and discovered that a number of them had closed down following the Abortion Act of 1967. So many young girls and women had chosen to abort in relative secrecy rather than wait nine months to give up their babies for adoption. The Catholic societies were still operating, but Jerry and Isabel would not convert to Catholicism as a requirement to adopt a Catholic baby.

Co-operative rather than keen, Jerry went along with all the research, but basically left the work to Isabel. He often travelled abroad, and she was able to set the pace of her enquiries from home. She wrote letters to numerous non-Catholic societies, enclosing information about themselves as individuals and as a couple, completing lengthy forms and phoning in as a follow-up. They were rejected by many societies on the grounds that Isabel, aged thirty- six, had been married before, and Jerry, aged forty– three, was not only too old but non-British. It all seemed impossible and hopeless to Isabel who was convinced that no matter how hard she tried she could not have what she most wanted in the whole world: a baby of her own.

One solitary evening after her walk, she cried with frustration for the umpteenth time as she perused the list of adoption societies yet again, and discovered one society that she must have previously overlooked. Each society was provided with a short description of its location and requirements. This particular one, the Bellevue Adoption Society, was located in York, and Isabel wondered why she had not noticed it before; perhaps because York was not situated very close to their home near Macclesfield, but in the north-east rather than the north-west of the country.

Wonder of wonders! Divorced people or those from abroad were not necessarily rejected. The age limit was forty–five for men and forty for women. It all seemed too good to be true for Isabel, and she wondered how long it would be before one or other of the society's requirements would render Jerry and herself ineligible, once again, for adoption.

She sent off the usual letter of enquiry, filled out the anticipated forms, and within six weeks they were invited to a general meeting for married couples wishing to adopt.

It was an informal occasion, involving those from all walks of life. Social workers explained the particular philosophy and rules of that society: the current shortage of babies as compared with days gone by and the consequently longer wait for adoptive parents: the pre-natal nurture of birth mothers: what was expected of adoptive parents: and what they could expect in their turn. Questions were invited and tea was served, but at no time was the future adoption of a baby guaranteed. On the contrary, applicants could be eliminated from the waiting list at any time, if it was thought necessary to do so.

Isabel and Jerry looked around and noticed that they were probably the oldest couple in the room. Neither of them felt the least bit sociable since so far their path to birth and adoption had been littered with failure, and they felt disinclined to talk about it to strangers. If they were not to be eliminated, they would have a chance to discuss everything with the adoption workers at a later date.

Following that meeting, extensive form-filling was required of them, and searching questions had to be answered concerning their marriage, background, income and social life. References had to be obtained from professionals who knew them both well enough to vouch for their honesty, and stability as a couple. Full medicals were arranged at their local health centre and fortunately they both passed. In the following weeks, they were informed that two professional social workers would arrive to inspect their home as a suitable environment in which to bring up a child. Evidently, a spotless, luxuriously furnished home was frowned upon as much as a dirty, disorganized one. The first would represent perfectionism which children would have difficulty trying to achieve, and the second would encourage a lack of hygiene, disorder and bad habits.

The adoption social workers arrived individually on two separate occasions and appeared to approve of the warm, welcoming atmosphere of Jerry and Isabel's home, but emphasized that their wait would be long owing to the shortage of unmarried mothers. Isabel wondered if she and Jerry would exceed the age limit by the time a baby materialized.

Income was more important to the society than Isabel had imagined. The more a couple could give a child materially the more enrichment that child would enjoy, provided that ethical values with structure and a great deal of love accompanied the prosperity. Both Isabel and Jerry knew of wonderful, achieving human beings who had risen from a poor background, motivated by their own poverty, but these examples were relatively rare. On the whole, two or three children brought up in a financially stable home with two caring parents were more likely to develop to the maximum of their ability, and achieve relative happiness, than one of ten children reared in a tenement building by an overworked mother and an absent father.

Christmas and New Year's Day passed without contact from the society. Then, January 1975 brought a request for photos. It was explained that the Bellevue adoption policy was for birth mothers to choose the couple they wished to bring up their babies. This was aided by showing them photographs of the adoptive couples, together with a written description of their age, background, profession and hobbies. Clearly the adoption workers exercised some judgment in the selection, but Isabel groaned on receipt of that news, imagining that the average sixteen-year-old unmarried mum would scarcely approve of couples in their thirties and forties. What if nobody chose them?

The following April more forms arrived, involving questions about their exact income, their bank details, their status as house-owners, the size of the mortgage and other financial commitments. The final question asked whether they favoured a boy or girl, and the given advice was to make a decision one way or the other. Jerry and Isabel had no debts other than a moderate mortgage, and after a short discussion, they decided on a boy. Now that the adoption process appeared to be working for them, Isabel felt cheered, but also on a knife edge, for fear that rejection was perhaps lurking just around the corner to dash all her hopes. Jerry was much more cerebral about the situation, absorbed in his work or flying off to conferences.

It was arranged that one weekend when Jerry had returned from abroad, two retired adoption workers would interview them at home. Isabel, in an unusually optimistic frame of mind, thought their visit was merely a formality and nothing to worry about, but she was wrong. Retired, severe- looking and extremely exacting in their interviewing technique, these ladies held influential seats on the board of the adoption society, something which Jerry and Isabel were unprepared for. Questions poured out concerning their philosophy on child-rearing: on upbringing when the child grew older: how they intended to explain to the child that he or she was adopted: boundaries: difficulties with teenage adoptees: and how Isabel and Jerry would feel if the adult adoptee decided to discover his or her genetic parentage.

On that last point, one of the ladies added that few adoptees took up the challenge of finding their birth mother, and of those who did, the follow-up contact was generally intermittent or non-existent. The next question concerned how they would complete their family. Evidently couples were needed to adopt mentally retarded children, the physically handicapped, older children with emotional and behavioural difficulties and those of mixed race. All this was unexpected and an adoption version of the Spanish Inquisition, Isabel thought, her heart sinking as the minutes passed. Jerry left her to answer most of the questions, presumably because she would spend far more time with the baby than he, and she tried hard to stay calm and think clearly.

After nearly an hour of what seemed like interrogation, the more severe-looking of the two ladies asked, "How old are you?" Jerry and Isabel had never tried to hide their ages at any point, and were very cognizant of the society's age limit, however much they both wanted to lose ten years. When they revealed their birth dates yet again, a high-pitched voice rang out.

"You're old! We want our parents to be young."

Isabel was just about able to control her tears until after their departure. Doom and gloom descended. Jerry became silent and Isabel resumed her place on the emotional roller coaster, all her optimism dissipated. She was glad to immerse herself in end-of-term examinations, marking and writing reports.

To lift their spirits, they arranged a trip to Ireland for the beginning of September, and after flying to Dublin, they hired a car to cover as much of the emerald isle as they could in a week. Since the fateful visit of the retired adoption workers, there had been no contact from the society, but for courtesy's sake Isabel informed a secretary that she and Jerry were to go on holiday, and she provided the secretary with the date of their return.

Almost immediately after arriving back at their cottage, the senior adoption worker phoned with some very unexpected news. The unmarried mother who had chosen Jerry and Isabel to be the parents of her baby had actually given birth prematurely whilst they were on holiday in Ireland.

They were overwhelmed with disbelief and confusion, entirely unaware that they had been chosen by anyone. In fact, they were both convinced that they had been rejected after the latest depressing interview. More news unfolded. The birth mother was named Francesca Bedale, aged twenty-one years, and living temporarily with her brother and sister-in-law in York, but she had been born and brought up in Norfolk.

"The one drawback," explained the adoption worker, "is that Francesca was absolutely convinced that she was expecting a son, but last Thursday she gave birth to a baby girl, weighing just six pounds. I know you have chosen to adopt a baby boy, so you must discuss this with each other and reach a decision by Monday. If you decide to wait for a boy, that is fine of course, and your right - but you may have a very long wait."

The change from considering themselves on the rejection list to becoming adoptive parents was so sudden that Isabel's head was in a whirl. Initially she was slightly disappointed that the baby was not a boy, but she was elated that they had actually been chosen by Francesca to bring up her child, and excited at the prospect of caring for a baby of her own after all these years of waiting.

Surprisingly Jerry now seemed to be happier to adopt a girl than a boy, and Isabel soon became convinced that, chosen as they were by the mother, this baby was meant for them. On reaching this decision and informing the adoption worker, they were told to pay a visit to Mothercare as soon as possible with a list of all the items they would need for the immediate care of a tiny baby who would be placed with them the following Saturday.

Fortunately, they had recently decorated the small bedroom, though not in a nursery theme. They had not dared to tempt providence for fear of being disappointed once and for all. Nine months of pregnancy would provide an expect-ant mum with ample time to collect everything necessary to cope with the needs of a newborn baby, but Jerry and Isabel had far less than nine days, and they were novices in choosing babygrows, bottles, formula, nappies, plastic pants, a carry cot, matinee jackets and bootees. They were advised to buy essentials only for the time being. For instance, a cot was not needed at first because a new-born baby would fit more snugly into a carry cot which by day could be con-verted into a pram, fulfilling its dual purpose. Isabel checked and rechecked the society's list so as not to miss anything vital. Then both she and Jerry phoned relatives and close friends to break the happy news to them. Long conversa-tions of congratulation followed with promises to visit even from those living on different continents. It was a time of expectant joy, and Isabel found herself permanently smiling at the thought of a new beginning. Even Jerry looked hap-pier than usual.

Another interesting custom of Bellevue was for the birth mother to meet the adoptive parents in the society offices on the day of the placement. She would be given their first names, but not their surname or address. After the placement, letters could be exchanged through the senior adoption worker. It was emphasized that the birth mother could withdraw her consent at any time before the formal adoption procedure in court in three months or so. Isabel felt very uneasy about this, aware of the close bond between a birth mother and her baby which could influence her powerfully to change her mind.

Waiting for Saturday to come seemed like eternity in spite of the busy preparations for this tiny baby to become theirs, making them a real family. Their appointment was at 10.30, so they left home at seven o'clock to avoid as much traffic as possible, and did not stop for coffee until they were close to York, with plenty of time to spare. They both felt nervous as they approached the adoption society gates, realizing that this was such an important day in their lives. Sybil, the senior adoption worker, showed them to a waiting room, and explained that when Francesca came into the room, she would place the baby in Jerry's arms and not in Isabel's. This was to pre-empt any jealousy from arising between the birth mother and adoptive mother.

Isabel would never ever forget the moment when she first set eyes on Francesca - a young woman, scarcely more than a girl, of medium height with wavy, chestnut-brown hair and a clear complexion. Her deep blue eyes, her most distinguishing feature, were now red-rimmed and filled with tears. She placed her sleeping baby tenderly into Jerry's arms, and sat down next to Isabel.

After a brief moment of awkwardness, Isabel remarked how beautiful the baby was, and asked questions about her routine: feeding, sleeping and changing. Then she went on to say how happy Francesca had made them both, and that they would do all in their power to give her baby a really happy life. All the time that Isabel was speaking, Francesca kept her eyes on the baby, tears continuing to spill down her face. Jerry said nothing, but smiled down at the sleeping child. Sybil said nothing and there was silence. After a few moments, Francesca dabbed her eyes and then assured them that she thought they were exactly the right couple to bring up her baby. She cried again, and Isabel held her in her arms and cried with her, her tears expressing empathy for Francesca's pain and for the years of her own disappointment and misery.

The need to drive the baby home before the next feed cut the placement short, with parting assurances of their devoted care of the baby and promises to write about her progress.

Understandably, Sybil did not want to prolong the painful situation for Francesca, and within half an hour of their arrival at the society offices, Jerry and Isabel were ready to drive back to Cheshire with their precious treasure.

The return journey was quiet. Fortunately the baby continued to sleep soundly. Jerry silently concentrated on driving safely in traffic-laden roads, and Isabel's joy at becoming a mother was mixed with the memory of Francesca's sadness etched into her soul. Would she change her mind and want the baby back? The baby continued to sleep peacefully until the car finally drew up outside their cottage. Then a wail started, followed by many more. They were home just in time to satisfy those recognizable pangs of hunger. Isabel lifted the ten-day-old baby into her arms tenderly, but nothing would calm that tiny child until the mixed formula had been warmed and the teat was in her mouth. Then, magic! The concentrated sucking brought peace and contentment for a while, and the tears dried quickly

From being a complete novice Isabel followed a steep learning curve in the next few days and weeks. On her first visit the health visitor advised Isabel not to take the baby out until she weighed seven pounds or more. Friends called round, and those who had had children gave her plenty of advice. After much discussion, she and Jerry decided to call the baby Laura, after absolutely nobody,but because they both liked the name. Isabel happily organized a daily routine, and was surprised to find that baby rearing was a full-time job. Jerry's evening meals were sometimes served a few minutes later than was customary, on the dot of 6 p.m., which he quickly criticized and which Isabel equally quickly had to correct.

Whereas Isabel seized the role of motherhood with joyful enthusiasm, Jerry took longer to adjust to becoming the father of an adopted child. The first few weeks were difficult for him with the presence of a "strange child" in the house, and he seemed to resent the vast amount of time that Isabel spent with the baby. He did not take part in Laura's routine at all, although Isabel encouraged him to do so.

In practical terms this meant that when he was home, he did not feed her or change her, which would have hastened his adjustment, but on their frequent visits to Mothercare, he always bought the next round of baby items with interest and amusement.

When Laura developed daily colic after her 6p.m. feed and screamed the place down, despite Isabel's gentle efforts to burp her, Jerry's immediate conclusion was that somehow it was Isabel's fault as an inadequate mother. The repeated failures in Isabel's life had resulted in her having little confidence in herself, and Jerry did not improve the situation. Thankfully the doctor was able to prescribe medicine for the colic which he said would probably disappear at three months.

Aged six weeks, Laura passed her first check-up at the health centre with flying colours, and was a smiling, gurgling delight to have around. Isabel wrote a long letter to Francesca, expressing their happiness and gratitude, and giving her all the news of the baby's progress. It was sent to Sybil for forwarding and in the course of her regular visits to the newly-founded family, Sybil brought a reply from Francesca. Isabel remained terrified that Francesca would change her mind and claim Laura back, but Sybil reasoned that Francesca had no means to support a baby on her own, and additionally, she dreaded her parents discovering her secret because they would disown her.

Due to pressure of casework in the courts and subsequent delays, Laura was five months old before she was legally adopted by Jerry and Isabel and their relief was visible for all to see. They celebrated with their close friends. Isabel's mother journeyed up from the south for a second visit to her granddaughter and to join in the celebrations.

At the age of one year Laura was baptized at the local church and one of Isabel's close school friends acted as godmother. Together with other old friends, they spent the weekend celebrating yet again, delighted with Laura and thrilled with Carmen for skilfully producing six puppies the night before they all departed. Isabel did not dream that she could be so happy. Over the next two years she and Jerry relished their role as parents. They took Laura on holiday to Athens to meet her Greek grandmother and Jerry's brother and family flew over from the United States to spend a few weeks with them. At home on a day-to-day basis Isabel and Laura socialized as much as possible with other mums and infants.

Strangely, letters continued to arrive from Francesca through Sybil, which unnerved Isabel despite the legality of the adoption. Her confidence as a mother was undermined. In fact, she wondered who was now the mother of Laura. Was it she or Francesca? She wished the correspondence would come to an end. Evidently, Francesca had not returned to Norfolk and was keeping in regular contact with the adoption society, but for what purpose? Finally, by the time Laura had passed her second birthday, Isabel decided not to answer the letters, thinking that a clean break was better for everyone concerned.

At about the same time, Sybil visited them to discuss the possibility of the adoption of a second child to complete their family. She explained that since newborn babies were in such short supply, Jerry and Isabel might like to consider adopting a mentally or physically handicapped child, a child of mixed race or one with emotional and behavioural problems. These children were not in short supply, and furthermore they were in desperate need of loving homes. Clearly she did not expect Jerry and Isabel to make an immediate decision, but left them to discuss the options before letting her know at a later date. At no time did she comment that another new-born baby was totally out of the question; she simply emphasized the great need of the other children.

Jerry made it quite clear that he would brook no argument about adopting an Afro-Caribbean child, or one of mixed race. He had seen white parents adopt black children in the United States and fail miserably after an investment of much love and well-intentioned effort. The problems, he emphasized, were manifested particularly during and after adolescence when adoptees could have problems with their own identity. In his view, children with emotional and behavioural problems - in other words, older children - should be placed with families with their own genetic children, or with those experienced in adoption or fostering.

Isabel did not think herself heroine enough to provide a home for a seriously mentally or physically handicapped child with all the twenty-four-hour care needed to do the job properly. Hers was not a marriage able to take an unlimited amount of extra strain, and she was convinced that Jerry would not support her, practically speaking. Then again, all the time she would have to give to this new handicapped child would seem unfair to Laura whom they had promised to bring up with so much loving care and attention. Isabel felt that she might break under the strain of it all, and what would be the use of that? She would have been happy to adopt a child of mixed race and take the risk, but Jerry was dead against it, refusing to change his mind, And so it was that they did not complete their family. Laura remained an only child.

To compensate for this decision, at least to some extent, Isabel took Laura to playschool two mornings a week when she was not quite three years old, and invited children in to play and to have lunch or tea as often as possible. At Laura's third birthday party, a dozen playmates sat around the large kitchen table to sing "Happy birthday, Laura", before tucking into, or fiddling with, sandwiches, cake and ice cream. It was a happy time, generally.

Books had always been important to Isabel and she quickly realized how much Laura loved stories. She read to her every day and then again at bed time, kissing her tenderly as the story came to an end. It was at those times of special closeness that Laura would ask where babies come from.

Isabel explained to her in simple terms, always adding that she did not come from her tummy but that she was a chosen baby whom Isabel and Jerry had adopted; they had waited a long time for her and they loved her very much. This was all the information that Laura needed for the time being, and the adoption society instructions were to repeat the story regularly, until the child was ready for more information. Amusingly this was not a problem since Laura often asked to hear the "baby" story again and again, informing all her friends that she was a chosen baby.

From early on, when Isabel could tell that Laura was a bright child because she picked up new words readily, spoke in clear sentences and was quick on the uptake, she decided to buy her a clipboard with coloured, magnetic letters attached to it to see if she would enjoy the game of finding the right letter. If no enjoyment resulted, the game would be put away for six months or a year or longer. *L* for Laura, *M* for Mummy and *D* for Daddy were introduced, and then hidden amongst the other twenty-three letters for recognition. It was easy for her and became a chuckling success. More and more letters were added gradually, always connected with people or things that Laura knew well so that her confidence would develop and her enjoyment continue. Simple sounds and words followed letters, taught mainly by the phonic method, and with no difficulty at all Laura was able to read well, and within her own scope of enjoyment, by the time she reached school age. Isabel felt that the whole reading experience had bonded her ever more closely to Laura. In fact, it was one of the happiest and most satisfying experiences of her life.

Chapter 8
Difficulties

Despite being an only child, by the time Laura had reached the age to start her formal education, she was well socialized on a daily basis with numerous little friends at playschool. At the weekends she enjoyed romping with some of them and the current litter of puppies in the garden, or walking across the fields with Isabel and Carmen and sometimes even Jerry when he was not abroad.

Each summer Isabel's mother would visit for a week or two, and every other year, Jerry's mother would fly over from Athens to spend a month with them. Both grandmothers were elderly and disinclined to help or babysit on their holidays or at any other time, and unfortunately there were no members of an extended family to support the couple. In fact, when Jerry was out of the country, Isabel felt that she was not only mother and father to Laura, but auntie and grandparent too. She silently envied the family hierarchy of many of her friends, particularly those with three or four grandparents, aunts, uncles and cousins, all living relatively near to them and providing the children with a strong sense of security and belonging. For Laura's sake she tried to build bridges between herself, Clive and his new family;

with Geraldine, his second wife; and with Martin, Robert and Anna, their three children. They lived in the south and therefore could not meet up very often, but when they did, the children played well together and Isabel struck up a warm relationship with Geraldine. Clive and Jerry had little in common.

In due course Clive sought out trouble for whatever reason. An argument arose out of virtually nothing which Isabel could remember, but the upshot was that Clive decided there would be no further contact between the two families. It came as a shock and disappointment to Isabel because she knew that it entailed a future loss for Laura who needed to feel herself secure in a family within an extended family. Sadly, in May 1980 Isabel's mother sustained a stroke and died shortly after, leaving Isabel and Laura with no contactable relations in the United Kingdom.

The state primary school experience at that time proved less than satisfactory. The open plan design of the school, together with the large number of children on roll, helped to create a continuously noisy atmosphere where concentration became virtually impossible. Pupils had to queue up at the teacher's desk for too long to have the next page of a workbook explained. Isabel was criticized by the teachers because Laura could already read well when she started school. It seemed that their philosophy was to teach all children at the same rate from the beginning.

Consequently, at six years old, Laura took advantage of a lack of supervision to become mischievous and idle. Jerry and Isabel knew better than to withdraw her from the state system until the end of term which was also the end of the academic year, but they thought some out-of-school activities might trigger new excitement and interest in her. Laura chose to have piano lessons and swimming instruction. The swimming involved other children and their parents which was great fun socially, whereas piano lessons were on a one-to-one basis with practice at home to develop concentration. The teacher was kindly and strict, bringing out the best in her pupils, including Laura. Before long she was taking part in local music festivals and gaining her Grade 1 of the Associated Board.

Laura was just seven years old when she was enrolled at St Faith's independent school for girls between the ages of five and eighteen years. Unlike the state primary, the classes were small, no more than eighteen pupils, and often considerably less, and each classroom had its own door. Laura loved the bright blue uniform and the individual attention. She was an outgoing child, made friends surprisingly quickly and settled down, enjoying the richness of the curriculum, as well as the after-school activities such as brownies and ballet. Her academic progress developed well, in stark contrast to her previous performance. She took first place in the end-of-term examinations.

Shortly after the beginning of Laura's second year at St Faith's, Isabel was advised to have a hysterectomy. As soon as one period was over, another started within a few days, sometimes lasting for six weeks. Consequently, she had become rather anaemic and felt tired all the time. Before the operation she made a wall chart, listing all Laura's needs on each day: who was to take her to school and collect her when Jerry could not. Friends had become amazingly supportive with offers of keeping her for the night, or for tea, until Jerry was able to collect her. Meals were prepared ahead of time, and a cleaner who worked for them three hours a week was able to do the washing and ironing until Isabel returned home after eight days.

Jerry's attitude to Isabel was souring. Undoubtedly it had something to do with her hysterectomy, the final confirmation that she would never produce the child he wanted. He refused to speak about his true feelings, assuring her authoritatively that talking about problems usually worsened situations rather than improved them. She did not agree, which was a reason for argument in itself.

The surgeon had suggested to Isabel that she should convalesce at home for two weeks before taking on the lightest of household duties, but Jerry refused to cook or clean, convinced that such work was beneath him, so Isabel had no alternative but to cope with everything domestic as soon as she returned from hospital. As soon as the chores were finished in the evening, she would retire to bed exhausted, sad about her loss of femininity and her sterile relationship with Jerry.

When he was not abroad, Jerry's evening ritual would be to bury his head in the *Financial Times*, or watch a television news programme and crack caustic jokes about British politics, or retire to his study to carry on writing his articles rather than open up to Isabel who was invariably ironing or tackling some other chore which could not be left. No intimate exchange of problems, worries or even joys passed between them in the hours before bedtime. Isabel felt isolated in her own marriage and desperately needed to confide in someone. She fervently wished that that person could be Jerry, but he was living a disappointed life and unreachable. When Laura was not in earshot, he would accuse Isabel of not providing him with the family he wanted so much and now it was too late. He said the situation was hopeless and he considered himself to be far less fortunate in every respect than most of his friends. It became quite clear to Isabel that had she been wealthy or had presented him with three sons, he would have felt very differently about her.

Jerry was also disappointed in British salaries, which motivated him to seek temporary consulting work abroad in Madrid, Helsinki or Paris. When he was away, Isabel and Laura were free to invite friends and be invited which was something of a relief and at night time, after a tearful release of the worries about her stale marriage, she would try to think of ways to revitalize it. She suggested that, as a couple, they could perhaps spend a regular evening out in Manchester at recommended Greek and Armenian restaurants which he liked. It would involve hiring a baby sitter occasionally, but that would not create a particular problem. Some of her friends were mothers of responsible teenage daughters eager to earn extra pocket money. Perhaps a carefree evening out would reignite the old spark that had unmistakably been there when they first met. Isabel was saddened by Jerry's lack of interest in the idea, feeling it to be a rejection of her.

Her second suggestion was that she should join the local amateur operatic society, enabling her to have one evening each week free to be herself and enjoy learning more repertoire. It would remind her of her operatic days in Philadelphia. Jerry's reaction was more hostile than she expected. His voice rose in anger and indignation that she should dare to suggest such an idea when it was her job to stay at home all the time with Laura. In his opinion no babysitters were required, particularly when he was abroad, and he completely disapproved of music entering Isabel's life again, unless it meant supervising Laura's piano practice or listening to a record. The threatening, glowering look he gave her filled her with anxious yet defiant thoughts for the future.

Usually Jerry's various trips abroad lasted six or seven days or less, until an offer for a lecturing-cum-consulting job took him to Helsinki for three weeks, leaving Isabel with a tight budget, and half an acre of gardening to organize. Her life revolved round Laura, dropping her off at St Faith's and collecting her before the various weekly activities of piano lessons, swimming and brownies. The enjoyment of reading flourished, as did their involvement with dog shows at certain weekends. It provided Laura with another absorbing interest, as she loved animals, and Isabel felt less lonely about her marriage if she kept busy.

She had realized for some time that she was being controlled and that money was not abundant, particularly now that Laura was attending a fee-paying independent school. The fees would not only increase with inflation, but also with her progression into the senior part of the school. One morning, after a brief and matter-of-fact phone call from Jerry in Helsinki, Isabel decided to contact the education office to try to obtain a part-time teaching post. Fortunately for her, language teachers were in demand. She was successful in gaining a temporary post for only four mornings a week, but she was thrilled to be starting the following Monday, to return to the profession she really loved, to gain some independence, to earn some money and to be truthful, to defy Jerry just a bit.

The job involved teaching French to GCSE groups whose teacher was taking maternity leave, as well as additional classes lower down the school. For Isabel it was a godsend. She had wisely kept *au courant* with her knowledge of French, listening to Radio France Internationale broadcasts, reading books in French and the occasional copy of *Paris Match* and *Le Figaro*. Conveniently, she was able to drop Laura off at St Faith's each morning before proceeding on to her own place of work, and collect her at the end of the school day without a problem.

For the first time in years Isabel radiated the joy of gaining a little independence and self-esteem. The general satisfaction which teaching always gave her, together with the added responsibility of preparing pupils for public examinations, boosted her confidence more than she would have considered possible.

"What the hell do you think you're doing taking some two-bit teaching job while I'm away, and without my permission," raved Jerry on return from Helsinki.

"It's only a temporary part-time job," replied Isabel, "and in no way interferes with you, or inconveniences your life or Laura's, come to that. I feel a whole lot happier working, and frankly, you should be glad for me. Anyway we could do with the extra money."

The mere mention of needing Isabel to provide extra money for the household was like paraffin to a lighted match as far as Jerry's temper was concerned. He screamed out a string of swear words and insults with such threatening ferocity, before slamming the study door so hard that the cottage shook, that Isabel wished he had stayed in Helsinki indefinitely. Since there was to be no social or musical enjoyment in her life, teaching was her only outlet, and she refused to be bullied out of her newly-acquired job.

Miss Hills, the headmistress at St Faith's, was a charming, dedicated teacher with over twenty years experience and sound ideas about developing each pupil to the maximum of her potential. As the numbers on roll were very manageable, she was able to get to know and understand each child really well, something lacking in the previous school where far too many pupils in a class were taught by young inexperienced teachers intent on organization and discipline rather than individual attention. It was, therefore, quite a shock to Isabel to receive a phone call from Miss Hills one Friday afternoon requesting her to come to her office at 3.30.

As she replaced the receiver, Isabel's face blanched with fear and anxiety. Her heart beat faster and her mouth went dry. She had been assured that Laura had not been hurt in any way, and it surely could have nothing to do with her academic progress because she had just won the form prize. So, what on earth was it? Deciding not to phone Jerry at the university because he would only curse her for interrupting a lecture or tutorial, she jumped in the car and drove straight away to St Faith's in the hope of seeing the headmistress before the classes were dismissed. As luck would have it, Miss Hills was herself teaching a class for the last period and was unavailable, so Isabel was forced to wait until 3.45 when pupils and parents, for the most part, had gone home At that time Miss Hills appeared with Laura and her form mistress.

Evidently, the headmistress's office was usually left open or unlocked. Laura had walked in uninvited and stolen pens and pencils from her desk. Someone had seen her enter the office and the items were later found in her possession. After some initial denial, she admitted that she was guilty.

When asked the reason for taking property that was not hers, she simply said that she liked and wanted those pens and pencils.

Whilst Laura waited in the classroom with her form teacher, Miss Hills suggested to Isabel that perhaps the nine-year-old did not have enough stationary of her own, but Isabel knew that the packets of pencils, pens and coloured pencils both at home and in school proved otherwise.

This unfortunate episode coincided with Jerry's imminent flight to Athens to visit his mother. He was aghast to learn that his daughter had been stealing from the headmistress, utterly appalled, in fact. He lectured her on what petty stealing can lead to before disappearing to the airport, whilst Isabel withdrew Laura's privileges for a week and organized her into writing a letter of apology to Miss Hills for the following Monday. She talked to her about respect for other people's property, which included everyone, adults and children alike, and to her distress, Laura claimed that she had never been instructed not to take things that did not belong to her. Isabel was sure she had not hammered the point, but when she had invited children to her home, she had taught them to respect each other's belongings. She was certain that honesty and respect for property would definitely have been on the teaching agenda of a Church of England independent school with religious education lessons and a visiting chaplain.

That night, lying in bed sleepless, feeling that she had failed yet again and this time with Laura, Isabel thought back to her own childhood and tried to imagine a similar situation after the war in her old state primary with fifty in a class. Her fierce Welsh teachers were ready to wallop anyone who stepped out of line, maintaining a high level of discipline in spite of the overcrowded classrooms. It was utterly unthinkable that anyone would consider, let alone dare to steal from the headmistress, and Isabel imagined that if she had been such an unlikely culprit, she would never have felt able to raise her head again. Laura was different.

During the weekend, when writing the letter of apology to Miss Hills, Laura did not cry or show signs of penitence, although she was quieter than usual. When asked, she agreed that she was happy at St Faith's, and when told that thieving again might lead to expulsion from the school and consequently a return to her former state primary, she slowly realized how her own dishonesty could affect her in the future. Whilst Jerry was still in Athens, Laura asked more questions about her birth mother. What was her name? What did she look like? Where was she living and why had she given Laura up for adoption? Was she ill, and did Isabel like her? Had she not loved her baby?

Isabel had regularly answered her questions on the subject, and the chosen-baby story had been much loved for a long time, but these questions were more detailed and insistent, and she knew that not only was honesty the best policy, but she should pass on the information in terms right for Laura's age. She explained that Francesca had given birth without being married and had loved her very much, but because money was short and work was a necessity, she thought it wise to give up her baby for adoption to a married couple who would be able to give her a better life and who would also love her very much indeed. Yes, Isabel had met Francesca, she liked her and she described her appearance. Laura became pensive as she listened to the answers to her questions, and as she left the kitchen, she asked,

"How much did you pay for me?"

"You're priceless" replied Isabel quickly, and then_"Daddy and I love you very much, you know."

"Yes, I know."

Jerry's mother lived in a small flat in the centre of Athens not far from relatives. She had brought her two sons up in the United States, and having divorced their late father for violence and desertion, she had decided to retire to Greece to live in greater safety, closer to the rest of her family where the cost of living was lower. Unfortunately, she had not worked throughout her life, other than in the home, so she was not in receipt of a pension. Her two sons, therefore, were obliged to support her financially as well as emotionally. They had sent monthly cheques to her for years ever since obtaining their doctorates, and whenever the opportunity arose, she would enlighten them about inflation and the need to increase her allowance. Her attitude was, "I brought up my sons. They are now big deals, so why shouldn't they keep me?" Delivered with a Greek accent, the comment usually brought a laugh.

Jerry returned to England after spending ten days with his mother. He had combined his stay with attendance at a conference, thus avoiding hotel costs, as he was quick to point out. However, after his arrival, Isabel learned that her mother-in-law had claimed that she could no longer live on her present income and that he would have to increase her allowance yet again, this time by a substantial amount.

Isabel felt her heart pound and the blood rush to her ears in annoyance. She wanted to shriek at Jerry that not only had he not told her of this financial burden until years after their marriage, but that he had also done his best to obstruct her from continuing her career on a part-time basis, and from earning money which they, as a family, needed. She knew well that expressing her anger would provoke a far worse outburst from him, and more importantly, Laura could hear, so she satisfied herself with one remark only.

"I'll carry on with the two-bit job, then."

Jerry made no reply, but on Monday morning Isabel felt more confident about continuing her job without further aggravation, and when the term ended, along with the maternity leave of the teacher she was replacing, she had no difficulty in finding another post. This time it was part-time and permanent.

Over the next two years Laura progressed well at school and continued with swimming, elocution and piano. She caught the normal childhood illnesses - chicken pox, German measles and mumps -and enjoyed the usual school trips and holidays, as well as family vacations abroad to France and Greece. Jerry's brother and family visited from the United States for two weeks which gave them all an opportunity to explore the Lakes and Scotland together. Laura was sad when her cousins returned to New Jersey, knowing that such trips were expensive and therefore rare.

As Laura approached eleven years of age, Isabel noticed unexpected changes in her. Although she thought they had enjoyed a close relationship as mother and daughter, and felt they were really bonded, Laura was now becoming silent, defiant, and truculent and was developing a very short temper. When the slightest thing would trigger her temper, she would slam doors and then spend far too much time alone in her bedroom. Clearly, this was adolescent behaviour, yet Laura was barely eleven years old, and showed no signs of the physical development of puberty. Isabel was always demonstrably affectionate to her, yet she was convinced that clear boundaries of discipline should be maintained, and that she should encourage Laura to talk about any problems arising from school, friends and adoption, whenever it felt right to do so. She wanted to be there for her at all times without overdoing it. She felt quite strongly too, that Laura should perform simple tasks around the house, such as keeping her bedroom tidy and laying the table, or clearing it after a meal, particularly as she was expecting generous amounts of pocket money every week.

As far as Laura's upbringing was concerned, Isabel and Jerry did not sing from the same hymn sheet. He believed in providing more pocket money than was good for her without expecting her to do anything around the house or garden. Consequently, she did not learn the value of money, but she did learn to expect and demand more, her thirst for acquisition seeming unquenchable. Whereas Jerry was parsimonious with Isabel, he was ultra-generous to his daughter, fast turning her into a British version of a New York *princess*, that is, a spoilt young lady, placed on a metaphorical pedestal by her parents and wholly expectant of the very best at all times.

Since Isabel felt that she was losing the discipline issue, she tackled Jerry about it one day when Laura was at a friend's birthday party.

"Can't you see, you stupid bitch, that I'm generous with her so she won't start stealing again?"

"Well, you're giving her far too much. It would be better to develop your relationship with her, and teach her some values, rather than merely trying to feed her greed. She's completely overindulged in presents and pocket money every week."

With one swift lunge, he knocked Isabel to the floor, causing her to hit her head against the living room wall.

"How dare a thick cow like you criticize my judgement about anything?" In pain and shock she was intent on making her point.

"No prizes for self-control. You are wrong. If we do not act as one over the upbringing of this child, we are heading for trouble."

He pushed past her and out through the front door, jumped into his car and was gone, leaving Isabel in floods of tears, with a large lump on the side of her head and a bruised cheek.

The least of Isabel's problems was having to explain her bruises to her friends with a porky about falling from the low branches of a tree in her garden when trying to collect dead wood for their open fire, something which she had actually done in the past. She brushed off their raised eyebrows and suspicious looks by cheerfully changing the subject. She was far too proud to admit that she had serious problems. Not that this was the only time Jerry had shown violence towards her. The first time was in Philadelphia when he had been controlling and cantankerous about her singing at the opera companies there, but somehow he had not persisted with his tyranny in the United States, perhaps because he was influenced by his buddy, Sam, who thought that this was a golden opportunity for Isabel the immigrant.

Later in England there had been rows during which he had struck her, and on one occasion he caused her to sprain her ankle badly, requiring hospital treatment, strapping up with plaster, and crutches. He never apologized. Somehow she had made excuses for him in her mind without verbalising them. After all, he had had to acclimatize himself to a new job in a new country. Everything was different: customs, friends, house, culture, even the language. It was stressful for him and then again, he had had to come to terms with the idea of adoption. The monthly disappointment of her not conceiving had been very distressing for them both, too, and perhaps a reason for antagonism. Excuses, excuses, excuses. She had to admit that Jerry had never struck her in front of Laura. He usually waited until she was out of the house, but he regularly demeaned her in front of the child, sometimes to the point of humiliation. Isabel knew that retaliation in like mode would ignite that ugly temper smouldering below the surface into something Laura should not see. To prevent such an eruption from happening, Isabel became very quiet around the house, trying to be her normal self with Laura, but not rising to his taunts or saying anything provocative. In fact, communication between Jerry and Isabel was minimal which produced a sour, deadening atmosphere around the house, and was only slightly preferable to rows.

Laura watched her father's overt disrespect of her mother and copied him when it suited her. Noticing her parents' disunity in their upbringing of her, she played them off, one against the other, to her own advantage, as children of parents in conflict are wont to do. Over the ensuing months, Isabel tried her best to maintain the normality of the household, supporting Laura with her homework, music, hobbies and friends. Her efforts to improve her relationship with Jerry proved unsuccessful. She forced herself to act normally, to enjoy the challenge of teaching as she had always done and simply to tackle everything expected of her. Jerry commented that physically she was in the house, but mentally she was elsewhere. If only, thought Isabel, they could recover their love and affection for each other and present a united and loving parental front to Laura. It seemed not to be.

The final term of the academic year, when Laura had turned eleven, presented a reorganization of staff at Isabel's school, when teachers were told that for financial reasons part-time teaching was now being discouraged. This meant that part-time contracts were being terminated for some teachers, whilst others, like Isabel, were being invited to apply for full-time posts. There was little time to make her decision for the next academic year, but as soon as Jerry heard about the situation, he steamrolled her into turning down the offer in one infuriated blast of words.

"No, you aren't going to work full time. Over my dead body. Part-time is bad enough. Your place is here, not in a bloody school. I'm telling you lady, you take that job and I'll divorce you."

He picked up a dish of spaghetti and threw it on the dining-room floor to emphasize the strength of his feelings, and to instil fear in her.

Their summer holidays passed and in September when reality kicked in, Isabel found herself without a job and Jerry very much in control. She had some savings left from her teaching which would not last long, and she knew that sooner rather than later she would be dependent on him for every penny. Alone in the house during the day she would cry, dry her eyes, and then cry again. Try as she might, she could not raise her spirits. To make matters worse her hysterectomy had triggered an early menopause with its well-known symptoms: hot flushes, fatigue, sleeplessness and depression. A sense of failure pervaded her conscious thoughts all the time and she found herself crumbling emotionally, faced with Jerry's anger and derision. He clearly did not appreciate her current financial dependence on him, and never failed to remind her of it. Having opposed the idea of her working, even on a part-time basis, he was now dissatisfied with her being at home all day. He was impossible to please.

One evening, after returning home from a presumably difficult day of lecturing, he noted that his meal was served at ten minutes past six instead of six o'clock on the dot. He turned on her, his eyes bulging with fury and frustration.

"Shall I tell you something? You're not at work, you can't have children, and now you can't even cook a meal on time. What are you? I'll tell you. You are a nothing. You are a nothing."

He repeated himself in case she had not heard or had misunderstood him. With these words, she froze into silent non-retaliation, and wondered how she could bear living with him in the future. She left him alone in the kitchen, and went to hear Laura's piano practice as if nothing had happened.

Isabel persisted with her efforts to improve the marriage, suggesting that they seek the advice of a marriage-guidance counsellor who would perceive their problems objectively, and perhaps as a couple, they would gain some understanding of their failings, and make a whole-hearted attempt to improve their relationship. Jerry would not hear of it.

"I'm not going to have my private life dissected by some goddamn, thick, social worker," he snapped, and that was that.

Weeks passed and Isabel hoped for an improvement, but none came. Her mother's recent death, and her continued estrangement from her brother, combined with marital difficulties and no job, caused her spirits to remain low. Each day she felt trapped in a situation over which she had little control and at night she cried and cried until sleep took over from exhaustion for a few hours. In the mornings she would rise pale and listless, involving herself with Laura's and Jerry's needs, and trying to put on a brave face.

Her beetle was a great advantage, although she scarcely could afford much petrol, and now that she was no longer working, she worried about the cost of repairs, servicing and MOTs. One day when Laura was in school and Jerry was at the university, she drove the three miles to see her doctor, and poured out all her troubles to him in the unrealistic hope that he would provide her with the elixir of happiness. Instead he listened, examined her and prescribed hormone replacement therapy, assuring her that she would soon be feeling better. He did not give advice about the state of her marriage, but as he listened intently to the details of her distress, his face became grave, and he asked her to return to the surgery in three weeks' time. Later she told Jerry about her visit to the doctor, and the hormone replacement therapy, but withheld the confidential details.

Just as her doctor had promised, after taking hormone replacement therapy for a short time, Isabel began to feel better, less tearful and more able to withstand the pain of her deteriorating marital relationship. The departure of hot flushes and insomnia triggered a new cheerfulness in her or, as she saw it, the rebirth of her natural lively spirits. Whilst confined to staying at home, she was determined to continue the correspondence degree course she had started years before. If she juggled her time sensibly she would be able to study without provoking Jerry's wrath and unrelenting criticism, using a couple of hours during the day, and reading after Laura's bedtime. There could hardly be cause for his objection and then, of course, he went abroad regularly which would release a great deal more time.

Empowered by the restorative properties of hormone replacement therapy, Isabel even unwisely tackled Jerry about their marriage at six o'clock one morning just before he went off to the airport on one of his foreign trips. She told him that he should contact her by phone whilst abroad to assure her, for Laura's sake, that on his return he would make a whole-hearted effort, as she would, to patch up their marriage. She faced him and held his gaze as they both stood before the open cottage door. He roughly pushed past her into the black chill of that autumnal morning and headed towards his car.

His last words to her were, "You parasite! You loser!"
He was away for a week, but he did not phone. After he returned, she left the matrimonial bed to sleep in her tiny study.

For almost two years Isabel had grieved for her mother and missed her support, albeit mostly over the telephone, since 200 miles had separated them. She had been very aware of the couple's marital difficulties and of Jerry's glowering temperament, and had taken a special interest in Laura, although she had five other grandchildren. Isabel recalled someone's wise words about not really growing up until both parents had died. Then you really had to stand up and face the world on your own, perhaps sometimes with no one even rooting for you. She felt guilty about her second failing marriage, particularly since she and Jerry had adopted Laura on the strength of a lasting marriage. No matter how many times she spoke to Jerry about the seriousness of the situation, he would completely take control and treat her just as he liked.

"Where would you go?" he would gibe. "Who would have you?"

She had learned that it was not a good idea to give him a smart retort, no matter how great the temptation. Besides, it was true: she had nowhere to go.

A few days later a considerable morale booster arrived from her solicitor, and since the postman did not reach their area until mid-morning, she did not have to share the good news with Jerry. Her mother's house had finally been sold and together with a few investments she had owned, the sum total had been divided equally between her and Clive. After bills had been paid, tax and fees deducted, they each received a cheque for just over £40,000.

Isabel trembled as she held the cheque in her hand, feeling overwhelmingly grateful to her dead mother for supporting her again in her hour of need. Tears of love and thanks poured down her cheeks for a few minutes, and then after quietly sipping coffee, and thinking what a difference the money would make to her sense of security, she promptly headed off to the village to bank the cheque as soon as possible. The feeling of elation lasted the whole day and the next.

Jerry had always refused to have a joint bank account, wishing to remain in total control of his money. Now that Isabel was no longer working, he paid the bills and gave her cash each week for the housekeeping. She had her own bank account, and left the money there prior to finding safe investments, providing interest for growth. She did not feel the least bit guilty about not telling Jerry immediately, since she knew that he had numerous investments in the United States and Greece, which he would never share with her.

It was one of those rare magical days when everything goes right and she was left wondering why it had to be so fleeting. Amazingly for December, the sun was shining with no prospect of rain as she stepped out of the bank, having deposited her cheque and made an appointment to consult the bank manager about her investment the following week.

Having filled the petrol tank of her little beetle she decided to drive to the Macclesfield Forest area to walk Carmen, as a treat to them both. The housework could be put on hold, and it was not yet time to collect Laura from St Faith's. In spite of having felt lonely in her marriage for so long, on this day she relished being alone with the dog to wander amongst the trees, to think, to enjoy the sun shining on the reservoir with the hills of the Peak District in the distance. Somehow this attempt at thinking was unsuccessful and maybe it was because she felt so fortunate. Most of her constructive plans, she thought, were formed when she felt downright miserable.

After walking for almost two hours, she returned to the car and drove slowly in the direction of St Faith's, some five miles away, passing open fields, farms and numerous attractive cottages. The Macclesfield hills receded into the distance, and the flatter land of Cheshire came into view. Then, on the right side of the road, her attention was attracted to a long and high wall behind which she could glimpse oak and beech trees and mature rhododendrons in abundance. What a wonderful sight they would make in May, she thought, and is it an estate of some sort? Her curiosity was soon satisfied when she noticed a large board on which was clearly written, "Walmisley Hall Preparatory School." As if by reflex, she indicated right, although there was no other traffic on the road, and drove up the long drive leading to a large, elegant, early-Victorian house surrounded by glorious specimen trees and situated in several acres of very well-manicured grounds. She parked her car outside the front entrance.

When she returned forty minutes later, she was overwhelmed by what had transpired in that short time. At reception, a friendly and highly competent secretary ushered Isabel into her office where she was provided with details about the school. It was, indeed, an independent preparatory school for boys and girls between the ages of four and thirteen, including both boarders and day pupils. The headmaster, Mr. Hamilton, was teaching Maths until 2.30, but after that would return to his office if Isabel would like to have a word with him. When they had been introduced, Isabel explained that she was an experienced teacher, that she was close to finishing a degree in French, and since she lived within a few miles of the school, she would be grateful for his consideration of a part-time post should one become available.

He burst out laughing, which was an unexpected response, and then offered her a cup of tea. Unbelievably, a part-time post in French would become available after Christmas. He would like to show her around the school on another day when there was more time. She would have to attend a formal interview and bring proof of her qualifications and experience. Then he started a conversation with her in French, which she was delighted to continue until it was time for her to pick up Laura. Finally, they shook hands, and she glided past the open Victorian entrance door as if in a dream. In less than forty-eight hours, her prospects had changed for the better.

CHAPTER 9
THE MOVE

Laura's pre-adolescent tantrums and secretive behaviour became more frequent as the months passed. Anyone experienced in the troubles that life deals out to us might say that the child was reacting against her parents' disharmony, and justifiably so, but other inner conflict seemed to trouble her. Isabel, particularly, had always been open and honest about Laura's adoption, providing her with as much positive information as she could, but the child just listened with avid interest and made no comment. She seemed to be storing up information and ideas which she intended for herself only, but not for discussion, at least not with her parents. She had reached the stage in life when friends mean almost everything, and she found herself to be the only adopted child in the class. She definitely would have preferred to be like everyone else and not different in any way.

Each evening after returning from school, she would make a dash for her bedroom and try to spend as much time up there on her own as she could. On one occasion when Isabel entered the bedroom to announce for the third time that dinner was ready, she found Laura trying to insert tampons, although she was as yet physically undeveloped with no sign of menstruation. At times her face seemed inscrutable, at other times angry, and she told lies. She avoided her father most of the time when he was not abroad, but had developed a knack of manipulating him to her own advantage, mostly with money and presents. Despite having a Ph.D. in Economics, he fell for it every time, and Isabel was powerless to improve the situation. When she tried to make him aware of what was happening, he refused to listen, or he accused her of being a jealous bitch.

The fact that Isabel had become a well-liked member of staff at Walmisley Hall Prep, predictably did not gain Jerry's approval. He resented her having to attend the occasional parents' evening or concert, and rationalized his own frequent absence from the household whilst on foreign trips as a necessity to put bread on the table. In fact, many of his trips only involved attendance at conferences or networking, and he seemed to overlook the fact that Isabel's earnings paid for school fees, music lessons and clothes for Laura and herself, together with other necessities.

Isabel found herself having to remonstrate with Laura more and more about her disobedient behaviour and lies. She would talk to her about the absolute need for trust between them, and Laura would remain defiantly silent, her eyes cold and clinical. It was hard to come to terms with the fact that a loving child of seven years had turned into this calculating, manipulative, secretive, pre-adolescent twelve-year-old. Was this the effect of an unhappy marriage on her daughter? thought Isabel, racked with guilt, or was she disturbed by being adopted? However much she tried to talk to Laura, to show her love and affection and to persuade her to open her heart, the shutters came down. No deal.

Another worrying facet of Laura's emerging character was the untrustworthy influence she was having on some of her school friends, to the extent that their parents did not encourage the friendships to be fostered and developed out of school. In school she remained a pupil in the same form with them, but Isabel was alert to the fact that whenever Laura invited these friends for an outing or a sleepover, the parents were quick to decline the invitation with some plausible excuse of another engagement or visiting relatives. Word had got round that Laura, accompanied by Camilla, a school friend from a very respectable family, had blatantly defied Isabel on a visit to Rhyl Sun Centre. After spending nearly three hours swimming under Isabel's supervision, the two girls had asked if they might go to the fair, and Isabel had agreed, telling them to stick together, and to meet her at the cafe nearby at half past three. She wrote down the time and place where they were to meet on paper and on the palm of Laura's hand, checked that their watches were working and reminded them not to be late. When half past three came and went, with no appearance of the girls, and the time reached a quarter past four, Isabel became frantic for their safety. She rushed back and forth to the fair, enquiring if the employees had seen them, to receive only negative replies, and when the girls finally turned up at half past four, unharmed, Isabel was in tears. She had been entrusted with Camilla's care, acting in loco parentis, and this was potentially a disastrous scenario. She chastised them for their disobedience and Camilla was clearly sorry. Laura, on the other hand, remained defiantly uncommunicative and unmoved by Isabel's worry.

At home Laura's love affair with money continued. She never seemed to get enough of it. Isabel thought back to her own childhood, and remembered being given a small, regular amount, suitable for her age, and then she was encouraged to earn extra money for holidays, Christmas and birthday presents by doing jobs around the house. This was a sensible idea. It taught children the value of money, and she applied it to Laura's upbringing only to find that Jerry gave Laura so much money that she did not need to do jobs. She could choose to be lazy, and spend, spend, spend.

Jerry refused to discuss the pocket money problem rationally, and yet another row ensued. Laura was witness to it. She saw her mother knocked to the floor and she realized that she would continue to receive plenty of money for no effort at all. Isabel's growing realization that an impossible and unwholesome situation was developing which she was powerless to correct caused her to consider separation from Jerry even more urgently. Before his latest departure to Madrid, she warned him and appealed to him again to improve their relationship and be united in their upbringing of Laura. He was not interested. It was painful for her to realize that she would remain persona non grata indefinitely, and the fact that he had now struck her in front of Laura displayed a further deterioration in their relationship. Jerry obviously felt that he could continue to treat her badly because she had no other options.

Isabel made an appointment with Jeff Hamilton, the headmaster, to discuss her problems and her intention to leave Jerry. He was not surprised about her revelations since Jerry had always refused to appear on social occasions, and it was obvious that Isabel was given no support. The head suggested that if she was serious about her intentions, he could offer her one of the five staff cottages on the grounds at a low rent. It would be vacant for use at the end of the current term. As far as teaching was concerned, she would have to remain part-time for a whole term, and then she would be appointed as head of department. She would be free to take Laura to and collect her from St Faith's, but once a week and occasionally at the weekend she would be required to undertake boarding school duties.

Whilst Jerry was away, Isabel took Laura to a school production of *H.M.S. Pinafore* at Walmisley Hall for the first time. It was an ambitious feat for thirteen-year-olds, and thoroughly enjoyable in every way. The drama and music departments had combined their impressive talents, and parents had dutifully helped with costumes and scenery. Laura's face was a study of enthusiastic interest, and not just for the production itself. The nature of boarding-school life enabled the staff to combine together like a large family, and to know the children really well beyond the confines of the classroom or the sports field. This warmth of laughter, support and supervision permeated the whole atmosphere of Walmisley for all to feel, and Laura felt it too. She laughed at the stage antics of the sailors, giggled at some of W. S.Gilbert's lyrics and at the occasional soloist singing under the note. She was reluctant to take her leave that evening and interested to know when she could return.

Laura was far too intelligent not to have realized that her parents' marriage was in trouble, but Isabel soon took the opportunity of speaking to her about her unconfirmed decision to leave Jerry, and asked how she would feel if the decision became a reality. Laura's happiness was of optimum importance to her, and could certainly influence the outcome one way or another.

In a rare moment of frankness and enthusiasm, Laura burst out. "I would really love to live in that school. There's so much going on and everyone looks happy!" Isabel explained to her that she would not become a pupil of Walmisley Prep since education finished there when pupils reached thirteen-plus years, but children of staff members could certainly take part in after-school activities and at the weekends. Nor would Laura and Isabel actually live in the school, but in a cottage on the grounds. Above all, she pointed out that no decision had been made yet.

When Jerry returned from Madrid, he was only in the house three days before heading off to Helsinki for three weeks. It was enough time for Isabel to wash and iron his clothes, cook his meals and become his object of ridicule once more. Again she warned him about the consequences of not trying to repair their fractured relationship, and again he pushed her aside roughly and laughed at her with contempt. He did speak to Laura, enquiring about her progress at school, and gave her three weeks' pocket money. Strangely, although Isabel had not pressured Laura into keeping silent about the considered move, she remained totally unforthcoming about Walmisley to her father, not even mentioning the performance of *H.M.S. Pinafore*. Keeping secrets was second nature to her.

With Jerry gone for so long, it was the optimum time to make preparations to leave without encountering brute force and angry scenes. Laura was eager to leave the cottage and to become part of the Walmisley Hall family where she would be able to gain new friends of her age, without any loss of friendships at St Faith's. She and Isabel became closer to each other in the knowledge that their move was very serious, yet beneficial to them both. No child could be happy growing up between the silent hostility of her parents. Isabel was convinced that the situation would never change since Jerry refused to communicate and made no effort to improve the situation, but all the same she felt guilty about her decision to leave, no matter how justified it was.

As soon as Jeff Hamilton, the headmaster, had been informed of her decision, he took Isabel to see the vacated cottage on the grounds where she and Laura would be living. She had often wondered what it would be like inside, since the exterior, like that of the other cottages, was attractive in a rustic 1950s style. On entering, she was delighted with the layout; a large living/dining room with an open fire and bookshelves on either side of it, a small adequate kitchen, three bedrooms and a bathroom, plus outhouses providing storage in a small garden and a shed. She was even more delighted when Jeff told her that he would have the place decorated before she moved in. Within a few days, he was true to his word, and the decorators arrived. Isabel was then able to have the living room and stairs measured up for new carpet and to make several sets of curtains.

Laura approved of the cottage, especially the cosiness of the open fire and the fact that her new bedroom would be larger than her present one. Isabel's was smaller, but it faced east with sunshine flooding in in the mornings, and it looked out onto the rugby pitch. She loved it immediately.

To contact a removal company, Isabel did the obvious and looked through yellow pages, managing to spot a local firm offering reasonable prices and able to fit in with her time constraints. Then she had to select the furniture she would take: two single beds, the piano and two Victorian armchairs which she had paid for herself, her desk and record player, Laura's dressing table, desk and computer, and a few pictures and mirrors. Rather than take any more from the matrimonial home, she decided to buy a gate-leg table with four chairs, a settee and a television. With these additional items and side-lighting she would be able to make their new living room attractive and comfortable.

Isabel watched twelve-year-old Laura closely to detect if she had second thoughts about moving. There was not the slightest hint of reluctance, only enthusiasm to get on with the job. The moving day finally arrived. Fortunately, Walmisley Prep had broken up earlier than St Faith's for the Easter holidays, so Isabel was able to bring some sort of order out of chaos before Laura returned to her new home for the first time. As luck would have it, it rained whilst three removal men were struggling with her very solid piano down the drive and into the van, but the operation went off quite painlessly, and Isabel was able to meet Laura from school with a big smile and a loving hug, knowing that their courage had become a reality. She had done it! Life would not be easy, but she was determined that no man would tyrannize her again.

CHAPTER 10
JERRY AND LAURA

To return from Helsinki to discover his wife and daughter gone with all their clothes and nearly half the furniture, came as something of a shock to Jerry. He was well aware that Isabel had warned him several times to join her in trying to repair their relationship for Laura's sake, but his pride and arrogance would not allow him to agree, and anyway, he thought she would never have the guts to leave. Where would she go? The fact that he had completely underestimated her was hardly surprising since, with the exception of Margaret Thatcher, he generally held a low opinion of most women, including his own mother and other female relatives. Beyond admiring the physical attributes or bubbly personalities of attractive women, he was always slow to concede that some of them might be intelligent. Yet, he held a double standard for men, treating them all, dull and mediocre alike, with the utmost respect.

It seemed that for nearly three weeks he refused to answer the phone in the evenings, leaving it off the hook, and by day he was at the university. Although Isabel had written a note to say that she and Laura were now living at Walmisley, he paid no attention to it. There was no contact at all until finally, he replaced the receiver and decided to take incoming calls.

Isabel kept the conversation factual, giving him their phone number and the news that she had contacted a solicitor who would be arranging a legal separation in due course, and therefore he, too, would require legal advice. His voice was dry and unemotional. Whatever he had been feeling for the past three weeks was disguised as if nothing had happened. No dramatic outbursts from him, and no I-told-you-so attitude from her. Then he asked to speak to Laura, and they quickly arranged to spend Saturday together. The call ended as it started, in a low key.

Within a few weeks the legal separation was drawn up. After initially objecting to his required contribution to Laura's maintenance, Jerry finally agreed with the solicitor's advice. He was mainly concerned that although Isabel was currently working part-time on a low income, she would soon be employed full time and in receipt of a larger salary, but nowhere near as large as his. It was arranged that he would see Laura every Saturday and at other times if required. In addition, he would take her on holiday every year. Laura was in full agreement and seemed to take all the arrangements in her stride.

The final term of working part-time proved a godsend to Isabel. She was able to bring the cottage up to standard, to organize the dogs and garden, to write a French syllabus for the entire school, including an appropriate audio-visual course, and to learn about her forthcoming boarding-school duties. Above all, she made sure that Laura was happily settled in her new home, that her school work was progressing well and that the out-of-school activities continued without interruption.

Isabel thought it would be a good idea if they both joined the local church, All Saints, and become members of the choir. Not only was it something they could do together, but even better, members of Laura's class attended the church, and she would greatly enjoy their company. The choir had a decent standard, children were trained for the Royal School of Church Music examinations and attended cathedral festivals. She also thought the church's teaching would present the sound moral leadership which the wayward Laura clearly needed. As for herself, she had felt uncomfortably distanced from God for many years, and without vocalising the fact to others, she dearly wished that she could regain her faith, and find some peace in her soul.

The rhythm of daily life continued and Laura particularly enjoyed her first summer of after-school activities at Walmisley, learning to play tennis on the hard courts, rounders on the field and swimming in the outdoor pool with the boarders, often in the evening sunshine. Everything seemed to be going so well that it could not last. As an only child she relished all the company, both at St Faith's and at Walmisley. The daily atmosphere of non-communication between her parents was a thing of the past.

Jerry collected Laura regularly on Saturdays between 10.30 and 11 a.m. as arranged, bringing her back at about 9 p.m. At first she was not keen on seeing him - although Isabel insisted that she should - saying that she had a headache or some such minor ailment. Then her attitude completely changed. Each Saturday she would return with a plethora of sweets, stationery, books, games and clothes. Isabel used a generous allowance to buy her clothes, but all this was in addition, and it certainly gave Laura an incentive to look forward to the next Saturday. A watch, jewellery, and ear piercing followed with ever more liberal amounts of pocket money.

Predictably, Jerry would not cooperate with Isabel with regard to all this materialistic spoiling of Laura, but other developments followed. Towards the end of the summer term, Laura reported triumphantly that her father had confided in her.

"You are ten times more intelligent than your mother," he had said. He then referred to Isabel as a bitch in Laura's company, and tried to discover if there was a new man in her life, failing to grasp that she had not the stomach for further emotional involvement or tyranny. Unsurprisingly, a now adolescent Laura treated her mother with indifference or total disrespect unless she wanted something. Why should she listen to a mother her father despised? Homework became a chore, and music practice a drudgery. Isabel tried again and again to reason closely with her, and to set boundaries of behaviour, but it was like preaching capitalism to Stalin. *Nyet.*

Then Jerry suddenly produced glamorous holiday plans which thrilled Laura to bits. They spent two weeks at Disneyland in Florida, and a further two weeks in New Jersey to reunite with his brother and family. Shortly after their return, Laura resumed her schooling.

For the next two years, Laura associated her mother with direction and discipline, her father with the acquisition of material goods combined with expensive holidays and she knew which she preferred. The Saturday visits to her father continued without interruption, except when he was abroad. It was Isabel's responsibility to take Walmisley pupils to France every year as part of their education, and Laura accompanied them, glad of their company and of the French environment. She also visited La Rochelle for two weeks, with other young people of her age, staying with vetted French families. Unfortunately, when Isabel and Fay, Laura's godmother, met her off the boat at Portsmouth, she was rolling drunk, even though a courier had accompanied the youngsters.

Within those two years Jerry managed to sell the family home on a booming sellers' market. The money was divided and he moved into a town property in south Manchester. Isabel, too, was convinced that she should buy a house, so as not to be left behind on the property market, and there were other reasons. Laura had now outgrown the children at Walmisley, and as much as Isabel adored her job, she now wished to return to her own home in the evenings, to be temporarily liberated from life behind the rhododendrons! She chose a newly built house on a private estate.

It was an exciting time organizing their new home, and Laura was especially glad to move into a bright and spacious bedroom which they decorated together. A carpet, Laura Ashley curtains and duvet cover to match completed an attractive room. Laura could now take a short train ride to St Faith's which gave her some independence, as did doing her homework upstairs at her desk in her room, away from her mother. It was worth trusting her at first, but parents' meetings, which Jerry never attended, and follow-up reports, proved that Laura was very definitely slacking. A fierce argument broke out when Isabel remonstrated with her about relaxing her efforts, offering to help with the language subjects, and if Maths was really a problem, private tuition could be the solution. Laura became so angry with these suggestions that she kicked a large hole in the bathroom door, and pushing past her mother, she leapt down the stairs and out of the front door, slamming it as she went. The house shook. At teatime she returned all smiles, having made some friends on the estate, but when Isabel told her that she was grounded until the end of the week for having ruined the bathroom door, another violent outburst followed.

Interestingly, Jerry would claim that no such outbursts occurred on Saturdays when Laura was under his supervision.

So that Laura could have the company of both her parents for a few hours on Christmas Day, Isabel invited Jerry to lunch and prepared the turkey and trimmings the day before. Christmas Eve fell on Saturday that year and Laura returned from her father's at 9 p.m. in a blatantly rebellious mood. As members of the church choir, she and Isabel were both committed to sing at the Midnight Eucharist, for Laura a duet with Madeleine and Isabel had a short solo. For some reason Laura appeared not the slightest bit tired, but definitely disinclined to get ready. By eleven o'clock, Isabel had let the dogs out and in, dressed, and reversed her car ready for departure. All the time Laura was clearly procrastinating in defiance of Isabel's efforts to be on their way.

The minutes passed and when Laura finally decided to get in the car, she sat in the front seat, instead of in the back as usual. Isabel pointed out that it was safer to sit in the back and would she please move? Laura refused. Isabel asked again and Laura refused again. Then raising her voice, Isabel told her firmly to sit in the back of the car. No. Isabel realized that it was impossible to pick up a teenager and place her in the back seat. She was definitely in a difficult situation. She glanced at her watch: 11.20. Heavens! They had to be in church and robed by 11.30. For that evening she would have to overlook the defiance, and take up the disobedience issue when Christmas Day was over. For two figs she would have liked to drive the car back into the garage and refuse to go, but it would have meant letting so many people down that she could not do it, and Laura knew that.

They were both silent as Isabel drove the three miles to the church in pitch, country darkness. On their arrival she saw a car in the distance giving her, as she thought, plenty of time to turn right towards the church car park. The bells were ringing and other cars were filtering in ahead of her. She was stationary. Suddenly there was a crash. The glass on the front-passenger side shattered and the car spun round. Isabel felt the steering wheel jam into her ribs, and when she looked at Laura, the child was bleeding from the face and quite still.

After that, her memory of events was not clear. She was helped out of the car into a nearby cottage, whilst a doctor from the congregation thought it best to leave Laura in the car and stayed with the child until the ambulance arrived. In the cottage Isabel was stunned and felt the need to close her eyes as her head spun round and round. Then she became aware that the other driver had also entered the cottage. An unmistakeable smell of whisky permeated the atmosphere, but she thought, it was Christmas Eve and the cottage owners might have taken a night cap. She could not tell. She was too shaken up to be able to judge. Neither she nor the other driver, who was unhurt, was breathalysed by the young policeman who arrived on the scene shortly before the ambulance took Laura and Isabel to Macclesfield Hospital.

Laura had sustained numerous gashes and abrasions to the left side of her face, requiring plastic surgery. Isabel was beside herself with worry and guilt, and felt as if she wanted to die, but she had to be strong for Laura, even when Jerry screamed out his filthy-whore abuse. His insults were the least of her problems, but she could have done with a shoulder to lean on at this time of crisis. Her car was a total write off, but she noticed at the compound some weeks later that had Laura been sitting in the back seat she would have been unhurt. The rear part of the car was undamaged, and the window was intact.

Laura was absent from school for half a term following the accident, and required much tender loving care and support. Whenever Isabel was required to teach, she employed a baby sitter to keep Laura company for the hours she would be away and to provide a meal and hot drinks. The surgeon chastised her for allowing a child to sit in the front of her car, and Isabel cried bitterly, saying nothing, but remembering with overwhelming guilt the tussle she had had with Laura before the service, and giving in.

Jerry visited Laura, but was of little practical support. "You filthy whore, how could you do such a thing to her?" was repeated regularly over the phone, and Isabel wondered if she would crack under the abuse and guilt. She just had to remain strong for Laura's sake. The most depressing news from the plastic surgeon was that Laura would always carry scars on her face, though with time, they would soften and become less noticeable.

Predictably, Laura's behaviour became more volatile and aggressive as her health improved. Outbursts of fury happened on a daily basis, and she blamed her mother for all that had happened. Isabel thought it right to apologize for the accident and to say nothing of the events leading up to it. Perhaps Laura had no recollection of them. If she did, she certainly did not convey the truth to her father. In any case, the overall responsibility was Isabel's and she did not try to avoid it, but it weighed heavily on her soul. Sleep evaded her. The trauma of the crash was relived each night in her thoughts. She could feel the shock of the impact once again, and if she closed her eyes, she could see Laura's white face with the blood trickling down it. Thank God she was wearing her seat belt!

Each agonizing night she would leave her bed to check on Laura in the next room and find the child with the scarred face sleeping soundly. She would kiss her gently, returning to her own room to sob herself into a short and uneasy sleep. In the mornings she was exhausted, yet her days were demanding with oral examinations, listening comprehension, individual written work for those taking scholarships, Common Entrance preparation, marking, lesson planning, and boarding duties one day a week. Without help she knew it was a matter of time before her work suffered, and unlike the state system, private schools could scarcely afford incapacitated teachers. She made an appointment to see her doctor and poured out her troubles to him, crying in her distress and speaking incoherently until her sobs finally subsided. After listening with compassionate patience and asking an occasional question, he prescribed anti-depressants and told Isabel not to expect any improvement in her morale for about three weeks, but to book another appointment to see him in a month.

Fourteen-year-olds at St Faith's were covering a substantial amount of the curriculum in six weeks, so it was only sensible to find out what Laura had missed. Then came the unenviable task of catching up before she returned to school after half term. Isabel was able to help with French, English and Latin, but a tutor was needed for Maths and Chemistry. Laura could read up the Humanities herself. Jerry's passion was Economics, but since it did not feature on St Faith's curriculum, he could not help.

Fortunately, their friends and Isabel's colleagues were supportive, and gradually a semblance of normality returned. The weeks passed and Isabel noted that whereas other parents and their daughters were very affectionate with each other, and she was with Laura, the affection was mostly not reciprocated. The loving, cuddly child who was always saying, "I love you, Mummy", had become a hostile teenager. Yet she was pleasant enough to her friends. Some counselling was arranged for her at the health centre, in the hope that the situation would improve, but she refused to discuss the sessions with Isabel.

Almost immediately after Laura's fifteenth birthday, Jerry announced that he was taking a sabbatical from the university to spend a year consulting and writing in Cyprus. He provided them with few details, simply that he would return by the end of the year and would let out his house in the meantime. Within a fortnight he was gone. It came as a shock to Laura, but she did not openly express any emotion about missing the Saturday contact with her dad, the lunches out, the presents and the money. Instead she used the weekends to spend more time with her newly found friends on the estate. This all seemed innocuous at first. Fortunately, Madeleine's parents who lived in a large double-fronted Victorian house on two acres half a mile from the estate did not allow their daughters out on weekday evenings except for their pre-arranged activities such as choir practice and music lessons. Isabel fully agreed with this rule, considering that GCSE examinations were imminent, but as expected, Laura did not agree. Many arguments and rows ensued. The one thing that Isabel and Jerry had agreed about was that Laura should do her best educationally and now that support had disappeared. The very occasional, brief phone call from Cyprus was no help at all.

For the weekends Isabel set the rule that Laura should say exactly where she was going and with whom; that she should return by 10.30 p.m., that she should not return home alone; and if necessary, she should phone her mother to come and collect her. The rules were discussed seriously, and again Laura was reminded of the importance of trust, but it later became clear that she had no intention of being honest. One Saturday evening when Isabel checked the phone number of the house on the estate where Laura had claimed she would spend the evening under the supervision of her friend's parents, there was no answer. Three calls later, still no answer. She walked round to the given address. It was in darkness. She burned up with worry and fury that she had been so cleverly duped. At midnight Laura returned home drunk and alone, having been to a club in Manchester with her friends. When questioned by Isabel, she shouted and screamed expletives at her, and then vomited.

Isabel later emphasized to an unreceptive daughter that she could have been raped and murdered, and that she would be grounded until she changed her dishonest attitude. Laura was furious with her mother and their relationship deteriorated. She had not expected Isabel to check on her.

The lovely, spacious bedroom with the en suite and the Laura Ashley curtains had turned into a near slum. Congealed coffee cups lay on their sides where part of their contents had emptied onto the new blue carpet, together with half eaten food, dirty washing, litter, audio tapes, exercise books, crisp bags, Jackie Collins novels, all manner of boxes, tins, and jewellery, umpteen pairs of shoes and yesterday's clothes. If she were to be grounded and not given her own way, well then she would wreak havoc on the bedroom where she would confine herself.

Holiday time proved even more difficult to control. Isabel insisted that homework and revision were completed, but that still left plenty of time for Laura to mix with her friends. Isabel worried because she had no reason to trust her daughter who lied to obtain what she wanted, and then laughed when she was found out. Parenting proved to be very tough indeed.

On several occasions Laura would slip out of the front or back door to an unspecified address, and Isabel would spend the evenings driving or walking round the estate looking for her, not knowing whether to call the police. Sometimes she was out all night, and Isabel was almost beside herself with worry. She realized, too late, that buying a house on an estate had been a mistake. Church attendance was no longer of any interest to Laura, whether her St Faith's friends were there or not.

One day in the holidays when Laura was out of the house, and Isabel was attempting to retrieve some of Laura's dirty underwear for the washing machine, she spotted an unmistakeable packet of birth control pills. She was only fifteen. What was the GP thinking of? Isabel challenged him about it and was told that when teenagers asked for the pill, it was prescribed without their parents' permission.

"She will not have an unwanted pregnancy," he added.

Of course, Laura had cleverly tried to dupe Isabel once again, but when the truth was out, she became violent and abusive, accusing Isabel of invading her privacy. The fact that she was only fifteen was of no consequence to her. On one occasion when Isabel locked both the doors to prevent Laura from disappearing in the evenings, another row ensued with damage to furniture following physical and verbal abuse.

A few weeks into the first term of the GCSE year, Isabel was able to speak to the teachers at St Faith's during a parents' evening, and she received an accurate picture of how Laura was performing academically. "An able pupil who is slacking", summed up most of the comments. In case Laura was uncertain of her mother's love for her, Isabel sat her down, took her in her arms and begged her not to waste her life and opportunities. She told her that if she was still angry about the scars on her face, they were diminishing, and in the meantime she could cover them up with the special make-up she had been given; that she was an attractive, intelligent girl with a bright future if only she would calm down and work hard for her GCSEs; and that she loved her very much and wanted to be able to trust her.

Over the next few months, Laura slightly softened her attitude towards her mother, agreeing to do her homework and revise on weekday evenings. At the weekend, no such cooperation was evident since she had her own agenda. This included smoking, drinking and disappearing during the day, which probably included sexual activity, but could not be proved and was much more difficult to control. One evening Isabel invited Laura's estate friends over to listen to records, chat and have a bite to eat. She remained in the next room out of their way only to find later that cigarettes had been stubbed out on the upholstery and carpets, and drinks had been knocked over and left. The invitation was not repeated.

At Christmas Jerry invited Laura to spend the holidays with him in Cyprus, and she returned to England after the New Year, raving about the night clubs, the freedom, the boyfriends and the mild climate. It took a few weeks for Isabel to settle her down to study again, and time was definitely running out for examination revision. Jerry had promised her another holiday in the summer after the examinations. It became clear that his sabbatical had somehow turned into a permanent job. He had relinquished his employment at the university, and had decided to live permanently in Cyprus. It was no less than Isabel had expected.

Until the GCSE examinations arrived in the spring and summer, Isabel harnessed Laura's attention on study with some difficulty, and would not be fobbed off with slackness and mediocre efforts when she was capable of much more. As soon as the examinations were over, Laura went out every evening, and the situation reverted to Isabel losing track of her whereabouts. The usual trick was for Laura to spend an hour at the house of one of her girl friends, and then they would discreetly disappear to spend the evening with boys at another address, or in a Manchester club. In addition to her concern about the alcohol, sex and cigarettes which had been introduced to her daughter's life, Isabel was constantly in fear that Laura would eventually take drugs. Laura was now sixteen and was becoming increasingly out of control.

In Isabel's opinion the one hope of saving Laura's future was for her to do her A levels in a boarding school. There she would have to obey the rules and accept discipline like all the other pupils, or face the consequences for not doing so. When she suggested the idea to Laura, and then to Jerry on the phone, it was well received by both, so three potential schools in Yorkshire, Lancashire and Shropshire were selected for a visit, and then Laura could make her choice. Isabel was acquainted with each of these institutions because of the Common Entrance links between prep schools and public schools. Jeff Hamilton was very helpful in setting up the visits for Isabel, reminding her that as a daughter of a teacher, Laura would be eligible to receive a bursary. That was good news indeed. At the time, the country was in recession, house prices had collapsed, businesses had folded and jobs had been lost. In this financial climate numerous parents were unable to continue to pay private-school fees and withdrew their children in favour of state education. Consequently, some public schools increased their bursaries in order to attract intelligent pupils to swell their numbers.

Having enjoyed three informative visits to these boarding schools, Laura finally chose the one in Shropshire, which had a fine reputation and Isabel was in full agreement for various reasons. Within the co-ed structure of a Christian school, a firm but unoppressive house system flourished in a good academic atmosphere rather than an excessively high-flying one. The A-level subjects Laura wished to choose featured on the curriculum, and she could add to her GCSEs if she wanted to at the end of Lower Sixth. She would be able to continue with her music lessons free of charge, having already reached Grade 7, together with singing tuition. Sport was encouraged on most afternoons. Concerts, theatre trips and educational visits were available throughout the term, and sometimes in the holidays. Laura's life would be full and directed to enjoyable, worthwhile pursuits. The school was only an hour's drive from Walmisley. Mother and daughter were optimistic about the future.

Whilst a number of Laura's school friends were finding jobs in the summer holidays, making money and keeping out of trouble, she was not the least bit bothered about work, since her father continued to send her money in addition to the modest weekly allowance from Isabel. Nevertheless, now that she was sixteen, two requests for babysitting occurred, and she accepted both. The first was from a prosperous couple, the Wilsons, whose son Isabel had taught at Walmisley Prep. Whilst the son was off on a canoeing trip in North Wales, they wished Laura to babysit their nine-year-old daughter one Saturday evening whilst they were dining out with friends. Isabel would drop Laura off at their house, and at the end of the evening Mr Wilson would drive her back. Isabel warned Laura to cooperate with the parents' wishes about house rules and bedtime.

According to Laura, everything went well, but the very next day, Isabel received an irate phone call from Mr Wilson accusing Laura of having corrupted his little girl who he said resembled a Mabel Lucie Atwell cherub with fair hair and blue eyes. He claimed that Laura had explained graphically on paper with notes and diagrams how the act of sexual intercourse was performed, and that she was a totally unfit influence on young children. He had the evidence to prove it and Laura later agreed that it was true. She also said that the child had asked her to do it.

The following day Mrs Wilson phoned to say that it was unfortunate that Isabel had to work so hard that she could not be at home with her daughter and look after her properly. Isabel was fit to burst with anger at this remark, but had to remember that Mrs Wilson was a Walmisley parent, and therefore blandly assured her that she virtually had no social life, and was at home every evening. Much to Isabel's shame and chagrin, the scandal was passed round Walmisley Prep.

The second request for babysitting came from a church couple with a young baby who was too young to be corrupted. Leo was a gurgling one-year-old, a joyful late arrival to his middle-aged parents, Mr and Mrs Broadwater, who were both heavily into their careers. Consequently, as Leo was looked after by his elderly grandmother all the working week, the parents felt they could not ask her to babysit on Saturday evenings too. Suffice it to say that the Wilsons had no connection whatsoever with the Broadwaters. The latter phoned and Laura took the call, agreeing to babysit Leo the following Saturday. When she was brought home at around 11.30 p.m., again everything seemed to have gone satisfactorily, but the next day, Mrs Broadwater phoned Isabel to ask irritably if Laura was a diabetic? Isabel replied in the negative, and was summarily informed that when the couple returned home just before 11.15 p.m., Laura was deeply asleep to the point of snoring and had to be shaken awake. Anything could have happened to little Leo, they told her. Babysitting was no longer on the agenda and Laura could not have cared less.

The next few days were spent preparing for her two-week holiday in Cyprus and finally the day came for Isabel to drive her to Manchester Airport. She kissed and hugged Laura goodbye. Laura showed very little response and did not look back once she had passed through the ticket barrier, as so many other travellers did. Isabel returned pensively to her car, gulping back her tears. Would their relationship ever improve? she wondered. She had told Laura many times that she loved her very much, but it seemed not to make the slightest impact on the girl.

Halfway through Laura's stay in Cyprus, Jerry phoned Isabel to confirm the date and time of her return flight. He also made a cryptic comment about her active hormones, and that she was smoking like a bonfire in damp weather. Isabel asked him to take good care of her and he rang off. As soon as Laura arrived back in England ready to prepare for her entrance into the sixth form of Belmont School in Shropshire, Isabel felt that their relationship had taken yet another turn for the worse. Laura was clearly thinking about the freedom she had enjoyed during those two weeks, sunbathing on the beach, frequenting night clubs, going out with boys, smoking and drinking, and was now more than ever irritated or exasperated by her mother's presence. The arrival of her GCSE results, though, was a relief to them both: to Laura who had managed to achieve six As and three Bs, and to Isabel for her efforts in trying to harness Laura's concentration and application during the preceding months. She suggested a special celebration one evening, but Laura turned it down.

At the start of term, Isabel drove Laura together with all her numerous pieces of luggage to Belmont School, where they were re-introduced to Paul Sharpe, the house master, and his wife, Karen. They were an alert, friendly couple, well experienced in the education of teenage girls. The usual procedure on the first day, always a Sunday, was to leave the luggage behind in the room allocated to them in the house, and then congregate in the main hall for registration, followed by an information session and then tea. Parents had to say their goodbyes at the main hall. In Laura's case, despite a valedictory hug from Isabel and a promise to phone her at the end of the first week of adjustment, she barely said goodbye and disappeared without a backward glance, eager to explore her new environment.

A week later and wondering how Laura had settled, Isabel phoned her to discover that she was fine; that she was sharing a room with a girl named Rachel; and that she had got to know a dozen other girls in the house. She had started on her three A-level subjects in addition to learning Japanese and the history of art. Drama had become a passion, and her piano and singing had been organized. She sounded excited and happy, although not overly keen about sport on wet afternoons. Isabel felt reassured and promised to visit her the following weekend, bringing one or two items overlooked in their packing.

On Monday evening the phone rang. It was Paul Sharpe and his tone was terse. He quickly revealed that the previous Saturday evening Laura had been seen copulating with one of the Belmont boys in the semi-darkness of the rugby field. Bottles of ale had been found nearby, and a description of the two pupils had been provided by a local resident who happened to be passing by with his dog. The offence, if it were proved to be true, would be punished by immediate expulsion. Evidently this serious incident was even more embarrassing for the school because it involved the son of a member of staff. The housemaster informed Isabel that he would contact her again towards the end of the week when investigations had been finalized. Then he phoned off. Isabel suddenly felt faint and sick, her knees trembling uncontrollably as she fell onto the nearest chair.

Trying to control the turmoil in her mind, she phoned through to Laura to hear her version of what happened.

"We are both swearing it did not happen," she said.

Somehow Isabel knew that their defence was not based on innocence. She assured Laura that she would visit Belmont the next weekend regardless of the outcome. It was too risky to confide in anyone but Jerry on the phone. He was totally appalled that such a thing would happen at all, least of all in the first week of the first term in her new school. Isabel emphasized that no restrictions had been placed on Laura's movements in Cyprus. Whilst he was absorbing the finer points of the *Financial Times* and *The Wall Street Journal*, she was out all times of the day and night, returning to his flat at 5 a.m. or sometimes not at all, so why should he be so surprised that this might happen in England? Clearly her sexual appetite was raging.

After nearly a week of acute anxiety about Laura's potential expulsion, Isabel was informed by Paul Sharpe that since both pupils had vehemently denied that sexual intimacy had taken place between them, the headmaster and the two house masters were inclined to disregard the observation of the passing resident whose eyes could have been deceiving him in the darkness. Both pupils were solemnly warned that if either of them were to be involved in any such scandal in future, they would be expelled forthwith.

With help, understanding and vigilance from the Sharpes and a great deal of support, love and encouragement from Isabel, Laura settled down over the next two terms into the cheerful rhythm of boarding-school life. There were occasional blips, such as being caught smoking in the house, a forbidden fire hazard, and slipping out to the local off-licence one Saturday evening after the controlled social drinking time. Mercifully, these misdemeanours were not punishable by expulsion. Isabel visited her regularly, taking her out to tea and places of interest, and remained in weekly contact by phone. She attended her concerts and drama productions, relieved to be doling out praise rather than reprimand. Academically, Laura was progressing well with French and English Literature, but struggling slightly with Economics. Socially, she was interacting well enough with the other pupils, but inevitably as teenage girls do, some quickly fell out with each other for seemingly minuscule reasons

In the summer term, to her great delight, Laura was informed that she would receive the Lower Sixth French Prize at Speech Day. Having seen her daughter so close to expulsion earlier in the year, Isabel felt truly emotional with pleasure and praise for her. Then Laura mentioned sadly that Rachel, one of her house-mates, had commented bitchily that whereas both her parents would be attending Speech Day, she believed that Laura only had a mother. She must be, therefore, from a one-parent family. Isabel was immediately incensed by such mean-spiritedness, and assured Laura that she would invite her father over from Cyprus to attend Speech Day. Then Rachel, amongst others, would witness

Laura receiving the French Prize in a new dress of her choice with both parents in attendance. That would show her, and more importantly, it would boost Laura's confidence.

And so on a sunny Saturday afternoon in mid-July, Jerry and Isabel sat together in a marquee at Belmont School with scores of other parents and their progeny, and smiled with some relief and satisfaction as Laura, looking happy, confident and very attractive in her new dress, went up to receive her prize. After saying her holiday goodbyes to friends, she joined her parents for a celebratory evening meal during which Jerry said that he would like to take Laura for a few days holiday in the Lake District whilst Isabel was finishing her term at Walmisley, and before he returned to Cyprus. It seemed a reasonable enough idea, and the next day they set off northwards with a small amount of luggage in Jerry's hired car.

When Walmisley's own speech day finally ended a few days later, Isabel arrived home to find the hired car parked outside her house. Laura and Jerry were inside waiting for her. She felt a sudden sense of foreboding that something was wrong. A cold shiver crept up the base of her spine and her heart started to pound as Jerry spoke quietly to his daughter. "Laura, would you mind going to your room? I have something important to discuss with your mother."

Uncharacteristically, Laura obeyed like a well-instructed sheep dog straight out of training, and triumphantly, Jerry observed the magical effect his words had on her. God, thought Isabel, what in heaven's name has happened?

She sat in silence, waiting, but not for long. Jerry's familiar, transatlantic drawl took on a patronising tone.

"Whilst on holiday Laura told me that she is not happy at Belmont School, and would like to finish her A levels in Cyprus with me."

Isabel was totally aghast, quickly pointing out that as closely involved as she had been with Laura and her progress over the past year, she knew that the teenager was basically settled and happy. The teachers thought so too.

"Well, she says not, and she wants to be with me in Cyprus," he repeated. As calmly as possible Isabel retorted that it would be crazy to withdraw her from Belmont then, a mere nine months from her A– Level examinations. How much better to wait, and then perhaps offer her a gap year in Cyprus before university? When she added that the examining boards in Cyprus would almost definitely be different from those used at Belmont, and therefore Laura would be expected to repeat Lower Sixth, and consequently spend two years with Jerry rather than merely the one year he anticipated, he truculently replied, "You don't know what you're talking about, and anyway I've already made a promise to her."

The shock increased for Isabel when, a few days later, Laura, inscrutable, and reluctant to speak to her mother, left for Cyprus with her father, leaving Isabel duped and broken-hearted.

CHAPTER 11
CYPRUS (1992)

The phone rang. It was Jerry, and he wasted no time with greetings.

"Well, we've scoured Nicosia for high schools, three in fact, and unfortunately none of them will accept Laura unless she repeats Lower Sixth. Surprise, surprise. Silence.

"… Soooooo," he continued, "she's chosen the one nearest to the apartment which makes sense since I have to drive to my office every day in the opposite direction to the other two. Same subjects, English, French and Economics."

"You do realize that we owe Belmont School £2,000?"

"What do you mean? Didn't you pay last term's fees?"

"Of course, but we are legally bound to pay next term's fees unless a term's notice is given."

"I don't believe you."

"Look, up and down the country parents are being sued for that very reason. I work in independent education, remember, and I know about this, same as I know about examination boards."

Long silence.

"Well, you can pay for it. I am supporting her here and there's all sorts of expense."

"How is Laura? Can I speak to her?"

"No, she's out with her friends, and I'm very busy just now." Click went the receiver.

Rejection, manipulation and now a financial stab in the back. Well, it could have been worse without the bursary, thought Isabel, and dried her eyes. Then she wrote a letter of explanation to the headmaster of Belmont, enclosing a cheque and thanking all the staff, especially the Sharpes, for their care of Laura over the past year.

Each night as she lay sleepless and tearful in her bed, she wondered how permanent this separation from Laura was likely to be. Would she ever see her again? Jerry was so stony-hearted, and Laura so headstrong that she could not rule it out. Yet Jerry was keen for her to benefit from a university education, and as far as Isabel knew there was no university on Cyprus. That provided reason for hope. Meanwhile she had to try to explain Laura's absence to friends without bursting into sobs. Not an easy task. Tears were never far from the surface.

In September Laura phoned to say that she had started her new school. She sounded far from enthusiastic. The teachers were hard. Some of the instruction was in Greek and she had piles of homework. Apart from that, she was ecstatic about the friends she had made and a boyfriend in particular. Before Isabel had a chance to comment, Jerry took over, informing her that his firm was able to pay for Laura's belongings to be shipped to Cyprus. Then he added that since furniture was expensive in Cyprus, he and Laura would expect her furniture to be included in the shipment: Victorian dressing table, cupboard, piano, chairs, bed, desk, trunk and coffer. Isabel literally could not believe her ears.

Now they wanted to strip her house of the furniture. She took a deep breath.

"I will,by all means,prepare her personal possessions for removal, but no furniture is to leave this house. I suggest you buy your own. There was a loud click from the Cyprus phone, ending the conversation.

A fortnight later Laura phoned, interested not so much in her mother's health, but in talking exclusively about the furniture. When Isabel reiterated that it would not be shipped to Cyprus, Laura refused to continue the conversation. Isabel heard nothing more from Jerry and Laura for six months including Christmas. Her own communications were ignored. The removal company arrived one weekday after school and Laura's possessions were loaded into a crate.

The following February (1993), Jerry finally made contact, frantic with worry, to inform Isabel that Laura had run away. She had been gone a week, he had no idea where she was, and evidently the situation had been triggered by a furious row between father and daughter. Jerry had objected to Laura returning to his flat from night clubs and dances at all hours of the morning, even on school nights, refusing to do any study and leaving her room like a pigsty. Laura could see no wrong in her behaviour. Had she not come to Cyprus to enjoy herself? Isabel suggested that she was probably staying with friends and to try to contact them. Perhaps the school could help. Jerry had no phone numbers to call and certainly no addresses, but doubted whether she had left Nicosia unless she had decided to take a holiday break with friends to Limassol or Ayia Nappa without telling him. He kept repeating that Cyprus was a safe place compared with the United Kingdom or the United States, and that he felt she would come to no harm. No, he had not informed the police yet, but he would keep Isabel abreast of the news.

Jerry's anxiety was palpable, and Isabel tried, in spite of everything, to calm him down. Finally, she replaced the receiver, shivering and feeling slightly dizzy. So much of all this worry and heartache was unnecessary. Laura could have been completing her mock A levels at Belmont School by this time, with a mere few months to go. The structure and discipline from the school, together with Isabel's love, support and understanding could have brought about successful results, she was certain. Instead, everything was going from bad to worse.

Feeling glum and frustrated, she urged her dogs into the back of the car and drove them off to Walmisley Prep with no reason but to walk. The place was silent owing to an exeat weekend. Not a boarder was in sight, so she was able to roam the acres freely with her dogs, exuding health and the canine joy of living, racing ahead through the great mass of rhododendron woods behind the staff cottages so familiar to her, beyond the rugby pitch and the sports field to the woods in the distance.

Once there, she sat down in a clearing and breathed in the stillness, hearing only the occasional caw-cawing of a rook high up in the elm trees above her. The tranquillity somehow unleashed the pent-up trouble in her soul, and she found herself racked by deep sobs of uncontrollable distress. Without realizing her similarity to the psalmist, she called out loud to God to help her, to protect Laura, and that she couldn't cope any longer. When at last her sobs finally subsided, she rose exhausted but calmer, and calling the dogs to her, she started on the homeward walk. It was dusk, and she suddenly felt very alone.

The following day, eight days after her disappearance, the mother of one of Laura's friends phoned Jerry to say that Laura was safe. An extremely stressful situation had aged Jerry, by now over sixty, and when Laura finally returned to the apartment, he was so exhausted from the experience and so relieved to see her unharmed that she was able to impose her own views of personal behaviour and rights on him rather than the other way round. He still had leverage regarding her funding, but subtly Laura hinted that she had made many generous friends in Cyprus, and therefore often did not need his money. He agreed to take her to Ayia Nappa for a few days for some much needed father and daughter bonding.

In thankful relief Isabel realized that she was unable to influence Laura's life on a day-to-day level from such a distance, knowing that she might not see her daughter for months, if not years. With renewed energy and commitment she threw herself into her teaching and pastoral care at Walmisley in her capacity as head of department and senior mistress. She believed that this was what God wanted her to do: teach, guide and nurture all the children in her care to the best of her ability, from the smallest, homesick and vulnerable seven-year-old boarder of divorced parents to the most gifted and confident thirteen-year-old preparing for a scholarship to public school. Her spare time was spent occasionally socializing or walking her dogs, singing in choirs and studying sacred music which absorbed her more and more. Her life was active and fulfilling, yet lonely. Her sadness and failure as a parent never left her. She had wanted to be the best and most loving mother in the world and yet it seemed that she was the worst

Laura had become a very attractive girl. Although the scars on her face were fading rather better than the surgeon had predicted, they were nevertheless still visible, and Isabel had realized two years earlier that some sort of financial compensation was in order. Using money that her mother had left her, she invested several thousand pounds for Laura in National Savings Certificates which would mature in five years free of income tax. This nest egg would perhaps be useful as a down payment on her first flat.

Back in Cyprus the father-daughter bonding sessions had produced no positive results in Jerry's view, since both Laura's behaviour and her attitude had not changed. In fact, her repeat of Lower Sixth was rather worse than her first attempt in Belmont School had been. All too often she returned from restaurants and nightclubs at three in the morning, creeping barefoot up the stairs to the flat, carrying her high heels. Jerry became almost apoplectic with fury, screaming curses and expletives at her, slamming doors and throwing crockery at the wall in his rage. He was up against a powerful problem. Not only was Laura allergic to rules, but she was also in love with the most gorgeous Adonis ever to be born on the island of Cyprus, and she wanted to be with him all the time. Jerry saw nothing of this hunk of masculinity, no matter how hard he tried to persuade Laura to introduce him. She was always up and off to meet him at this bar or that club, never ever telling Jerry exactly where she was going, only to comment briefly that all her friends would be there and that Dimitri adored her company.

Dimitri had managed to secure a place at an American university in order to pursue business studies and sport, and was preparing for his imminent departure with parties and celebrations. Since Laura was so besotted with him she had indulged in unprotected sex several times, so it was hardly surprising that she became pregnant, unfortunately without even a Connecticut phone number to fall back on.

"I will call you from the States," he said.

He left to begin his new life in New England and never contacted her again. Somehow she had failed to continue taking the birth pills started when she was only fifteen, and just before her eighteenth birthday, she had an abortion. She found it impossible to tell her father, so she borrowed the required cash from a Cypriot friend who was also familiar with the location of the abortion clinic. The whole sad and degrading procedure was completed whilst her father was at work. The thought that her own birth mother could so easily have aborted her could not have escaped her.

During the summer Isabel spent seven days on holiday in Larnaca. Her purpose was to spend time with Laura and to discuss her future education with her and Jerry, telling him well ahead of time the date of her arrival and the location of her hotel. Only one meeting took place at the beginning of her stay, a lunch in a small family-run taverna close to the beach. Isabel hugged her daughter tightly when she first laid eyes on her and thought that she looked pale and wan. During the meal Jerry spoke as little as possible. It was clear that he did not want to discuss Laura's education and had no intention of doing so in the future. After two hours they said their goodbyes and departed. Isabel had achieved virtually nothing on her Cyprus visit, so in a moment of spontaneity she decided to take a boat from Limassol to Israel for a short trip, mainly to see Jerusalem and Bethlehem. It was an unforgettable and cathartic experience.

Laura relaxed by the seaside as often as she could during the hot summer months, and by September she looked suntanned and restored to health. Before the term started, Jerry impressed on her that she should make an all out effort to raise her academic standards and achieve good A-level results for university entrance. This, after all, was her last year and equivalent to Upper Sixth. By the middle of October a number of blazing rows had occurred over predictable problems: too many late nights, or rather early mornings, and insufficient study. Her teachers were unimpressed with her efforts so far. To make matters worse she ran away again, but this time only for six days. Perhaps she imagined that on her return her chastened father would concede to her every wish again. She was in for a shock.

During those few days, Jerry paid a regular visit to his doctor, and was advised to undergo a thorough medical examination. His blood pressure had risen to frightening levels and treatment was prescribed, but he became increasingly convinced that for his own health's sake he had to make a hard decision. He could not live with Laura any longer. In her absence he rented a tiny flat for her, located near her school, moved her personal possessions to that address and changed the locks of his own apartment. When she finally decided to come out of hiding, he drove her to the new flat, explained the medical reason for his decision, gave her a food allowance and promised to do the same in the months to come.

For the first time he toughened up his attitude towards Laura, for reasons, as he saw it, of his own survival. The future was entirely up to her, he said. She could waste her time and talent, and produce lousy results, in which case he would disassociate himself from her, or she could study seriously for her A levels in preparation for university entrance in England which he would fund. He agreed to take her out for a meal once a month until the end of the academic year to check on her progress, and he would pay for her rent and food. She was, after all, now eighteen years old, an adult.

Laura was incandescent. How dare her father, so easy to manipulate for so long, outwit her and give her an ultimatum? She was bitterly angry about it, and this anger had not subsided when she stayed with Isabel during Easter 1994 to visit universities and fill out Universities Central Council on Admissions forms. It was also at that time that she confided to Isabel her sad account of the abortion almost a year earlier. They were sitting together on the settee in the living room as Laura revealed the details to her mother. Isabel took her in her arms and held her tightly in silence, aware that she had bottled up the pain for many months and needed to talk about it. They both cried. Laura did not mention the painful subject again, though Isabel often thought about the little grandchild who might have been.

Before Laura returned to Cyprus to take her examinations, she told Isabel that living on her own had been tolerable although she felt lonely sometimes and would have liked more money to spend. Between lessons and study, she had made friends with a group of Pakistani students who lived in an adjacent block of flats, and she had become close to one in particular, Saeed. As a Muslim, he had received permission, presumably from an imam, for a temporary marriage to take place between himself and Laura, providing some sort of respectable legality to a relationship which might not last.

The examinations came and went, followed by another blisteringly hot summer. In the middle of August the results finally arrived, bringing Laura three Cs, hardly the product of an all out effort from an able student, but enough to be accepted at Plymouth University to study Economics with French. She flew back to England and after two weeks of shopping and preparation, Isabel drove her and a variety of luggage down to Drake's town for the start of term, passing row upon row of Victorian terraced houses, for the most part let out to students.

Laura adjusted quickly to a new situation with easy confidence, and after they had both offloaded all her paraphernalia at the correct address, it became obvious to Isabel that Laura no longer required or wanted her presence. Isabel hugged her, gave her a cheque, wished her good luck for a new start, promised to phone soon and departed. As she drove back to Cheshire, with the window down and the radio for company, she felt a profound sense of relief.

It was clear and understandable to Isabel that during the last two Cypriot years Laura had become exceptionally independent and secretive. Although she had opened her heart on one occasion about the abortion, it seemed that when life was going tolerably well, she did not confide in Isabel much about anything. Fortunately she had made friends, and perhaps her peer group provided all the emotional support she needed. Isabel thought back to her own life as a student, thirty-odd years before, and remembered keeping in regular touch with her parents and even more so once her father had died. She had cared and felt a sense of responsibility. Was that a quality missing in this generation, or was it peculiar to Laura? Isabel would phone the student accommodation regularly, but not too often, and send money every month, whereas Laura would phone for various requests to be sent on to her.

In November she announced that she had invited Saeed for Christmas, and hoped that was all right. Isabel was slightly surprised, thinking that Laura would grab the opportunity of spending the holidays in Nicosia again. Jerry had clearly not extended the invitation.. Isabel said she was willing to welcome Saeed for five days of the Christmas holidays so long as they both agreed to sleep in separate bedrooms, with all that that implied. Laura claimed that Saeed would be flying in from New Jersey and therefore it would be preferable for him to stay two weeks. Isabel pointed out that he would be able to stay with other relatives living in the United Kingdom and that she needed to rest after a hectic term and then prepare for the next. Laura was irked to have to compromise her arrangements.

Just before Christmas 1994, Saeed flew to Heathrow, and then from Euston took a train to Macclesfield where Laura and Isabel were waiting for him. Isabel was immediately struck by the warmth of his personality and his intelligent sense of humour. His conversation was stimulating, and he was always smiling. What beautiful manners he has, thought Isabel, compared with some of the bovine teenagers she had had the exasperation to meet on the estate in the recent past. He appreciated that she had bought halal meat instead of Sainsbury's, and when showing him to his room, that she indicated the direction of East for when he would say his prayers five times a day. Instead of expressing irritation at her no-sex-in-this-house-rule, he observed her

request with the utmost respect. He told her that he was a
Sunni Muslim, not that she understood what that meant at
the time, but she could not imagine Laura wearing the veil
and becoming a submissive Muslim wife. She was a free
spirit if ever there was one.

Smiling to herself, she was pondering the thought of
Laura in full Muslim dress, when Saeed placed a Christmas
present in her hands. Inside a beautifully wrapped box she
found small, carved figures of the holy family in the stable
at Bethlehem: Mary, Joseph and the baby Jesus, with the
shepherds, the ox and the ass. She gasped in delight, and
then was so moved by the generosity of spirit of this young
Muslim to his Christian hostess that tears welled up in her
eyes and flowed down her face before she had a chance to
wipe them away. She squeezed his hands, and whispered her
thanks, and knew that she would never forget his kindness,
and his warmth and respect for a religion not his own.

Laura and Saeed departed a few days after Christmas
to visit his cousin and his cousin's wife who were living in
Bayswater. They did not approve of Saeed having a non-
Muslim girlfriend and told him openly. So,after staying
with them for a couple of days in an atmosphere of disapproving silence, Laura decided that friends of hers living in
Leamington Spa would be more enthusiastic hosts. There
they stayed until early in the New Year (1995) when Saeed
boarded his flight to New Jersey.

Once back in Cheshire, Laura suddenly and brusquely
asked Isabel for the name, address and telephone number
of the Bellevue Adoption Society so that she could contact
her " real"mother. Isabel had been expecting this request
for some time, and had wondered why Laura had not

mentioned it before. Clearly, spending two years in Cyprus had postponed any such possibility for contact. She went directly to the file in her study and presented Laura with all the information she required, knowing that this search was inevitable, that many adoptees would want to discover their roots and their medical history at the very least. Laura declined Isabel's offer to help and returned to Plymouth for her second term, taking the information with her. She contacted the adoption society from there.

CHAPTER 12
FRANCESCA AND LAURA
(1975-1995)

The Bedale family had encountered many changes since Francesca had moved up to York twenty years earlier to give birth to her illegitimate baby, and to live there temporarily with her eldest brother, Sebastian, and his wife, Heather. After giving up her child for adoption, Francesca stayed with them for a few months, grateful for their support when she was feeling so emotionally vulnerable. Each year as many Bedales as possible enjoyed a family day in August, a time when Francesca's parents, brothers and sisters, uncles, aunts and cousins would gravitate to the Norfolk farm and exchange family news around a sumptuous barbecue. It had to be a sacrosanct date in the diary for all the family, and for the first time ever, Francesca dreaded it. She dreaded becoming emotional in front of everybody and most of all she dreaded that they would discover her secret, that Sebastian or Heather would inadvertently let slip a revealing word and her Victorian JP father would uncover the truth.

Francesca did not have to suffer what she most dreaded, and slowly and painstakingly, her dressmaking business took off in a modest way. She was convinced that returning to Norfolk permanently would be a bad idea. Instead, as her finances improved, particularly with initial help from Sebastian, she was able to afford a deposit on a small flat in the city centre. To pay the mortgage she worked in a music shop, just as she had done in Norwich, and her skill as a dressmaker was soon recognized by certain ladies of York who were disenchanted with the usual fashion labels. With Francesca's helpful designing ability, they could aspire to wearing unique garments without being confronted with the national debt. She worked long hours, and when orders started to accumulate, she was able to employ Mary, a young seamstress, to help her with the sewing. As business improved, she worked only part-time at the music shop. The pain of losing her baby lessened as the years went by, but she would never forget her, staying in regular contact with the Bellevue Adoption Society.

Just before her thirtieth birthday, Francesca met Bill, a concrete spreader for a construction company. Although he had one failed marriage, he nonetheless appreciated the value of family life, and was eager to settle down again. Francesca had socialized very little during the past ten years, in spite of vehemently wanting to marry, settle down and have a family. Bill was seven years older than she, a warm hearted, gentle giant of a man whom her parents would not have considered an ideal choice. He was barely educated, his conversation ungrammatical and he totally lacked ambition. He was at his happiest relaxing with a lager in front of a football match on television. Francesca's father and mother would have erupted with indignant snobbery ten years earlier, yet when they observed how generous a spirit he was and how their youngest daughter appeared happier in his company than she had been for a very long time, they said little, smiling their acceptance, and within a year Bill and Francesca were married.

Francesca produced a son, John, after one year, and then William two years later. She had been able to confess to Bill how she had given up her first baby for adoption and sworn him to secrecy. He was totally loyal, and she often thought that had she kept her baby girl, they would have had the perfect family. In his phlegmatic, good-natured way, Bill allowed himself to be dominated by his wife. It was easier. Each week she took his wages, allowing him a small amount of pocket money, and budgeted for everything else. He not only decorated their house to her high standards, but was also willing to help out with DIY jobs for the rest of her family who treated him with grateful affection, his skills being much in demand.

Shortly after William's birth, Francesca's father died, and her brother Robert took over the Norfolk farm completely. All the other children had married, moved away and were pursuing their careers in various parts of the United Kingdom. Francesca was the last to marry. Following her husband's death, Francesca's mother, now over seventy, moved up to York to live nearer to Francesca, Bill and the children, but also closer to Sebastian and Heather. They had prospered, but had not produced a family, though it was not clear whether that was due to failure to conceive or a decision not to have children. Heather had become senior partner of a thriving law firm, and Sebastian was now a highly successful barrister. They still adored their spacious and substantial Victorian house in Heworth, York. Its stunningly designed garden made visitors catch their breath in admiration when viewing it for the first time. They had made close friends in York, were comfortably settled there as well-liked and respected members of the community. Since York was easier for most members of the family to reach, family day was now held in Sebastian and Heather's house where there was plenty of accommodation.

Francesca, with her husband and two young sons, had not only developed confidence, but had grown to enjoy those annual reunions. Although some of the family members now lived in the home counties and even Edinburgh, the Bedales were basically a very united clan. In the Norfolk days, when some trouble occurred, they all adopted an us-against-the-world attitude, and would help each other out in difficult times. Perhaps unusually for England, family members were always far more important than friends, and Francesca derived great comfort from all the members of her family. They were her friends, in spite of her secret.

The recession of the early to mid-nineties brought a rise in unemployment throughout the country. The housing market slumped, and Bill was forced to accept a four-day week, with the consequent loss of income and worries about paying the mortgage on their three-bedroomed semi. With two young sons to care for, Francesca had long since given up her work at the music shop, and had considerably reduced her dressmaking activities. She now used that skill to provide clothes for the family. To earn extra money she prepared dishes such as shepherd's pie and Lancashire hot pot for the local pub's lunchtime menu, which enabled her to collect the boys from school without a problem.

In 1995, after ten years of marriage, she no longer enjoyed an intimate relationship with her husband. In fact, they had shared precious little physical contact since the birth of their second son, William. Bill was a good, stable, caring father, but after the children were born, she no longer found him attractive and was disinclined to have sex with him very often. Then it stopped completely. In many families rejection would have brought about rows, bickering, querulous accusations, adultery or a permanently cold atmosphere, all of which would have adversely affected the children. Bill reacted differently. He continued to be his old phlegmatic self, but watched sport and drank lager even more often. He gained weight.

Francesca longed for a love affair, but could do nothing about it. She had waited a long time to marry and she had no wish to cause unhappiness to Bill and the boys, or cause the disapproval of her relatives if they ever found out, but she was aware of a constant yearning in her heart which never seemed to leave her. The memory of Michael kept coming hopelessly into her mind.

On a sleety morning in February, when she had packed the boys off to school after a week's half term, she returned from shopping and slumped into an armchair with coffee on her mind, allowing the heavy shopping bags to half spill their contents onto the living room floor. Then the phone rang. The caller was a social worker from the Bellevue Adoption Society.

Their reunion was simple to arrange since Francesca had remained in regular contact with the society over a period of twenty years and her phone number was on file. The social worker advised them to meet at more or less a halfway point between York and Plymouth, where Laura was studying. A hotel in Salisbury became the approved location. Francesca felt she needed some support, so for the first time in twenty years, she revealed her secret to her sister Caroline, who readily agreed to accompany her, but was shaken to the core not only by such a delayed revelation, but also by the fact that Sebastian and Heather had remained loyal to the secret for two decades. Laura went to Salisbury on her own. That was her wish.

Tears of joy and sorrow flowed, and the inevitable questions followed until it was impossible to stay in the hotel any longer. Laura listened intently to Francesca and searched every feature of her face to recognize their similarities. Promises to remain in close contact by phone were followed by an invitation from Francesca for Laura to visit York and meet the family during the Easter holidays. This would give her time to reveal her twenty-year secret to them all and prepare for a later extended family reunion.

Just before Easter Laura returned to Isabel in Cheshire with time enough to do her washing and packing before setting off to York. She was overwhelmed with excitement to be spending the holidays with her birth family; not only her birth mother, but also two half brothers whom later she very quickly adored. By now, John was ten years old, and William, who was barely eight, reminded her very much of herself at the same age. She found herself forming a special bond with him. The boys slept in a room with bunk beds, and got on well together, so Francesca reserved the small remaining bedroom to become Laura's den for whenever she came home. She had newly decorated it and made an attractive quilt with curtains to match. Bill gave Laura a warm welcome, too, and then returned to watching his sport.

In the few days that Laura spent with her birth family, she felt very much at home, and as if her life were beginning all over again. These were her roots, and although Isabel and Jerry, her adoptive parents, truly loved her and had supplied all her material needs and a good education, they had not provided her with a family. This was her family, and although they were new to her, she was strongly drawn to them. Why, why did her mother give her up for adoption? She found the story of Francesca's having to choose between her family and her baby because of her father's Victorian attitudes sadly convincing, especially after seeing him in a few photographs. She even told Francesca that she had made the right decision at the time, but this was now, and everything had changed. Before Laura left for Cheshire they hugged each other tightly, promising that when Laura returned to Plymouth they would write and phone until the big family day in August.

Back in the mêlée of university life, Laura phoned Francesca a couple of times and then she stopped. Too much was going on in her life, with the discovery of her birth mother and family, as well as a new boyfriend, Alan, and yet she was supposed to be studying for a degree. She felt tossed about on wave after wave of mixed emotions and had difficulty sleeping. She wanted to empty her mind of all the conflict, and be peaceful, at least for a while, but she could not. The whole reunion plan was gathering momentum. Francesca continued to phone and write three or four times a week, proving that now she had found Laura she would never let her go. As the examinations approached, Laura felt unprepared, anxious and tearful about them, so she sought the advice of a university student counsellor who helped her and interceded on her behalf to the examiners.

Isabel continued to absorb herself in all the teaching, pastoral and organizational demands at Walmisley, but in her free time she felt very uneasy indeed. Yet she recalled the advice and reassurance given to her and Jerry twenty years previously as if it were yesterday: that a low percentage of adoptees seek to find their birth mothers, mainly for medical history reasons, and usually they do not pursue the relationship, certainly not beyond the exchange of Christmas cards. Some adoptees, they were told, were even very disappointed with the birth mother they had discovered and wished they had not bothered. Others were resented for having disturbed the past, and were rejected for a second time.

From the little information that Laura had imparted to Isabel before returning to Plymouth, hers was a very different scenario and one which Isabel was not prepared for. Still she hung on to other snippets of advice that she had been given in 1975: the whole reunion experience might well not last long: adoptive mothers do not have the nine months of preparing for the birth as birth mothers do, but the upbringing of an adoptee is just the same as that of any other child..

She thought about all the tantrums, the violence, the lying and thieving, the bad influences and the cold clinical attitude, the duplicity, the sex and its consequences, the smoking and drinking, the accusations and the treatment as if she were a wicked stepmother, and wondered if this was normal behaviour for all children? Of course it was not. What on earth had she done to deserve it? It had been such a struggle, and still continued to be. For all her love and efforts over the years, she must have been a very inadequate mother. Who else could be to blame? She thought again. It seemed to her that Laura was becoming ever more distant from her, and if the rows and antagonism stopped temporarily, they were replaced by a great wall of silence. The closeness they had shared when Laura was under the age of ten had gone completely, and for the most part, hostility had taken its place.

She considered the grown-up children of her friends, some of them Laura's friends, who had received a similar loving upbringing, a private education and many opportunities to develop and gain confidence. Yes, as teenagers, they gave their parents a slightly rocky ride, and problems arose, but unlike Laura, they seemed to have passed through the topsy-turvy, aggressive behaviour of adolescence, and were now settling down as students with a career before them. Some were even aware, if not grateful, of their parents' efforts to provide them with a good start in life. *Grateful* was not in Laura's vocabulary, and furthermore Isabel felt she was permanently losing her to Francesca. Jerry remained in Cyprus and said little.

Family day in August proved to be an overwhelming experience of welcome for Laura, more wonderful than she could ever have anticipated. Every single member of the family and extended family had arrived in York to greet her, each one bringing her a gift for the occasion. It was like the most exciting and unforgettable birthday she had ever had, only it was not her birthday. Apart from Sebastian, Heather, Francesca, Bill, John, William and her new grandmother, Francesca's other two brothers and two sisters were in attendance with their husbands and wives, and no less than ten cousins between them. They all welcomed her with great warmth and Laura revelled in the feeling of inclusion into this new family - her family. She felt right, she felt happy, and wished that life could be as perfect as this all the time as she moved among her relatives at the barbecue in Sebastian's idyllic garden. Her natural ways and sense of fun endeared her to them on that sunny August afternoon, as did her quickness to learn their names, and she hugged them all with thanks.

Tears of gratitude were wiped from Francesca's eyes several times during the party - gratitude to her family for this unanimous welcome extended to her daughter. Twenty years earlier it would not have been possible, but their father was now dead, and her darling had come home.

Isabel knew that her future with Laura would never be the same again. Changes were developing at speed in her daughter's life and she had become a paragon of privacy, revealing only the odd titbit of information. It seemed that at all costs she wanted to be in control, to keep the news of her new family completely separate from Isabel and Jerry, to become less involved with them and more involved with the Bedales. However much that fact was to be expected, it filled Isabel with a profound sadness which all too often overflowed into bitter tears.

Another crushing blow was the arrival of an attractive, carved wooden box left open on Isabel's desk in her study. A pile of neat handwritten letters were clearly meant for her to read, and had been left there by Laura before her second visit to York for family day. They were all recent letters from Francesca, filled with intimate news of the family, how she was spending each moment thinking about Laura, how she hoped to welcome her home again as soon as possible, and how the boys loved her. The den was waiting for her. She thanked Laura again and again for having the courage to come home, and told her that she would be there for her always. In one letter she advised Laura to give Isabel time for her wounded feelings to heal a little before leaving her completely, signing herself yet again with the words, "Your loving mother".

Anger, sorrow and disbelief overwhelmed Isabel. How could this happen? How dare she? It was as if all those years of love and care of Laura had been swept away and come to nothing. She wanted to tear all the letters up into tiny pieces in the spurious hope of making all that she had read in them untrue, but she did nothing. She just sat down, staring hopelessly into space.

The seeming futility of the past twenty years cut deep into Isabel's soul and embittered her. What was the point of anything? She dreaded any well-meaning person asking her how Laura was, and being forced to lie about her if the questions became too penetrating, or to tell the truth and break down in tears yet again. She could feel herself sinking into depression. She struggled to get out of bed in the morning, and felt exhausted from doing nothing, grateful only that it was holiday time, and hoping fervently that she would feel better once the new term had started. Her mind was in a turmoil. Was God laughing at her? Did he find her infertility and the loss of her only adopted child a joke upon a joke?

Then there was the potential finger pointing. When adoptions were unsuccessful, the critical, uninformed public would think that the adoptive mother, not the father, was at fault, and that she had not loved the child enough, or had been unkind or neglectful. They would be able to comment that so-and-so was adopted and he or she was well adjusted, and then think, so what did Isabel do wrong?

When, unexpectedly, two years later, a social worker from the Bellevue Adoption Society wrote to invite her to a meeting, Isabel was both curious and negative about it, but agreed to attend. Perhaps the experts would be able to enlighten her as to why this had happened, and what had gone wrong? They certainly had not prepared her for the possibility of this outcome, and she felt duped.

The meeting was with two social workers only. One was the senior adoption worker who had actually placed Laura with Jerry and Isabel over two decades earlier and had come out of retirement to attend the meeting. The other was much younger, currently involved with placements as well as organizing a quarterly magazine for the society. Isabel supplied them with some details of Laura's upbringing and the not-so-recent reunion with Francesca, and added that she had received no warnings of potentially extreme behaviour nor the possibility of a permanent transfer to the birth family.

Mrs. Sybil Dobson, the older social worker, replied uncomfortably that in the past such reunions had not happened and certainly were not the norm. In her view, the success of an adoption placement was mainly based on whether an adult adoptee was independent, able to earn his/her own living and form relationships. The fact that Laura was studying at university was proof enough. She clearly did not want to continue the conversation, but the younger lady, Miss Binns, was keen to invite Isabel to write an article for the magazine. Isabel warned her that she would write the truth as she saw it which might not be palatable for the society's readership, but Miss Binns encouraged her to go home and write the article for submission within three weeks, promising not to alter it in any way for publication. Six weeks later a copy of the magazine including her article was posted to her.

The circulation was intended for the adoptive parents, birth mothers and adoptees, past and present of that society. The article was entitled "One Point of View".

I am an adoptive parent with a daughter in her early twenties who has recently completed a degree course. Over three years ago, whilst in her first year at university, she decided to contact her birth mother. The prospect of this was never a taboo subject in our household. In fact, we had discussed it several times, and both her father and I realized that she would want to discover her roots at some point in her life. I had offered to help her, but I wondered about the timing of it. How would she cope with the inevitable emotional upheaval of it all and be able to concentrate on her studies? However, she was adamant. She would do this without my help, other than by obtaining the address and telephone number of the Bellevue Adoption Society, and she would not wait until she had finished her degree.

Things took their course, and although I felt insecure, I comforted myself with the guidance provided all those years ago. Of those adoptees who did seek out their birth parents, I had been told that some do not want further contact after the initial meeting, whilst others gain the information they require and maintain occasional contact thereafter. I could cope with that. Yet with all the years of love, devotion and care, wondering whether after the turbulent, teenage phase there would ever be a time of relief and satisfaction, my spirits sank lower and lower as events unfolded.

Before very long, she was reunited with her birth mother and then welcomed into a very large family of grandmother, cousins, aunts, uncles and half brothers. Education and a great deal of love and support we had given her: a large family we had not, and so this new experience of finding so many relatives was both overwhelming and fascinating to her, as she was welcomed into the family and showered with presents.

My daughter later told me that ever since she had been adopted, her birth mother had kept in contact with the adoption society with an exchange of letters and telephone calls spread over a twenty-year period. It was clear, therefore, that although the birth mother had given up the baby physically, she had not done so emotionally. This would not augur well for the future, at least not from my point of view. I wondered about the adoption society's wisdom with regard to this point. Surely it would have been better for both sides to have had a clean break? With hindsight, I can see how potentially dangerous this seemingly harmless practice was.

Three years later my daughter left an open box of letters in my room for me to read in her absence without giving me any explanation regarding what her birth mother had written. Letter after letter ended with the words, "Your loving mother". Some included thanks to my daughter for "having the courage to come home", and "I will be here for you always."

In another letter, she advised my daughter to maintain contact with me only until my wounded feelings had had time to heal to some extent.

I struggle to remain objective, but I cannot imagine that the birth mother has played fair. She has other children, yet she has made me feel that after twenty-three years of so much input of love, devotion, time, effort and monetary sacrifice, I have only been a custodian mother to this daughter, and she, the birth mother, is justified in being able to claim her daughter back.

I do not know how all this will end, but the same questions persist in dominating all others in my mind. How did I fail so badly after trying so hard? I naively thought that if you applied your whole heart and mind to something you would surely succeed. Incorrect. Counselling has been a great source of constructive help and support to me because I am determined not to emerge from this experience bitter and twisted, so to speak, but if anyone were to ask me at this moment if I would repeat the adoption experience, the answer would have to be in the negative. My mind recalls what a college lecturer had once wisely commented to me years ago: life owes us nothing, and we should accept it on its own terms and not our own. Correct.

If I had my time over again, when faced with infertility, I would undoubtedly have other options available to me in this day and age, but given that all possibilities had been tried and proven unsuccessful, with hindsight I would not purposely offload so much pain onto myself again. Adoptive parents, like all sensible parents, have to let go when the time is right, but unlike natural parents, they may have to share their children or simply hand them back.

Fostering would be a viable option, because you can provide love, care and stability to a human soul, but at the same time keep a check on your emotional involvement. I did not in my wildest dreams imagine that my daughter would return to her birth family on anything but a temporary basis for information: that she would develop an ongoing relationship with them all for years: that they would accept her with open arms and claim her as one of their clan: that the birth mother would disregard my feelings: that their various family meetings, celebrations and reunions would all take place regularly in my ignorance, and in all likelihood will continue to do so into the foreseeable future: and that I would have to ask myself who would be the bride's mother at a future wedding and who would be the grandmother later on. Not, not in my wildest dreams.

In my grief, for such it is, and particularly at times like Christmas when she does not contact me, I recall how life with her used to be and how bonded we were as mother and daughter. With nostalgia I cherish a Mothering Sunday card, inscribed with her nine-year-old handwriting, "To the loveliest of all mummies", and yet realistically, I fear that in the future I may have no part to play in her life.

CHAPTER 13
TOM (FROM 1995)

Isabel attempted to renounce self-pity, knowing full well that suffering was universal and not peculiar to her. So,she no longer railed against God for not having provided her with a happy family life. Instead she gained comfort from talking to him when she was feeling lonely, as well as from attending church and from singing church music. She had always had a soft spot for the French writer and philosopher, Voltaire, who in his book *Candide* had advised mankind, "Il faut cultiver son jardin." In other words, find fulfilment in doing what you enjoy, be it writing, a craft, gardening or whatever.

In Isabel's case it was her absorbing interest in church music. There was so much of it to delve into: all the English repertoire from before and after the Reformation, as well as the European traditions, both Catholic and Protestant. Although teaching and interacting with her pupils was a therapy in itself, music was her great solace and compensation once work was over. It could touch the soul more deeply than any other art form, and enhance the spiritual atmosphere in services. A world without music would mean a life not worth living, in Isabel's view. Importantly, too, choirs provided friends.

She sang with a large church choir in the next town. The singers were competent enough to tackle different mass settings and anthems or motets each week. It was challenging and satisfying. The choir master, being a professional musician, was well able to elicit the best work from his singers. She also joined the local choral society to gain knowledge of major works for large choirs, and tackled Bach's B minor Mass, the *Christmas Oratorio*, Handel's *Judas Maccabeus,* Fauré Requiem, and of course, the beloved *Messiah.*

On free weekends she would join musical friends from all over the north-west who, like herself, had become addicted to singing early music. Day or weekend courses were organized and directed by a musical powerhouse of a man, small in stature but large in musicality, intellect and knowledge. On each occasion he developed in his devotees a deeper understanding of the music of different composers: Tallis, Byrd, Gibbons, Purcell, Palestrina, Arcadelt, Victoria, Lassus and so on, and heaven help anyone who sang under the note. A concert tour of two Italian cathedrals, namely Florence and St Mark's, Venice, was arranged, and included churches in those cities. In addition the choir was required to accompany the Mass. It was one of life's treasured and unforgettable experiences, not only for the sublime music, but for friendships formed and fostered.

A chamber choir of sixteen singers was set up as an offshoot from the main organization, and all members of this newly formed group had looked forward to the following summer of 1995 to fulfil their plans of touring churches and cathedrals in the Loire Valley when, with worrying suddenness, their conductor fell ill. Although his condition was not too serious, he nonetheless needed time to convalesce, and conducting was out of the question for several months. With disappointment the group realized their concert plans in France were to be cancelled unless another conductor could be found. Maggie and Robert Butler, a couple in the choir who sang soprano and bass respectively, had the good fortune to contact their friend, Tom Meredith, who had been a student with them at Liverpool University in the sixties. He agreed, much to everyone's relief and pleasure, to accept the challenge and join them.

Tom Meredith was an intensely musical man. He was in his late fifties, a retired architect by profession, yet experienced in conducting church choirs and madrigal choirs, as well as being a skilled organist and pianist. It became evident to the group that his loveless marriage of many years had ended eighteen months earlier; his wife had left him and he had sole responsibility for the welfare of his elderly mother who was now confined to a nursing home. The two grown-up children, a boy and a girl of university age, had chosen to live with their mother in the holidays, and so he saw little of them.

Tom organized a varied programme, and rehearsed the choir in churches three times before their trip, once in Rochdale and twice in Chester. The programme's first half would include motets and anthems by Tallis, Byrd, Palestrina, Victoria, Guerrero, Arcadelt, Lassus and Purcell, whereas the second half was devoted to later church music by Elgar, Stanford, Parry, Vaughan Williams and Rutter. Between the conducting of these two substantial groups, Tom was to play the organ, mostly works by Bach, Buxtehude, S. S. Wesley and Vierne. The concerts were in

Sens Cathedral, Anger and towns en route. Tom ably rose to the challenge of mastering the complexities of continental organs as yet unfamiliar to him. Miraculously, he succeeded in pouring music out from those instruments, whether four manual or single manual, and Isabel was filled with admiration for him. His conducting of the motets was clear and sensitive and his knowledge of entries and notes accurate, as was his observance of dynamics. The acoustics, particularly those in Sens Cathedral, enhanced the vocal blend, and the congregation displayed their appreciation with warmth.

An official welcome speech to the choir took place in the town hall. It was delivered by an exceptionally tall lord mayor and required Isabel to translate what he said in greeting. When the ceremony drew to a close, champagne and canapés were passed round as the French and Brits mingled with an abundance of entente cordiale. Tom moved through the crowd to Isabel and took her hand in his.

"That took courage," he said, "you were quite wonderful."

"Not nearly as wonderful as your playing in the cathedral."

As Isabel smiled back at him, he bent forward, kissing her lightly on the cheek, and she felt a frisson ripple through her. She had not felt such joy for years.

It was incredible to Isabel that they both felt this growing, mutual attraction. Tom would sit next to her in the minibus as they were ferried from one town to the next and held her hand as they talked animatedly to each other, sharing appreciation of music close to their hearts, or information about themselves, followed by the inevitable exchange of jokes. Tom was endowed with an infectious sense of humour, displaying qualities of a real raconteur and had

Isabel and the group in peals of laughter. One joke triggered off another, and more followed until her sides were aching. In fact, she hadn't laughed so much since viewing *Beyond the Fringe* with Peter Cook and Dudley Moore in the sixties. She could not understand why she felt this way about him. She was no longer young and she had not intended to feel this way. In fact, she had wanted no more complications in her life, and considered the men she knew simply as friends or colleagues. Yet, she could talk so easily to Tom about virtually anything, it seemed to her. She recalled the stilted conversations she had had with Jerry on so many occasions in the past, the awkward silences, the lack of empathy and the non- meeting of minds, and here she was on a singing holiday feeling that she had met her soul mate.

The tour was a resounding success on all levels: giving concerts, joining up with French choirs, visiting the sights, eating outside on warm summer evenings with wine flowing amid joyful repartee. Unfortunately, it all had to come to an end and Isabel was privately terrified that her holiday romance would disappear into oblivion once they all returned to England, but during the Channel crossing she and Tom exchanged phone numbers and addresses, promising to keep in touch. He lived near Oxford which he jokingly said would mean taking the M40, the M42 and the M6 if he were to drive up to Cheshire for a visit. Her heart skipped a beat when he mentioned that, and she immediately invited him.

Within two weeks of their return to England, he had spent a weekend with her. Their attraction had turned into passion, their need for each other was strong. At her home he would play the piano, she would sing and they would make music together for hours. She cooked for him and he enjoyed her food, the Greek and Italian dishes particularly. He was always most welcome as a reliable bass to sing for Evensong on Sunday evenings in her choir, and then they would visit mutual friends for supper, or enjoy a curry in a favourite Indian restaurant. It was a time of extreme and unexpected happiness for them both, and as the months went by, separation from him became increasingly difficult. Early on Monday mornings he would drive back to the Oxford area and she would return to Walmisley. On Monday evenings she yearned for him in the loneliness of her empty house and cried. Then the phone would ring.

It was comforting for them both to exchange sadnesses of the past and receive supportive understanding. He listened to the details of Isabel's broken marriages, traumas and the continuing saga of sorrow with Laura, whilst he confided to her the truth of staying in a loveless marriage for so many years for the sake of the children who now had both gone. James and Julia, his children, were about to leave university and had their own lives to lead, he commented. There was an occasional meeting, but few letters or phone calls were exchanged. Their imminent graduation ceremonies would mark the end of their passing from childhood into adulthood and sadly, he expected to see even less of them.

When Laura spent a few days in Cheshire during the summer of '95, Isabel told her about Tom, and that she would have the opportunity of meeting him in due course. Laura seemed mildly interested and did not object in any way. She was busy preparing to spend a fortnight's holiday in Cyprus with her father. The remaining part of her vacation, she pointed out, would be spent at her boyfriend's flat in Dulwich and then at Francesca's in York. In fact, she did return to Cheshire a few days before the start of term in Plymouth to go shopping for clothes in Manchester. This was particularly important since she was to spend an academic year in Paris to fulfil the language requirements of her degree.

Even living in university accommodation in France seemed to be an expensive business, so both Jerry and Isabel provided extra money and neither had managed to teach Laura how to budget. Money continued to slip through her fingers like sand through an egg timer. That aside, it was fortunate that she had the support of friends at Plymouth who, like herself, would be transferred to Paris for a year. During the first term, Isabel phoned regularly, and Laura returned the call when she needed something parcelled up. Everything seemed to be going smoothly. Then in the second term, she phoned unexpectedly.

"Mum, I've been raped!" She started to cry over the phone and was virtually incoherent, but Isabel did catch that she had seen a doctor. Isabel told her that she would travel to Paris within the next two days. Fortuitously, half term had just begun and she would easily be able to travel to Euston and then from Waterloo to Paris on *Eurostar*. Once she had arrived she managed to find a room in a hotel conveniently situated near the Gare du Nord.

Two days later, at ten o'clock on a Sunday morning, Isabel arrived at the student accommodation in a northwest suburb of Paris to find that Laura did not answer the door. She continued to knock and ring. Still no answer. She checked her address book. Yes, this was the correct number. After knocking and ringing again, the door opened and a sleepy looking student in a short nightie peered at her. She introduced herself as Viv, one of Laura's friends, but frustratingly she didn't know where Laura was. Later, over a coffee, when she observed Isabel's anxiety, she volunteered that Laura had gone out the day before with Frank, another student boyfriend, and would return later that day. Isabel gave Viv the name, address and telephone number of her hotel to pass on to Laura and thanked her before saying goodbye.

She had expected to find a traumatized daughter confined to her room, scarcely able to go out, and certainly not at night. Instead she had stayed out all night a short time after being raped, aware of her mother's arrival, and this time with yet another boyfriend. She waited several hours for Laura to contact her, telling herself all the while to keep calm, supportive and non-judgemental. Finally, she could wait no longer, and phoned the student accommodation. Lo and behold! Laura answered and claimed not to have received the message from Viv.

Evidently the rape had taken place two weeks earlier and Laura had not told Isabel immediately. That Saturday evening Laura had been invited to a pub on Boulevard Saint Michel with a local business man she knew and spent most of the evening drinking with him. Later, when he suggested taking her home, she refused, having struck up a conversation with someone else who had no contact with the university. When it became too late for her to travel home on her own and she realized that she was no longer among friends, she accepted the offer of her new friend to put her up for the night. He showed her to a bedroom and left to go to his own. Laura had drunk a great deal throughout the evening and when she found him on top of her in the early hours of the morning, she was unable to prevent penetration from taking place. She had had sex without her consent.

The next day she reported the rape to the police in her suburb and said she had received little or no support. She was given a morning-after pill and told where to receive checks for HIV. She was also told that a prosecution could not be brought since the crime had not been committed on their patch. One policeman added that it was extremely unwise to accept an offer to stay the night from someone unknown to her, and she had therefore brought the situation on herself. When she returned to the police station close to where the rape had happened, she was told that it was too late, and that it would be impossible to prove that Monsieur X had raped her. It would be her word against his, so that was that.

Isabel remained in Paris for the rest of the week and each day saw Laura out of lecture time for meals. She appeared to be neither traumatized nor depressed, but Isabel had no experience with rape victims to know what was normal, yet she was aware of the same old walking-on-eggshells policy when talking to her. Any suggestion was interpreted either as criticism or control; any wrong word could produce an outburst. On the evening before her return to England, Isabel, as always, told Laura how much she loved her, only to receive a hostile response, more hostile than usual. That evening Francesca had made her usual weekly phone call, and on this occasion it was to tell Laura that the supposedly anonymous article, 'One Point of View', appearing in the Bellevue Adoption Society magazine, had obviously been written by Isabel, and she was hurt and upset by it. Laura shouted her anger in protection of her birth mother, uncaring about Isabel's pain or her right to give her opinion. It seemed not to count. Interestingly, Laura admitted that she had not told Francesca about the rape.

A half hour later, when she had calmed down, she claimed that she had spent all her money, and could not survive until the end of the month. Smoking and drinking were expensive habits and Isabel told her so. Nonetheless she could not see her daughter go short of food, so she gave her yet another cheque together with her remaining currency. The next day, Saturday, Isabel made her way to the Gare du Nord to catch the *Eurostar* at 11a.m. Laura did not see her off.

At the end of the academic year Laura celebrated the first of her two graduation ceremonies: the French one, in the university great hall. The whole procedure was naturally conducted in French, and Laura looked vivacious and jubilant as she went up to receive her award. Afterwards, surrounded by her student friends, she quite obviously wanted to see the departure of Tom and Isabel as soon as possible with a flippant goodbye and no mention of thanks for attending. Jerry stayed in Cyprus. The following year when she graduated from Plymouth University, she was able to control a situation of secrecy by withholding the date and time of the graduation ceremony from Isabel. She invited Francesca instead. One of her memorable remarks from the previous French trip was, "Why don't you stop talking about emotions and all that stuff, and just talk facts like Dad?"

By the spring of 1996 Isabel and Tom could scarcely bear to be parted, realizing that they needed to be with each other permanently, to face together whatever life might fling at them, joy or sorrow. They both felt that no previous love in their lives could match the depth of their feelings for each other, and Tom was certain that God had meant them to find each other to be a mutual source of love and comfort in their latter years. Aware that time was precious, Isabel took early retirement from Walmisley Prep, amid fond farewells and gifts of appreciation, to join Tom near Oxford. It took a few weeks to organize the move and to let out her house. It was only slightly sad to say goodbye to her friends since she was sure she would see them again for future musical events. It was easier for Isabel to join Tom, and not the other way round, since he was responsible for his elderly mother in a nearby nursing home.

For the next five years Tom and Isabel lived happily together in his village near Oxford, a lovely part of the world unfamiliar to Isabel and so all the more exciting to her in its potential for discovery, especially the city of dreaming spires. Isabel was introduced to all Tom's relatives, and quickly entertained his children James and Julia, and Julia's boyfriend. Tom relished introducing her to all his friends, and involving her in his well-established life. Together they enjoyed so many musical events, both in Britain and abroad, making new friends and reuniting with old ones. Isabel helped Tom with the care of his mother, as well as nurturing his neglected garden with new plants, shrubs and trees. Her dog, Fifi, a smooth dachshund, eventually learned to respect Tom's two cats.

After their marriage in a registry office during the autumn of 1998, Tom and Isabel received a marriage blessing soon after in the church where he was organist and choirmaster. As they walked hand in hand down the aisle to the chancel, to be greeted by the priest to the strains of Elgar's "Salut d'Amour", their friends and the smiling choir awaiting them, Isabel's tears of joy flowed freely. It was a day memorable in its cup-runneth-over happiness for them both.

CHAPTER 14
MICHAEL

Laura returned to England to complete her fourth and final year at Plymouth University, and Francesca continued to keep closely in touch with her, writing regular letters and phoning each week. Laura no longer spent her holidays with Isabel - and now Tom - or with Jerry in Cyprus, but divided her time with Francesca and family or with boyfriends. It seemed that she required only financial support from her adoptive parents and little else, though Isabel phoned as she had always done, and jotted down news which she thought might interest her daughter. As sad and difficult as the situation was, she thought that giving Laura some space without pressing her with questions or demands to visit might give her the peace to sort out her feelings.

By now Laura had become an accepted member of the entire Bedale family: aunts, uncles, cousins, and half brothers alike, and of course, grandmother. When on holiday in York or in Plymouth during the term time, she received invitations from various parts of the country to spend a weekend or attend a wedding, particularly with cousins who were more or less her age and whose company she enjoyed. She was related to them by blood, and she drew confidence from that fact, but the discovery of her family was as yet incomplete.

The desire to meet and get to know her birth father incited Laura to want to gain as much information about him as she could. Francesca had narrated the whole Norwich saga to her at the time of their reunion, but without an address or telephone number, little progress could be made as to his whereabouts. After all, he was last known to have dashed off to France over twenty years earlier and was likely to be living abroad somewhere.

During her year of study in France, Laura had taken the opportunity to search for the name *Michael McKenna* in the Parisian telephone directories, but without success. With reluctance she realized that like thousands of other adopted children, she might never find her father. Despite his rejection of her all those years ago, she still wanted to meet him, and she felt saddened and incomplete that this was not possible. Both she and Francesca finally realized that he would remain out of touch, which for Francesca might have been the wisest thing since her husband, Bill, would not have welcomed Michael McKenna re-entering her life. His patience had already been stretched to the full.

Francesca enjoyed her stable life in Heworth, York, working part-time, bringing up her boys, treating Bill with passionless civility, and satisfied that her relationship with Laura was deepening, despite her daughter's mercurial temperament. Each week she relished one day of freedom in York city centre to shop whilst John and William were at school and Bill was working. On those occasions she felt almost fulfilled and content, even though her life with Bill was boring and sexless. On this occasion, as she wandered along the narrow, cobbled, medieval streets, glancing in the quaint shop windows, she felt a sense of triumph that after giving Laura up for adoption well over two decades ago their reunion had not been short lived, but had developed into something of a mother and daughter relationship, and with a caring, supportive family around her, she felt happy.

With a sudden urge to express her gratitude, she slipped into the church of All Saints, and sat down in one of the pews to rest. Her decision to enter the church surprised her as she had not been a churchgoer for many years, not since the adoption. She stayed in the pew for about ten minutes just looking at the altar, silently praying her thanks, and then she rose up, turning towards the west door and pausing by the notice board. One particular notice clearly listed visiting organists scheduled to perform in York churches the following week with the dates, times and locations. Halfway down the list, was the name *Michael McKenna*.

Could it be the same Michael McKenna who had abandoned her in Norwich and broken her heart; her darling, whom she had loved so much? She could never forget him. Surely the coincidence of finding him so close to home was very unlikely, and yet finding two organists with the same name was just as unlikely. Her mouth went dry and her heart beat faster with excitement as she noted the dates and times of his concerts, both lunchtime and evening. It would be unwise to tell Bill that she was attending an evening concert and much easier to combine a lunchtime recital with shopping. No explanation would be required. She would discover the truth without fuss.

Waiting for the week to pass seemed like an eternity, particularly as she could tell no one: not Bill because his jealousy might not be contained: not Laura, for fear of raising her hopes needlessly: and not Sebastian who would present her with a piece of unwanted advice.

Eventually, the day arrived and when Bill was safely out of the way, she took extra care with her clothes, hair and general grooming, ready to be in time for the 1.30 lunchtime concert at the church. When she arrived at 1.20 she chose a seat near the back, not wanting to appear conspicuous, noting that the church was surprisingly full. After the vicar had spent a short time introducing the organist, and a longer time informing the audience of a voluntary collection at the end of the concert, the musician himself appeared, bowed and moved to the organ console.

Francesca had to suppress a gasp. It was unmistakably her Michael McKenna, with the same almost fluid ease of movement, and of course, the memorable smile. He was slightly heavier, and his shock of chestnut-coloured hair revealed a little grey at the sideburns, but there was no doubt about it. As short as was this lunch-time concert, devoted to works by Bach, she could scarcely wait for the end to come. His nimble use of the pedals and filigree finger work were lost on her as the music evoked all the memories of her past bereavement, both of him and her baby. The thought of how different her life might have been caused tears to well up in her eyes and spill down her cheeks. After the final applause, the audience filed out through the porch and away, whilst Francesca waited outside for several minutes. Michael eventually emerged and she came face to face with him. For a split second he stared at her, and then in recognition, his face became a study of incredulity and embarrassment. He softly spoke her name,-"Francesca"- and speechless, she just stood looking at him.

They took tea in a nearby cafe, grateful to be on their own without the complications of family or friends, and each poured out a summary of what had transpired in their lives over the intervening two decades. To his surprise she enlightened him about choosing adoption over abortion, and he sadly revealed a failed marriage with no children and that he was now living in Dublin, merely spending a few weeks giving organ recitals and concerts in English cathedral cities as a music holiday.

Instead of feeling anger, she now understood why he had not wanted to settle down with a family in his early twenties. He invited her to meet him the following evening after a recital in the minster, but when she explained why that was not possible, he suggested lunch for two days later. She felt the magic of his attraction rising in her, almost compelling her to accept.

Where was all this going to lead? She did not care, and after they had met for lunch in a small, intimate restaurant in Stonegate, he invited her back to his hotel for coffee. The remembrance of their old romance reignited the strength of her renewed passion for him and emphasized the rightness of their physical union. She had long since silently and guiltily admitted to herself that she had married Bill to have a family of her own, but now she could not bear him to touch her.

If Bill required an explanation as to why she was spending more time in the city centre than usual, her excuse would be that she was choosing and buying more fabric from various shops in York, and needed time to be sure of exactly what she wanted. In any case, excuses or lies would not have to last long because Michael was due to move on to Peterborough in a week's time, and then later to Exeter. They met as often as they could, spending their time indulging their passion and sharing their private thoughts. Francesca could remember when she had last felt so deeply happy, and that was at the beginning of their relationship in Norwich. Yes, she had felt content with her children, and was grateful now that she was older to have such a large, supportive family. Bill was a decent if boring husband, but it was only with Michael that she felt truly in love and alive as a woman.

On their last day together Michael confided to her his sadness and regrets about not having a family. It seemed as if providence was taking revenge on him for having rejected their child in Norwich, for which he felt deeply remorseful. Had it been up to him, their baby would have become simply an abortion statistic, and with mature hindsight, he could appreciate how painful it must have been for Francesca to bear the baby full term, and then give her up for adoption, to lose her forever. He hung his head in despair for a few silent minutes.

Francesca could stand his dejection no longer. She flung her arms around him and whispered,

"She's not lost forever, darling. She's alive, well and studying at university." She watched his eyes glisten at this news, withheld until now, and his facial expression change to pure joy as she explained to him the details of the reunion with her daughter and Laura's subsequent welcome into the Bedale family: that they both remained in close contact: that Laura spent much of her holidays with the family: and that he would be able to meet his daughter who had given up hope of ever finding her birth father. What a revelation! He could scarcely believe it, and all this had developed simply from Francesca spotting his name on a notice board in a York church. It was surely meant to be.

After spending the next week in Peterborough, continuing his organ-playing holiday, Michael was due to travel on to Exeter which, after all, was at least in the same county as Plymouth and therefore not so very far from Laura. It was arranged that Francesca would phone the astounding news to her, and then she and Michael could make contact. Unfortunately, Francesca would not be present at their reunion. It would mean leaving the family to travel to Devon, and more importantly, to be forced to give Bill all the details of how she had met Michael. It would be easier later on, if necessary, to tell Bill that Laura had done some paternity research on her own.

Francesca's final leave-taking of Michael was both passionate and tearful. Although he tried to reassure her that they would find ways of seeing each other in the future, she could not imagine how that would happen. After all, he did not even live in England. She was at least comforted, knowing that she had made him happy. Laura was their daughter and by meeting her father and forming a relationship with him she, too, would be happier and feel more confident. Her genetic puzzle would be solved and who knows what the future would bring?

Laura, studying for her finals, was understandably amazed and intrigued with the news. Francesca's voice revealed her obvious involvement with Michael. It took several minutes for her to explain the details of how she had, by chance, discovered Laura's father, how he would phone her at her student accommodation, and how Bill must never know about their affair. It was all impossibly exciting, and they started to giggle like school girls over the phone. When Laura finally replaced the receiver she could no longer keep her mind on economics. Every passing minute she anticipated a phone call and could not settle. An hour later when the phone rang, she heard a resonant male voice, as excited as her own, introduce himself as her father, adding that he was dying to meet her. They arranged that he would travel from Peterborough to his hotel in Exeter, and before his final programme of concerts was due to begin, he would take a train to Plymouth to spend a few hours with her before returning later in the evening. Then they would take it from there.

Laura was awake all night, unable to sleep for the excitement, and in the morning she was so tired that she missed her first lecture. She needed to study, but her powers of concentration were at a low ebb.

She met him at the station and, from Francesca's description, she recognized him as soon as he stepped off the train. Somehow his eagerness to see her helped to cancel out the fact that he had rejected her so totally in the womb. She had had her own experience of abortion in Cyprus and understood how a baby would not have been welcome in her own life at the time. So, despite everything, she returned his hug, as he swirled her around in his arms on the station platform.

How good looking he is, she thought.

The slight gap in his front teeth, the dimples which helped to light up his face when he smiled, and the curve of his eyebrows were so like her own. He was definitely her father and she was so glad to have found him.

She showed him around the student accommodation whilst her friends were at lectures, and he laughed at the undergraduate mess which reminded him of his own University of East Anglia squalor in the seventies. Then they walked through the town towards Plymouth Hoe in the cool breeze and the afternoon sunshine, each asking and answering questions about their lives in the intervening twenty-three years. The conversation went on and on. Over a meal in a restaurant near the Hoe Laura could scarcely believe how easy it was to talk to him. The hours passed all too quickly for her. Before he left her to take the train back to Exeter, he took her hands in his, kissed her on the cheek and invited her to his valedictory concert the following Saturday. She would be free of lectures and they would be able to spend the weekend together. He gave her the money for the train fare, assuring her that he would arrange the accommodation. He would meet her off the train at 4.05 in the afternoon, and they would have a meal together in his hotel before the concert.

Laura wished the days away until Saturday, with no thought but Michael in her mind. During the week Isabel phoned to ask how her studies were progressing and to wish her well for the examinations. Laura mentioned nothing about Michael and ended the call with lighting speed. She had already spoken to Francesca in great excitement about attending the concert on Saturday evening.

The concert was presented by three organists, including Michael. The cathedral was only half full, but it was Saturday evening, and perhaps the residents of Exeter had other forms of entertainment on their minds. Michael played the Fantasia and Fugue in G minor by J. S. Bach, as he had done in York, the Prelude in F sharp minor by

Louis Vierne and finally, *Choral Song* by S.S.Wesley who had been director of music at Exeter Cathedral in the mid-nineteenth century. Laura beamed with pride at her father's skill, though disappointed that the cathedral was only half full. After the concert he introduced her as his daughter to the other organists and cathedral officials, and after a brief, congratulatory conversation, Michael and Laura wended their way back to his hotel. He suggested a drink or two before retiring.

As Laura sipped gins and tonic in the subdued lighting of the hotel bar, she felt important, relaxed, dreamily happy. She was with her musical father who loved her and she loved him. When eventually it was time to leave the bar, she went to claim her overnight bag from Michael's bedroom only to be told that he thought it pointless to reserve more accommodation since his was a double room, and there was plenty of space for them both.

Overpowered by the alcohol and her attraction to him, she was unable to resist as he slowly removed her clothing and helped her naked into the double bed. She lay there silent and sleepy for a minute with her eyes closed, until she became aware of his naked body astride her and his urgent need for oral sex. He called her his precious, his darling, as he took her full breasts in his hands, and reached his climax. They must have slept for some time afterwards, entwined together, but then she felt the urgency of his penis entering her vagina with powerful thrusts, until he brought her to the fleeting paradise of orgasm, followed by his own. Then they slept until morning, and he repeated the lovemaking as the sun rose.

Later, Laura awoke with a sick headache and looking at her father who was dressing silently, realized the enormity of what had happened. He asked her if she would like breakfast, but she refused, adding that she needed to revise and had to return to Plymouth on the earliest train. Her final examinations were to start the very next week. He tried to dissuade her, but she was adamant, keen to leave the hotel as quickly as possible.

He said he would contact her shortly, and after a brief goodbye, she ran out of the hotel and up to the railway station to find that the early train was on the point of departure. Few people were around and she managed to find an unoccupied compartment. She slumped onto the familiar upholstery, and cried bitterly.

CHAPTER 15
THE PRIMAL WOUND

It is certainly true that our actions can alter the course of other lives, like a dropped stone in a pond with its rippling effect spreading wider and wider until it reaches the bank.

Laura was horrified by what had happened, angry with her birth father for his seemingly planned seduction of her and ashamed, guilty and appalled that she had been unable to resist his powerful sexual attraction. She now felt disgusted with herself, particularly because she had secretly admitted that she had enjoyed the orgasmic excitement of those few intimate hours which had been missing from her previous sexual encounters.

She phoned Francesca, knowing full well that her birth mother had fallen in love with Michael again, if indeed she had ever fallen out of love with him. She had had several clandestine meetings with him in York, was hoping for him to return to her and was wondering what the future would bring. Laura felt uneasy about Francesca's reaction when she told her the news. Would she abandon her again? Would her love for Michael be more important to her?

Needing immediate support, she phoned Isabel, blurting out what had happened and temporarily stunning her adoptive mother. It was useless for Isabel to say, how dare Francesca and more importantly, Michael, bring turmoil to Laura's life in such a repellent way, right in the middle of her final exams because the damage had already been done, and anyway, she had no contact addresses or phone numbers for them. Would Laura like her to drive down to Devon to give her some comfort and support? No. She assured Laura that she loved her, no matter what, and that she should try to knuckle down to finish her examinations. Four years' study should not be wasted and if necessary, she should lean on the support of a university counsellor. Other than that she could phone Laura each evening during the examination period, if that would help.

Off the phone, Isabel felt out of her depth with the whole ugly mess, and Tom was utterly aghast when she shared the news with him. She cried in his arms for a long time, and then fell asleep from exhaustion. Yet, wakeful in the early hours of the morning, she could not fathom how this painful situation had come about. Although Laura was now an adult, she had loved her, nurtured her and mothered her, so therefore, to some extent, she must be at fault. Guilty again.

During the following week, phone contact was made between Francesca and Michael who had left Exeter. He had travelled back to York where they met for the last time. She told him that their affair was over and that they, together with Laura, could no longer be a family trio. She knew that she would have to choose between her lover and her daughter, and she chose her daughter. She had abandoned her once and would not do so again.. She added that Laura no longer wanted any contact with him.

Michael looked dejected. Perhaps realizing what he had lost and that nothing could rectify the situation, he quietly settled the bill in the cafe where they had met, muttered a sotto voce goodbye, and strolled off down the Shambles without looking back, hands in pockets, head down and shoulders hunched. Francesca could only imagine that he would return to his hotel, and maybe, within the next few days fly back to Dublin. She didn't have his address there and neither did Laura. They knew just as little about his status or circumstances in that city. He had come into their lives again by coincidence, and would now disappear, having provided them with a general outline of his life, but few details.

During the summer, Jerry phoned from Cyprus, and receiving the latest news from Isabel, remained remarkably controlled, almost reticent. He was much more interested in Laura's examination results and what she was going to do with her future. She had, in fact, gained a lower second, humorously known off and on campus as the drinkers' degree, which was unsurprising considering all her emotional upheaval in the run up to the examinations.

Laura had made contacts during her year in Paris, and on leaving university she decided to return to Paris to search for a job, with interim financial support from Jerry and Isabel. She loved the city and French culture..Life there would offer a way of perfecting her French, as well as a means of cooling down the atmosphere between herself and Francesca, following the disastrous sexual encounters with Michael. The money which Isabel had invested on Laura's behalf as a result of the traffic accident years before had now matured, and Laura was advised to re-invest and draw on it when necessary. She was keen to take the money, amounting to £8,000, before making a short, unemotional farewell to Isabel and planning to join two other graduate friends sharing a flat in Montmartre. Now life could really begin.

Isabel, accustomed to her deteriorating relationship with Laura, and consequently demoralized by it, contacted an adoption advisory agency for help. One afternoon a counsellor sympathetically listened to her story, interrupting her narrative from time to time with specific questions about Laura's upbringing, progress and behaviour. The agency often assisted adoptive parents with the care and discipline of uncooperative toddlers or rebellious teenagers, or birth mothers with the loss of their babies, or adoptees with the search for their genetic parents. Since Laura was an adult who had already been reunited with her birth mother, little could be done. Short courses could be attended occasionally both in London and the provinces, and then, of course, a number of books had been written on the subject. A recently published work by Nancy Newton Verrier revealed information about adoptees, collected in America over a ten year period, which would revolutionize the way society looked at adoption. It was entitled, *The Primal Wound*.

Some twenty-five years earlier, Isabel and Jerry had been informed by adoption social workers that the only difference between adopted children and one's own biological children was that adoptive parents do not conceive and wait nine months for them to develop in the womb. There was no other difference, they were told. The upbringing and expectations of these children would be identical to those of their peer group. No one at the time suggested that raising an adopted child would be any different from raising a biological child, but now this book told her the reverse.

Psychologists and doctors now knew that the bonding between mother and child began in the womb, physiologically, psychologically and emotionally, continuing after the baby was born. When, therefore, the baby was separated from the birth mother, a feeling of abandonment and loss remained fixed on the unconscious mind of the child who was subsequently adopted. The abandonment by the birth mother caused the 'primal wound.'

Clinicians noted that whether children had been adopted at birth or much later, or whether the adoptive family was functional or dysfunctional, a definite consistency of behavioural problems arose; the same issues concerned them. Adoption was considered in the past as the best way to solve the problems of birth mothers, abandoned children and infertile couples, but research concluded that it was by no means problem free. It had been proved many times that a newborn baby knew its own mother, and that following separation, both would experience grief. In the child this grief could be manifested in a sense of loss, mistrust, anxiety and emotional/behavioural problems, and sometimes in depression or difficulties with relationships, as well as a loss of self-esteem.

As Isabel continued to read Nancy Verrier's book, so much of what was springing out at her from the pages could be identified with her upbringing of Laura. She learned that adoptive children fell into two broad groups: those who acted out their pain with temper tantrums, hostility and behavioural problems towards the adoptive mother, as a means of expressing their anger about having been abandoned by

265

their birth mothers. Interestingly, this hostility was not projected towards the adoptive father. The second group of adoptees were compliant, anxious, more withdrawn. Both groups feared being abandoned again, and their problems usually increased during adolescence.

Laura had acted out from the age of eighteen months, but Isabel had not associated her temper tantrums with pain - more as a sign of natural development; and yet they had continued, testing Isabel almost to breaking point sometimes, and often triggered seemingly for the slightest reason. She had showered Laura with loving affection throughout her childhood, remembering particularly all the books they had read together when she was a little girl, and as she turned a page she would kiss her curls. How many times had she told Laura the adolescent how much she loved her, and had tried to create a happy and fulfilling life for her? This research revealed that no matter how much or how often an adoptive child was shown or told that she was loved, she would be unable to believe it. Parents who believed, as Isabel had believed, that their love for the child was all that was needed, were mistaken.

Isabel had wondered why Laura, as a child, often had not returned her kisses and cuddles at home, yet became more affectionate in outside company. Evidently adopted children did this because they knew their parents would not dare to reject them in public. She could only imagine the depth of Laura's pain, and hopelessly wished that she had known about the primal wound in 1975.

This distancing can also affect compliant adoptees and interestingly, in every case within Nancy Verrier's experience where there were two adopted children in a family, one took on the acting-out role, aggressive, provocative, even anti-social, whilst the other remained compliant and acquiescent regardless of gender or birth order.

Isabel had always given ninety per cent of the love and nurturing in Laura's childhood. Jerry was often away working abroad, and was, anyway, more cerebral and emotionally distant as a type, thus placing most of the responsibility for Laura's well-being on Isabel. She was silently hurt, therefore, when she noticed that the relationship between Jerry and Laura was more straightforward and she was unable to understand why. Now it was clear that all Laura's feelings of pain and loss had to be worked out on Isabel, the adoptive mother, who was not responsible for the abandonment. She realized that even though the child did not consciously remember the separation, its painful impact should not have been minimized. She remembered many occasions when she was subjected to undeserved hostility from Laura, and then more criticism from Jerry who was not on the receiving end of this trouble and would consequently accuse her of provoking situations. In fact, in adolescence some sort of father/daughter alliance was formed against Isabel which gave Laura the control she craved.

Research had shown that since many adoptees considered that they had been manipulated at birth, and placed in an alien family against their will, they felt compelled to gain control over every conceivable situation which presented itself. Studies showed that adoptive children had a tendency to steal and hoard things, which Isabel could identify with as well, remembering how Laura had stolen pens from the headmistress's office when she already had plenty of her own. Some adoptees explained their feelings of being stolen as babies, and therefore considered that stealing must be all right.

The adoptees' problem of making and maintaining relationships was not evident in Laura's early childhood. Isabel had frequently invited many little friends around to play and in turn, Laura was invited back to their homes over a number of years, with no detectable problems. However, she later claimed that her high-school years were not particularly happy regarding friendships, since she felt different from the other girls, whereas her time at university was more successful socially, and she was never without boyfriends. They came and went with no greater speed than those of her girl friends.

Adopted children placed in families with biological siblings often seemed to demand ninety per cent of the parents' attention. Again, Isabel could not identify with this fact. Laura was an only child to whom, if anything, she had devoted too much love and attention. For all that, as a parent of an adult adoptee, she experienced a whole mixture of emotions, something akin to being an evil stepmother.. She felt totally inadequate and deeply hurt. Ironically she had a sense of abandonment, and she had no doubt that she was considered by society to have had an insufficient love for Laura.

This book was, indeed, a revelation, and if the research had come too late to influence Laura's upbringing, it could at least provide a little solace and understanding now. A particular comfort was the fact that not only did Nancy Verrier conduct her research in conjunction with other psychotherapists, psychologists and doctors in the United States, but she was also the mother of an adopted daughter.

Her studies had enabled her to understand fully the pain of the adoption triad: birth mother, adoptee and adoptive mother.

As soon as Isabel had finished reading *The Primal Wound*, she read it again, this time jotting down the important points in note form, feeling a need to familiarize herself completely with the new research. To raise her spirits Tom suggested taking a short holiday near the Norfolk Broads, to enjoy the wide skies, beach walks and perhaps messing about in boats. After quickly searching for a bed and breakfast in the area, and swiftly packing a case, they were off.

The bleak wildness of the north-east coast of Norfolk attracted them, and in the early morning sunshine they walked hand in hand along the five miles of sandy, dune-backed beaches between Winterton and Waxham with scarcely another human soul around. Occasionally they used binoculars to spot cormorants and oystercatchers. Before stepping down to the beach, Tom had seen a barn owl, but inevitably as non-twitchers, there were birds they could not identify.

As they continued walking, an unexpected colony of grey seals came into view which delighted Isabel, though she knew better than to venture too close to them. She and Tom rested a while on a nearby breakwater to observe them all basking in the sunshine close to the water's edge. One or two burly males would pick snarling, half-hearted fights with each other, and occasionally, amid snorts and grunts, younger ones would return for a dip in the sea to catch fish. They seemed to be problem free. As Tom and Isabel resumed their walk, two youngsters started to swim towards Waxham parallel with the shore, keeping up with them and displaying a curious interest. Isabel stopped and started to sing Schubert's 'To Music' to them. One in particular seemed attracted by the sound and swam a little closer, then closer still.

Isabel felt she had made contact with this wonderful, wild creature of God's creation and it gave her great joy. She realized more than ever that she truly loved life despite the deep, incomprehensible pain it can bring. Seals must face storms, wind, cold, all kinds of danger and the loss of their young, yet they carry on. She would do the same, riding the rough waters and, in turn, enjoying the calm. She flung her arms around Tom, thanking him for bringing her to Norfolk and telling him how much she loved him. Completing their walk, they scrambled up the dunes to discover the stark and lonely outline of Waxham Church. No doubt it had an interesting history, but it was locked due to the early hour, so they headed for where breakfast awaited them. The walk had been special in every way, so they did not repeat it the next day. Instead, after spending time at nearby Hickling Broad, they drove to Sheringham Steam Railway, one of Tom's favourite places.

The few days in Norfolk were a tonic to them both, and as the magical wildness of the area so appealed to them, they knew they would return.

An unexpected call from Laura in Paris brought bad news. She had run up debts, and the support she was receiving from Jerry and Isabel was insufficient. Worse still, most of the compensation money had been spent in paying off debt, or stolen. On leaving Montmartre, where the theft had taken place, she had chosen to live on her own in a more expensive area near St Sulpice, and could not afford the rent. Despite sending off copies of her CV to numerous firms, she had not managed to find permanent employment. She had taken up bar work three evenings a week, but the pay was poor and she could be asked to leave at any time. She sounded desperate, and clearly needed help as soon as possible.

Within two days Isabel had booked hotel accommodation and had prepared some meals for Tom to consume in her absence. After promising him that she would phone from Paris, she took the London train to Marylebone and made her way to Waterloo and *Eurostar*. As soon as she arrived at the hotel near the Gare du Nord, she phoned Laura who arrived soon after. She was in considerable distress, and every now and then paused to wipe away her tears, mentioning repeatedly that she was terribly hard up, as if to impress the fact on Isabel's consciousness. Isabel put her arms around Laura and assured her that help had arrived. They went down for a meal to a local brasserie where Laura was quick to order wine and even quicker to drink it. Isabel remained unflinching as smoke was blown into her face between courses.

The latest piece of news was that Laura had lost the bar job and was now totally without work. She started to cry as she opened her cigarette packet yet again and then gulped down another glass of wine. Isabel quietly pointed out that drinking and smoking were expensive habits which she could ill afford, to which Laura replied that she was attempting to reduce the drinking, but found it impossible to give up smoking at the same time. Before they parted it was agreed that Isabel would find her way to Laura's flat at twelve noon the next day, and in the meantime, Isabel gave her money for immediately necessary groceries.

Arriving at the flat at 11.30 with a copy of *The Primal Wound* in her bag, Isabel noticed a young man about to leave. Laura introduced him as Sean, a friend of hers from Cork. She was clearly irked that Isabel had arrived too soon. Sean quickly disappeared, and Isabel needed some sort of agility to edge her way into the tiny room with an even tinier shower and toilet. The living space was filled with clutter, dirty washing, papers, cigarette packets and empty bottles of wine. A single bed against the wall was covered with grimy sheets and pillow cases and a heavily stained quilt. Several pairs of shoes, dirty cups and ash trays could be seen under it. In a corner opposite she noticed dirt and grease spattered all over the small stove, sink and surrounding walls. The fridge was filthy and empty. Evidently the grocery money of the previous evening had been spent on buying drinks for her friends.

How in heaven's name did she get into this state? thought Isabel.

Interestingly, on the wall amid all the chaos were numerous photos of Francesca and Laura with the entire Bedale family; two of Laura with her genetic father, Michael McKenna; a small one of Jerry; and an even smaller one of Isabel. Even more interesting, was the fact that she had not revealed her plight to the Bedales.

Laura started to cry again about what she owed: the rent, the electricity bill, the Barclay card and the mobile bill. The landline in the flat had been cut off due to non-payment, and she was carrying such a heavy overdraft at her French bank that no more money could be drawn. Immediate action was required. Isabel paid a cheque of £1,000 to the bank and settled the electricity and the mobile bills. Then she bought cleaning materials, and ignoring lunch, they set about purging the flat of all the dirt, dust and grease. The bed was stripped, the rubbish disposed of, and the launderette did its job while they cleaned and cleaned again. Isabel noticed how creased and untidy Laura's clothes were, so she purchased an iron and an ironing board. A few hours later when she had filled the fridge with food, and the bed had been made with clean sheets, they realized how hungry they both were. A small nearby restaurant serving excellent food at moderate prices was their next port of call where Laura, with all the confidence of a much-travelled princess, ordered three courses and then proceeded to leave substantial amounts of each.

They returned to the now pristine flat where they discussed new places to send Laura's CV, the need to take pride in her appearance and to present herself for interview in clean, well-pressed clothes. It would help to make a list of achievable tasks each day so as to promote order and progress in her life.

Then Isabel produced from her large handbag a copy of *The Primal Wound* for Laura to read in her absence. She explained the research into adoption in the United States over a ten-year period including the primal wound which accounted for much of her difficult childhood and anti-social teenage behaviour, and that she could not have behaved any differently then. Isabel added that now Laura was an adult of twenty-four years, she was responsible for her actions, and she loved her very much. Laura burst into profound sobs which went even deeper than her earlier worries about unemployment and debt. She grabbed the book to her, as if it were a precious love letter from her sweetheart which she could not wait to read. Isabel knew it was time to leave, so she kissed her lightly on the forehead and said goodbye.

The next day they met in a restaurant known to Laura on the Boulevard St.Michel. She looked pale and tired, having been reading most of the night. Over the meal she commented that the book was like a best friend who knew everything about her, more especially the growing up with a false sense of self, and anger within, which she had been unable to understand or explain before. Isabel added that what had impressed her most of all was the importance of the mother/baby bonding, and that she understood and empathized with Laura's need to have Francesca in her life and to be part of the Bedale family.

Laura was silent for a few moments and then muttered that it was Isabel who had mothered her in the past. That morning, Laura had received a letter from the personnel department of a firm based in Paris, inviting her to interview. She was understandably pleased and encouraged, and after lunch, Isabel bought her a new suit and shoes for the occasion. Then Laura claimed to have her own plans for the evening, though she did not reveal what they were, and they said their final goodbyes. Once again, Isabel was due to return by *Eurostar* the next morning.

She needed to phone Tom and to pack her case, but she welcomed the chance of walking back to her hotel to clear her mind of the mishmash of thoughts crowding into it and to gain some perspective. Suddenly feeling desolate, she could not wait to return to her beloved. She had failed to recognize the depth of Laura's pain and sorrow as a child. How could she understand? She had never lost her own mother so early in life. Well, after reading *The Primal Wound*, she had given Laura her full support to bond with Francesca and the Bedale family, to heal the wounds of their separation. Yet, she knew that it would be at her own expense and it was a pain that would not go away. She was losing her only child whose life had become a closed book to her except in times of need or emergency when she was called upon to help and then quickly forgotten, or so it seemed to her. Laura was reluctant to provide her with any details of the Bedale family, or to let her have contact with them.

CHAPTER 16
CONCLUSIONS

During the next four years, Laura managed to gain temporary employment in finance companies in Paris, but nothing permanent. As she was ambitious to be a high-salary earner, she finally succumbed to Jerry's suggestion to study for a Masters of Business Administration degree. In his opinion that qualification would guarantee her the kind of job she wanted. It would involve a year of intensive study which he decided to finance, telling her that the high cost of the course together with accommodation and personal expenses would represent her inheritance. She could not expect an additional legacy at the time of his death since he had acquired new responsibilities in the form of a Cypriot wife and two step children. These arrangements were organized by phone, post and e-mail, but he remained reticent about inviting her back to Nicosia.

In those years the contact between Laura and Isabel had been maintained almost overwhelmingly by Isabel with periodic phone calls and letters and, of course, presents at birthdays and Christmas. When Laura suddenly announced that she would like to visit Isabel and Tom in their new, retirement country cottage, they were both surprised and pleased. No doubt she was eager for them to meet her French boyfriend, Alain, during a summer weekend. She was now twenty-eight years old, and Isabel hoped that she had gained some maturity and confidence from her regular contact with Francesca and family, and perhaps had softened a little.

Isabel shopped thoroughly, making careful preparations for their visit, and both she and Tom were delighted to greet Laura and Alain when they arrived in Alain's Peugeot on a sunny Friday afternoon in August. Alain was tall, dark and charming, with a keen sense of fun, and easy to talk to in either French or English. His work was concerned with computer problems, and Isabel joked that he was a good guy to have around since she was a novice with computers and hers was periodically giving her a hard time.

It was clear that Laura and Alain were fond of each other and Isabel was glad. Laura looked well-dressed and happy, and anticipated her MBA course in Paris with nervous excitement. She scarcely mentioned the Bedales and, as always, she went immediately on the defensive with anything Isabel said, regardless of how innocuous the remark was. Isabel chose not to retaliate. The weekend, after all, was something to be enjoyed, and Laura was pleasant enough to Tom. She remembered reading that adoptees can carry grudges for the slightest reason and are ready to be offended by any harmless remark which the adoptive mother might utter. She had hoped, though, that with the passing of the years and Laura's gaining maturity, their relationship would have improved.

Alain was passionately interested in chess, and when he spotted a set on a table near the fireplace, he invited Tom to play a game. He obliged good naturedly, knowing that as a rare player he would be soundly beaten. Whilst they were both immersed in exercising their wits on the chess board, Isabel showed Laura around the large cottage garden, explaining the redesign and the acquisition of new trees, shrubs and plants.

Then they went back into the cottage and climbed the spiral staircase to discover the two quaint bedrooms in the roof, and the progress that Tom had made with the redecoration. Then they went downstairs to the living room where Alain was bordering on victory, through to the dining room, kitchen, bathroom and finally, the master bedroom. The view from it looked across to the dunes on one side and over the garden on the other. Up to this point, Laura had not really engaged in conversation with Isabel, but had just made the occasional remark. Then she turned from the window, her eyes cold and calculating, her face unsmiling, and looking hard at Isabel with one eyebrow raised, she asked, "When are you going to die?"

Isabel froze. She could scarcely believe her ears. Her knees shook as she felt the blood drain from her face. She sat on the bed to steady herself and to regain her composure, her trembling hands searching for an elusive handkerchief.

"Not yet," she answered finally, as tears welled up and flowed down her cheeks. She stared back at Laura, uncomprehendingly. This heartless question was totally unprovoked, and it certainly was not a joke. For interest's sake she had simply been telling Laura a brief history of the cottage, and what progress had been made since she and Tom had moved there several months earlier.

Then Tom smilingly popped his head around the bedroom door.

"Well, darling, predictably it's a French victory. I've been well and truly hammered."

He stopped short, noticing Isabel's distress, and was just about to ask a question, when she briefly shook her head at him.

Changing her attitude somewhat, Laura added,

"There, there, Mum. Now don't get emotional."

Isabel suggested that they should have a cup of tea, followed by a walk along the beach before she prepared the evening meal. She had no intention of spoiling the weekend for Tom and Alain, so she pulled herself together and donned a pair of sunglasses for the dual purpose of hiding her red eyes and protecting them from the sun. Tom held her hand tightly as they strolled along the beach, enjoying the late afternoon sunshine with the wind behind them.

Alain was very appreciative of the meals Isabel served, and his easy way of engaging in conversation and enjoying humour lightened the whole atmosphere. The rest of the short time which he and Laura spent at the cottage passed pleasantly enough until Sunday lunch. Tom and Isabel invited them for a meal in their local pub, well known in the locality for its good food. They knew the proprietor and his wife well. In fact, they had become friends. So, it was in a warm and welcoming atmosphere with plenty of humour that the four sat down to eat. Drinks were poured whilst Alain in nearly perfect and charmingly accented English told Isabel and Tom about his family, particularly his young five-year-old nephew of whom he was very fond. He added that he had really missed his family when he had studied abroad.

Laura interrupted the conversation with a non sequitur by saying enthusiastically that when she was seventeen she managed to manipulate her dad into withdrawing her from Belmont School to study in Cyprus because she was unhappy, and he had fallen for it. She claimed that she had not been unhappy at all, but simply wanted to enjoy the Cypriot night life. Having aired that little revelation, she glanced at Isabel triumphantly and then burst out laughing. Nobody else laughed. As if Isabel did not know. She had actually told Jerry at the time that he was being manipulated by Laura, but he had refused to listen. The subject was changed when local friends came to join them for a drink and a chat.

Later that afternoon, Alain and Laura said their goodbyes to Tom and Isabel before setting off to York to see Francesca and family.

Months passed, Christmas approached and there was no contact from Laura. Evidently she was immersed in her course and had no time for phone calls. When Isabel phoned on one occasion at the weekend, Laura quickly brought the conversation to a conclusion. Then three weeks before Christmas, Isabel sent her a gift cheque together with a card and a newsy letter. She waited. No reply. No card. No phone call. Although Isabel was troubled about it, she did not want to pervade Christmas with doom and gloom which would sadden Tom, so she mentioned little of her worries to him and fortunately, their lives were particularly filled with music, concerts and carol services.

However, on Boxing Day in the early evening she could contain herself no longer. She had to speak to Laura and find out if all was well with her. She picked up the phone and dialled her number. Surprisingly, Laura answered straight away, although her voice was barely detectable. Her speech was slurred, and the background noise of conversation and laughter suggested that she was either at a party or in a bar. It turned out to be the latter, but it made no difference to Isabel. It was, after all, Christmas, and why shouldn't Laura be celebrating? Then she asked her if she was well and how the course was going. Had she received her letter, cheque and card? Yes, she had. A very dangerous question followed. Had Laura any idea how sad it was for a parent not to have contact of some sort with their children at Christmas? Laura's reply was that she had sent no cards because she was studying, to which Isabel briefly pointed out that cards were of no particular importance. A phone call from her mobile with a brief ' Happy Christmas' message would not only have been enough, but would have made Isabel's Christmas, too. She wished Laura a happy time and rang off, and as she replaced the receiver, Tom remarked that the conversation had sounded low key.

Nothing more was said on the subject until early in the New Year when Isabel received a type-written letter from Laura in the post. It was most unexpected and as she read it, her surprise turned to horror. Laura stated categorically, in carefully constructed sentences, that she wanted their relationship to have closure and that this closure should have taken place years before. Counselling would do no good in her opinion. She had not asked to be born, nor had she asked to be adopted. Consequently she bore no responsibility for her decision. To make matters more un-palatable, she claimed that Isabel might hurt her relatives in the future, and therefore she wanted her to have no contact with them.

It was such a brutal blow that Isabel crumbled, heart-broken, into deep gulping sobs until she was exhausted, and then the whole cycle of grief began all over again. Tom brought her tea and then read the letter himself. It made him very angry, since he considered the reasons to be spuriously groundless and intensely cruel.

"You're better off without her," he remarked vehemently.

Isabel had never seen him so angry and yet, as loving and supportive as he was, his anger on her behalf did not compensate for the ongoing emptiness within her at the loss of her daughter. The effort and love of all those years had become a futile waste of time. Even though she had not given birth to Laura, she felt as if a chunk had been ripped out of her heart as she moved about her domestic tasks on auto-pilot.

It seemed on the face of it that Laura's reason for closure was because Isabel had criticized her thoughtlessness at Christmas and yet, the letter was carefully composed as if it had been prepared for some time, and it reminded Isabel of other instances in the past when Laura had covertly made plans in order to gain control. She had found out later that this behaviour was typical of many adopted children. Then the recollection of being asked when she was going to die, indelibly etched on her memory, supported this conclusion. Although Laura had claimed later that it was a joke, Isabel knew otherwise.

In a state of confused emotion, she was unable to write anything back for several days, but with all the events over the years leading up to closure, she knew the letter was deeply serious, not just a fit of pique, and required acknowledgement of some sort. It had been written by a twenty-nine-year-old after some thought and calculation, not by an eighteen-year-old on the heated spur of the moment. The letters between Laura and Francesca, written after their reunion, when Laura was nineteen, indicated that she wanted rid of Isabel. All the painful comments and events which had taken place subsequently only served to confirm the fact. It seemed that Isabel would have to accept closure, hoping that at some time in the future Laura might change her mind. In the meantime she could do nothing but reply.

Eventually she wrote that she had always loved Laura, but if closure was what she really wanted, then so be it.

What had become clear was that Laura had withheld all her teenage and adult disasters from Francesca: the near expulsion from Belmont School, the totally bad influence of a minor, the abortion, alcohol in very large doses, incessant smoking, rape, theft and promiscuity. Isabel knew about them all, but Francesca knew nothing. Laura had confirmed that. The only exception was the fleeting, incestuous relationship with her birth father, Michael McKenna. Francesca had to be informed.

It was as if Laura wanted to present a whiter than white picture of herself to her birth mother, and if Isabel remained in her life, the truth might get out. Then there was the problem of hiding all this history from Alain. In order for Laura to remain in control, Isabel would have to disappear from her life. Jerry did not present the same problem. He was still based in Cyprus, well out of the scene of action, and was almost totally involved with his new wife and step-sons. Having provided for Laura's second degree, he was philosophical about the little contact he shared with her. An e-mail or a very occasional phone call would suffice, but at least there was contact of some sort, and Laura had given him her address. It was now impossible for her to continue a relationship with Michael, her birth father, so she hung onto Jerry, albeit tenuously. She did not want or need two mothers.

As hard and unjust as the situation was, Isabel had to find wisdom enough from somewhere to accept what she could not change. She was determined not to burden Tom with her heartache, although he was always loving and supportive. Whenever he was involved with organ practice or one of his hobbies, she would sometimes walk alone on the dunes and cry out all her pain. Then she might spot a solitary young seal near the shore and run down to sing to it. Somehow her connection with wild life always comforted and inspired her. Gradually the pain would recede, at least temporarily, until something else triggered the anguish again. It was usually people's questions about Laura.

As the months changed into years, she had to en-lighten people that there was no longer any contact be-tween Laura and herself. She did not even have her address. Unsurprisingly, no one knew a thing about the primal wound and the monumental impact it had on the adoptee. It was generally considered that adopted children were just like any other children, and she could read on their faces fleeting looks of silent judgement. It made her feel both mad and sad. She certainly was not faultless, but deep inside she knew that she had been a better mother than many of those whose disapproval she had to tolerate. Right through Laura's childhood and teenage years Isabel had been devoted to her. Jerry was totally incapable of this kind of devotion and love, and yet he had triumphantly emerged as the good parent.

When Laura acted out as a difficult adolescent, Jerry had no trouble in creating further alienation between Laura and Isabel, presumably as a means of revenge. After the separation, it was done regularly in the form of verbal abuse which Laura reported back, and flagrantly over the telephone. He had not consulted Isabel about removing Laura from Belmont School to Cyprus which proved to be a total disaster, and they had both ignored Isabel for six months or more when she refused to expedite Laura's furniture to Nicosia. The traffic accident had also worsened the situation. It had been a difficult time, and without Nancy Newton Verrier's research, Isabel would have become embittered, incapable of understanding her failure and the purpose of her life as a mother.

Tom, the great love of her life, became her raison d'être. Like thousands of others all over the country and beyond he, too, had suffered family problems during and following a broken marriage, and as the years went by and old age beckoned, they clung to each other ever more closely for mutual comfort and support. They continued to be soul mates with music as their shared passion, and yet they enjoyed their differences. He took on the challenge of crossword puzzles; she read as many books as time would allow. He knew almost everything there was to know about steam railways; she relished travelling on them with him, especially if lunch or cream teas were served aboard. She enjoyed redesigning the garden, but he was happier tinkering with his vintage car in the garage.

Important to them both was holidaying abroad on music courses with mutual friends, or singing the services in some English cathedrals when the choristers were on vacation, or exploring Paris, Rome and Amsterdam. They were right for each other, and hopeful for a long and happy marriage. The fact that the past was painful to them both only increased their thankfulness for having found each other late in life. The words 'if only' came to Isabel's mind many times, but she knew that such thoughts were futile.

Tom's seventieth birthday was celebrated over three days in London with a slap-up meal at Simpsons in the Strand for the family: James, Julia and Julia's husband, Gavin. Then came a visit to Covent Garden for a performance of *Il Trovatore*, followed by *Xerxes* at the Coliseum, and finally, *The Mouse Trap,* left them culturally replete, with a host of happy memories.

Tom's high blood pressure had always been difficult to control and sadly, by late summer he sustained a transient ischaemic attack which affected his speech and one side of his face. Words of few syllables became a necessity for him, yet he managed to keep his sense of humour and love of life. Fortunately, his skills at the organ and piano were unaffected, but less fortunately, the diagnostic tests took many weeks to complete. The final MRI scan revealed a malignant tumour in the left parietal lobe of his brain. He collapsed on Christmas Eve just before the midnight Eucharist, and died on Christmas Day.

In a way it was a merciful release from all the lingering pain and disablement that might have been, and for that Isabel, together with Tom's relatives and friends, was grateful and relieved, but he had died much too soon, crushing her hope of a long and happy marriage.

After the funeral and all the organization of minutiae which follows a death, and when everyone had long since travelled back to their homes many miles away, Isabel found herself daily bereft in the cottage, staring into space and feeling the full impact of Tom's absence. The love of her life had gone. Would she ever see him again, or was this the end with no hope of heaven in the future? Doubts crept in and out of her mind. She wandered aimlessly round the cottage, holding his photo and wearing his dressing gown because it smelled of him. She clutched at the toy seal he had bought her as a memento of their visit to Lindisfarne and the Farne Islands, and gut wrenching sobs would overwhelm her.

Then perhaps the phone would ring and she would try to pull herself together for the well-meaning caller. Sleep evaded her. By morning she was exhausted and could see no purpose for getting out of bed. Food was of no interest. Her grief was inconsolable. If only she could feel Tom's spirit near her and the assurance of God's loving protection, but she felt nothing; just silence and emptiness. In losing Tom she also lost the will to live. Was there any point? She realized that throughout the years following Laura's rejection, Tom's love and belief in her had lifted her out of failure and melancholy - dearest, darling Tom.

As the months passed, the phone calls and visits became less frequent, and then all but ceased. Friends and her few relatives, understandably involved with their own lives, had either lost interest, or had guessed and hoped that she had emerged from her grief. Little did they know. Isabel wondered if she would ever recover from Tom's death. Her doctor, bereavement counselling, loving, supportive friends and relatives, together with her faith, all contributed to a gradual healing process over the years. It was a case of becoming better able to handle the grief, rather than getting over it.

Little by little she gained strength enough to visit and empathize with other bereaved or isolated people, and as often is the case, the support was mutual. Sometimes she felt humbled by the bravery of those who were far worse off than herself, realizing that she had much to learn from them. She also realized that the more we have loved a person, the more we suffer when that person dies: the closer the connection has been, the more devastating will be the loss. As C. S. Lewis said, "The pain now is part of the happiness then. That's the deal."

She immersed herself in music again, both listening at home and singing in choirs. It was what Tom would have wanted her to do, and as ever, it gave her great joy. She pottered about in her garden, enjoyed walking on the beach or in the countryside with friends, devoured books at every available opportunity and occasionally took a holiday. She supported her local church, and built up a life for herself within that caring community. Gradually she came to realize that all the American research on adopted children, particularly that of Nancy Newton Verrier, was a comfort sent by God, working through the minds and skill of those clinicians and doctors. Isabel drew strength from that thought.

Old age crept up on her stealthily and like other elderly people, she often wondered in the sleepless hours of the early morning how her end would come. Tom was always on her mind and she would pray for the repose of his soul, trusting in God that they would meet again in heaven. Then she would pray for Laura, living somewhere in Germany, that her life would be happy and fulfilled with Alain and whenever she saw Francesca and the Bedales. Perhaps, in time, she would realize that Isabel had had no clue at the time of adoption how the primal wound could produce such devastating effects of loss, and have compassion for her ignorance. She might even realize that Isabel had done her best.

She tried to keep the happy memories of Laura's childhood and the extreme happiness she had shared with Tom, her soul mate, her Mr Music, in her heart. She remembered, too, all the hundreds of children she had taught and mothered over the years, and she smiled at the thought of them, now grown up and guiding their own sons and daughters. Nobody could take those memories away from her and she was thankful. She had to come to terms with the fact that she might well die without seeing Laura again, and without being able to say goodbye to her. That was what closure meant, but she lived in hope.

Lightning Source UK Ltd.
Milton Keynes UK
04 September 2010

159372UK00001B/4/P